TI

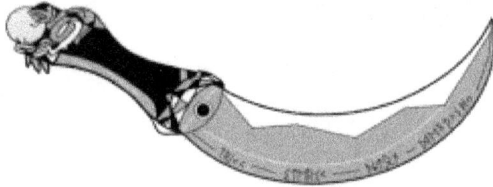

ASHLEY SCHELLER

Ashley Scheller

Content Warnings: The following work depicts, mentions, and discusses a coma, family loss, anxiety, the sustaining of injuries/blood, mild violence, and the effects of a natural disaster.

Editor and Sensitivity Reader Acknowledgements

Chealsey Thomas

Artwork created by

Ashley Scheller

THE WIELDER DIARIES: SHATTERED

2nd edition

Ashley Scheller

~Dedication~

In celebration of this new edition, I'd like to take this moment to thank those who have supported this series.

To my family and their terrific support, who always has my back, I love you.

To fellow authors, you're an inspiration and the world needs your story. Keep writing.

To my LGBT+ editor and friends whom I stand by their side, stay true.

To Ms. Amber Hill, my friend, thank you for your guidance. Stay amazing.

~ An Unlocked Reference ~

A)

Arinamo's Great Alchemic Designs – *(n.)* A cultural text of Genecia's foundation and principles

Title/Rank:

1. Calph – *regarded beginning*
2. Dissapha
3. Sephur
4. Coniphur
5. Fermuru
6. Distiphur
7. Colutia – *regarded life achievement*

D)

Dead Mountains – *(n.)* Landform, western range

E)

Elaiobus – *(n.)* Thing, a world force, a magical entity that thrives on stories and chooses the innocent who fulfills their role as a Saqui

F)

Foggy Mountains – *(n.)* Landform, eastern range

Folk-kin – *(n.)* **Hello. Known as the Crystal of Elaiobus, an Imogen-Kythe, I write the accounts of the Saqui and those close to the adventure. Reader, enjoy the following tale.**

G)

Genecia – *(n.)* Place, home world to the Genecians whose society is advanced in alchemy, transmutation, and equal change

Guardians – *(n.)* Title, a designation, of the Saqui's personal knights, viewed worthy of character by Elaiobus

I)

Imogen-Kythe – *(n.)* Thing, unique item or weapon, serves the Saqui to wield

J)

Johari – *(n.)* Place, located in the Masana Territory, home of the Royal Tribe of Lions

M)

Masana Territory – *(n.)* Place, the northern kingdom

O)

Overland Territory – *(n.)* Place, the southern kingdom

S)

Saqui – *(n.)* Person, Elaiobus' chosen, an innocent who will write their story with the Folk-kin and rule the Overland Territory

Z)

Ze – *(pron.)* singular they (Ze is over at the store.)

Zem – *(pron.)* singular them
(The shirt belongs to zem.)

Zir – *(pron.)* singular their (This is zir book.)

Zirs – *(pron.)* Plural they/them/their (Zirs need to go. -or-This library belongs to zirs. -or- Zirs food is good.)

~Acknowledging Our Story's Performers~

KAYLA ROYBISHKI: Saqui, a Wielder. The chosen to lead this Story transcribing within the Folk-kin. While rediscovering herself and her past, several pages of knowledge have been torn and stolen. Betrayed she seeks to know why.

Lute Gibe: Guardian, a healer. A young student of medicine. A witness to a betrayal, he seeks to retrieve what was lost.

Jacques Volt: Guardian, a swordsman. A young student of combat and weapons. A witness to a betrayal and seeks justice.

Jared (Unknown): Guardian, a (**Lost to Memory**) wizard. He seeks the truth behind the astrayed.

*Xenos (**Lost to Memory**):* Guardian, (**Lost to Memory**). Ze is guilty as ze flees.

Annika Eider: Mentor, a sorceress-medium of our world order. She set our Wielder and Guardians on their path. She now recovers from injury.

King Basi: Brother, a king of the neighboring Masana Territory. He governs those recovering from our last fight.

The Court of the Overland: Lords and Ladies who support their Saqui, in the Overland Territory. Today, they (**Lost to Memory**).

On this pivotal note, we resume our Story...

LUTE – 14 YEARS

"XENOS," JACQUES SHOUTED, running after the traitor who busted through the hospital window.

I rushed to Kayla, sprawled on the wood floor. "Oi, Jacques, she needs us first."

My friend kicked the wall and spun back around. "No, Kayla needs a doctor first. I'm goin' after that beast."

"I get you're frustrated. But, somehow, that so-called 'beast' *is* Xenos," I argued. "We can't run off and tackle a comrade."

Jared stood by my side with his boney hands gripped around his magic golden staff. "It is best we do not rush in blindly."

Jacques whipped out a thin, leather hair tie from his pocket and began pulling back his black hair. "Ya two do what ya must."

"Oi, listen to your friends, man." I shook my head.

"No time. I'm goin' after the stolen diary pages."

With a sigh, I checked Kayla's pulse and lifted her from the floor. "Go get 'em then, Captain Volt."

"Be careful," Jared warned as Jacques rushed out.

After placing Kayla on a bed to my right, Jared came forward and gently placed his hand on her pale forehead. He closed his blue eyes, and the staff's purple orb held upright in the jaws of a golden lion head glowed a matching hue.

"I can heal the bump, but she will remain knocked out until her mind is ready."

"Thanks, old man." I let out grateful sigh and looked toward the door. "When you're done, catch up with Jacques, okay? I bet he's not far."

After a few moments, the wizard took back his hand, opened his eyes, and gave me a nod before he left without a word.

I looked at Kayla's face.

Wake up already...don't do this again...

"Oi. Relax"—I muttered and placed a cool, damp compress on the top of her head—"it's a bump. No magical, sleeping curse this time." I pulled up a chair next to her bedside and took a seat.

It was one thing after another, wasn't it? She woke up; lost her memories. We were at peace, but the Dragon of Lightning Zar and a horde of Leaf Turners showed up at our door.

"Who knows how long this mess will take to clean up," I muttered.

And now? Kayla regained most of her memories yet lost the opportunity to gain them all.

I balled my hands into fists, zoning out the nurses and patients chatting and walking past the room outside. "Xenos..."

"L-Lute?"

"H-Hey." I sat up in my chair. "You, okay?"

Kayla blinked and turned her head from side to side. "Y-Yes, what happened? Where is everybody?" Her green eyes slowly grew wider. "Xenos—" She bolted straight up only to hold her head. "Ah."

I stood and held up my hands. "Oi! You're safe. It's okay."

"But—"

"No buts! Jacques and Jared are on it."

She swept her blonde hair out of her face. "Okay, um...what are they standing on?"

"Oh ha, ha. Gimme a moment." I turned around, looking for the blue Folk-kin diary. "There it is." I got it and walked back. "Please, stay here at the hospital and rest." I handed it to her. "Here."

Kayla frowned and rested the diary on her lap. "I don't know if I have it in me to read right now."

"Take a nap if you need to, but I would pick up where you left off. It could help us help Xenos."

"If it will help, then I'm on it."

I turned on my heel toward the door. "I have to make rounds in town, but please, Kayla, wait for Jacques and Jared to report back."

"Back from stopping Xenos, you mean."

"It will be alright." I looked over my shoulder. "Trust me."

BASI – Appears 31 When Furless

THE SUN WAS ALMOST right above us, and the pleasant wind rushed past my mane. The soil was rich and wet under my four paws. Looking south, it was odd feeling the warmth everywhere save for the cooler air across my face. I sniffed the ground. The tiny yellow and white blooms were refreshing but almost made me sneeze.

Tall trees of needles and brown cones to those bearing strange fruits left me wondering their names. One more step, and I'd cross into a whole other world.

I looked at my adopted sister, Kayla, beside me. Standing tall, she smiled back. Hope and happiness swelled in my chest for us; indeed, destined for great things.

Our procession arrived at the border, where the Masana tall grasses met the wild fields of the Overland. Although we celebrated Light Festival weeks early, Kayla and I agreed to fortify the ties between our kingdoms.

Kayla nodded at me and looked up to her friend Jacques upon his horse. With a raise of his hand, he signaled it was time alongside the elder from the Monkey Tribe, Baobi, and others. Tula and many of her Bird kindred chirped and trilled overhead, signaling people and respected Beasts alike to move as planned the night before. The excited humans of the Overland Territory cheered, parading past my sister and me in two parallel, single-file lines down the gentle slope toward their home.

The individuals who stayed at the border with Kayla and me were her Guardian friends, the Lords and Ladies of the noble Overland households, Baobi, Tula, and my bride-to-be Moli. Meanwhile, the Samaria Troops formed two lines to the north.

The Monkey elder came forward and sat back on his haunches. "Are you ready, my king?"

I nodded and took five strides backward from Kayla's side. In turn, she turned north and took five strides forward as both of our entourages gave us space.

Baobi raised his wrinkled hands toward the sky. "One for the dawn. One for midday. One for the evening. As foretold, passed down from one king to the next, each great family of the Masana Territory pledged this promise."

As he spoke, we sibling rulers of our separate lands walked in a circle, never breaking eye contact as we repeatedly crossed and left the borders of our home.

"May we trust. May we respect. May we prosper," Baobi finished, placing his hand over his heart, and bowed his head.

Kayla took out her Sword of Elaiobus and turned south while I turned north. I roared alongside her mighty cry. The crowds erupted with thrilled cheers of glory to each Territory and our official alliance.

I turned around and saw my sister smile at me over her shoulder. With the ceremony over, I pushed up off the ground with my front paws. Kayla's eyes sparkled as my point of view rose and passed hers. She was looking up at me when I had fully transformed. There I stood on my hind legs, regally dressed in unexplainable robes and jewels inspired by the blues and golds of our kingdoms. I held out my arms, and my surprised sister rushed in to give me a hug.

"Oh, Brother! You can change into your Furless form without me?"

"I feel we always could." I smiled and let her go. "You were always nearby back then, and we wanted to be there for you." I turned us both to face the Overland. "The world is changing, but Johari will always be here. I'm proud of you."

"You too." She squeezed my paw. "I'm not sure what to do first."

I chuckled. "How exciting."

KAYLA – 9 YEARS

"HOPE YOU'RE TAKING notes, Jared," I mumbled.

The wizard adjusted his cloak and discreetly leaned over. "Probably should."

Seated upon the uncomfortable marble throne, a turtle could go faster than the afternoon session with my events planner. He rambled with excitement about my Coronation as if it were days rather than weeks away. I didn't want to appear rude, squirming in my chair, so I focused on the three shiny rings on his fingers, the yellow diamond tattoos peeking around his left wrist like a bracelet, to the many bright colors on his tunic, half-paying attention. The tall man also wore a feathered hat upon his copper-black coiled hair framing his friendly face and green eyes.

At my limit, I looked at Jared in a plea for a break, hoping the wizard could help me.

My friend gave a quick nod and raised his hand. "Thank you, Sir Emil Haley. It is sure to be a great event under your supervision."

The planner gave a giant smile and bowed with such flourish I almost ducked behind my hand in embarrassment.

I'm still not used to that...

"Thank you, your highness Saqui. I look forward to designing your dress," he said, bowed, then strutted away. His heeled boots clicked with each of his steps crossing the floor.

Once he left the room, I jumped out of my seat. "Oof, finally." I stretched my arms over my head. "Thank you for the rescue."

Jared nodded. "Yes, the Ladies of Shellfore's cousin has much to say, but I am sure he means well."

"Right." I yawned. "Thanks for reminding me. I'm still memorizing the noble family lines in History, but I like him. He's nice."

"You saw Sir Haley's yellow diamonds on his arm. Have you learned all about the townspeople's marks yet?"

"The colorful shapes everybody has—who has what and why—are confusing, but I'm working on that, too." I smoothed out my soft blue skirt. "They aren't magical, right?"

"No, but Lord Quild had explained to me such was regained when you claimed your throne."

I sucked the air between my teeth. "Yeesh, yeah, no pressure." I exhaled and relaxed my shoulders. "One handshake and everyone went from looking like paper to having color—like finishing my drawings in Art."

"A curse broken, to be precise. Remember, you—"

"'Am the Saqui,'" I quoted. "I know, Jared, heh, I get it."

He gave a rare grin. "There is much to learn, but I know you will do your best. Now, may I be excused?"

I folded my arms. "Oh, stop. You know you don't need my permission."

Jared chuckled before he bowed then left, leaving me alone.

"Your highness?"

So much for a break...I just want to go on a walk...

"A-Ah, y-yes?" I spun around to face the questioner.

Her green eyes were unwavering. She bustled into the room straight toward me on a mission: my teacher, Miss Amelia Wanda.

Here we go again...

Small, turquoise stars marked her earlobes as she tucked her graying, brown hair behind them. "Forgive me, your highness, for startling you, but I require your presence for another lesson. It cannot wait."

I walked down the steps in front of the throne toward her. "Really? We went through all your lessons. You said we were done for the day."

My tutor clasped her hands behind her. "Yes, we have gone over your daily civics, reading, writing, and etiquette."

And speaking lessons and dressing lessons and history lessons...

"However, this is special and urgent. Until you formally create your Court"—Miss Wanda's muted-green skirts swooshed when she turned and walked away—"please, follow me."

I suppressed my grumbles and trudged along. Although she wanted to help, the speed Miss Wanda insisted on doing things drove me nuts. I missed talking and eating with my friends. Often, my head would hurt after a long day. Most days, there was no time or energy to go on a walk or even practice my magic with Jared.

Miss Wanda opened the polished doors which connected the throne room to the ballroom. An enormous, sparkling chandelier hung from the high ceiling. The floor made of gold and brown marble swirled together across the vast space. Across from the ballroom entrance, a flowing white curtain blocked off the wide balcony. The castle's second throne was off to the right, made of carved honey oak with comfy golden cushions and positioned before the kingdom's flag.

The deep blue fabric hung from the ceiling to the floor, bearing gray and snow white pictures matching my arm tattoo. Close to the roof was a male lion's head with a peaceful face. He wore a wreath of silver feathers on his embroidered head while an animal heart nestled within his mane under his chin. The pommel of a hilt appeared halfway in front of the heart, covered in silver stones. The white sword's blade went straight and narrow to the end of the flag.

Not at all freaky, Lady Annika...made before I got here...

"Your highness? Your highness," said Miss Wanda, poised beside me.

I straightened up right away. "Y-Yes?"

"It is time you learn what is known as the waltz."

Are...you serious?

Typical. I bit my lip, annoyed by Amelia's eagerness, all worked up over something so small. She pointed to a quartet of violinists walking into the room, followed by a familiar face.

I stepped forward. "L—"

"Oh, good. Over here," Miss Wanda waved.

Lute's freckled face lit up when he saw me. He walked over faster and hugged me without so much as a hello, ignoring Miss Wanda's protests.

I returned my friend's hug with a big smile. "Hello!"

"It's been two weeks since the Two Kingdom Alliance with the Masana Territory," Lute said and lifted me in the air a little. "Because I kept missing a chance to talk to you, I grabbed this opportunity."

"Oh, gosh," I chuckled.

"Sir Lute Gibe, honestly, I summoned you here to practice, not dilly dally," Miss Wanda huffed, folding her arms.

Lute set me back down. "Yeah, yeah...ready to dance?"

"Guess so?" I shrugged.

The now-seated violinists began their boring piece. The kind of boredom that made me sleepy. However, here we were.

"One, two, three and one, two, three—your majesty, let him lead, not you," Miss Wanda instructed. "Sir Lute, put your hand gently on the side of her waist, not flat on the middle of her back."

Lute's sly imitations of our teacher kept me from going berserk. Silently mocking her words with such funny expressions I once snorted, trying not to laugh aloud. Fortunately, Miss Wanda never caught on while our practice continued until there was barely any sunlight left in the windows.

"Is she always like this?" Lute whispered after Miss Wanda left.

"I thought she'd never wrap it up." I plopped to the ground in dramatic woe. "My poor feet...."

"Pfft~ relax, you're fine." He offered his hand. "To dinner?"

I giggled and took his offer. "You mean together?"

The doctor-in-training grinned. "Right? It's been too long, and the three of us miss hanging out."

"By the way, I didn't know you could dance," I said as we left the ballroom.

"Ha, you saw me. I was as bad as you were."

I laughed. "Bet Miss Wanda is kicking herself over picking you to dance with me." I joked as we made our way across the throne room. "You have, as Amelia put it, two-left feet, goofball."

Lute pulled the dining hall doors open. "Oi, just cuz you haven't grown taller these past couple of months, don't get on my case about my growth spurt."

I put my hand on my cheek in mock outrage. "How dare you?" Yet I broke out giggling.

"Oh? What's this?"

I jumped around. "Jacques! Hello!"

Lute gripped his chest. "Oi! Let's not sneak up like that."

8

Our friend smirked and pulled off his riding gloves, revealing his calloused, brown fingers. "Not my fault ya two weren't payin' attention." He shook his head and opened his arms to me.

"How was your day?" I gave him a quick hug.

Jacques let me go. "It's been long so far, but good."

We headed for the other side of the long room while servants finished setting up our meal of assorted bread, drinks, cheeses, and fruits.

"Is that all?" I asked.

"I'm serious. It hasn't been at all eventful," said Jacques. "Just more trainin'."

"Bet Jacky is tired of eating in the barracks," Lute joked.

Jacques pulled out a seat for me, but not before he rolled his pale blue eyes.

I took the offered chair. "I mean to make the food better soon and hope it's not too terrible, for now."

Lute took a seat on my right and shot an all-knowing grin, resting both hands under his chin and elbows on the table. "Might want to improve the recruitment list too."

Jacques glared at Lute for a moment, unhooking his sword from his hip, then hung the sheath's loop on the post of his chair on my left. "Can-it. We don't need a lot of people."

My friend leaned back and continued grinning despite Jacques' warning. "Yet the cases I've seen in the hospital, oh boy." Lute then whistled.

"Oh, jeez." I shook my head, unable to stop smiling.

"Be assured training our recruits is not hard for our captain to manage," Jared encouraged, strolling in.

"Ah, there you are." I waved. "How are you, Jared?"

He bowed his head in greeting, and took a seat next to me across from Lute. "I am doing fine, thank you." He took his napkin off the table. "Lord Blackfrost sends his regards."

"And how is he?" I unfolded my napkin in turn.

Jared passed a basket of bread to me. "He and his lady are looking forward to helping with the Coronation details with Sir Haley. Otherwise, all is well."

I took a piece of bread and passed the side dish to Lute. "Okay, good to hear—sorry, Jacques, has training been hard?"

He set his gloves aside on the table. "Well, I'd say, yeah, the recruits now squires are above idiocy but are clumsy. Fortunately, a fair number are from my old desert home, so not much to teach there. How to fulfill the duties of a guard shouldn't be too hard in general."

I helped myself to some sliced cheese. "I'm glad."

Our silence gave way to quiet eating.

Lute set his cup down. "We barely get together as is...is it bad I was hoping for more to talk about?"

"Besides saying it's been busy?" I looked up from my plate. "Ever since coming to the castle, it's been non-stop lessons before my Coronation in a few weeks."

Jacques laughed. "Silly. Ya can take a break."

Lute tore some bread. "I understand, though. We all got caught up in the castle life."

"Yes," I said as a servant refilled my cup. "But, the four of us should eat together more often. I miss you guys. Between all the lessons and planning, it's been hard. At least we have the Light Festival in the next dry season—when it's *supposed* to happen."

Jared nodded. "Of course, we had celebrated early this spring, didn't we?"

"Yeah...all growin' pains."

"Come now," said Jared. "It cannot be all bad, Jacques."

The captain swallowed his last bite of bread. "Right, nothin' but major adjustments. My problem lies with us bein' taken by the seat of our pants the moment we arrived here, asked to perform what the emblems of our uniforms suggest. Lute? Town doctor-to-be. Jared? Meet the Castle Advisor and a Warden of Magic. Me? Not a single lord or lady gave a second thought. Nope. I could have wanted to be a horse trainer, but, no, no, no, solely Militia as if ya call a bumblin' thirty soldiers an army. Kinda limitin', don't ya think? We used to have choices, but now it's about meetin' the town's expectations."

"W-Well," I coughed, feeling awkward. "Yes, I would love to visit the Masana someday."

Jacques winced and shifted in his seat. "Oh, yeah...sorry, Kayla, I'm sure we will be able to."

I smiled and leaned forward to pick up my cup. "It's fine. Do you do anything after your duties? Do you want to be a horse trainer?"

Jacques wiped his mouth with his napkin. "Yes to the first, no to the second. It was just an example. I've been workin' on my calligraphy under Lady Blackfrost."

"Interesting. Can I ask why?" I asked.

"Want to write my own story, my tale, considerin' I'm already a part of the Folk-kin's grand plan."

Jared set down his cup. "You speak as if the diary is our puppet master. You know it is not. It is—"

"'It is what it is'?" I cleared my throat. "I hear that a lot. Sometimes, that feels a bit—"

"Convenient," Jacques finished and rubbed his temples.

Jared picked up his fork. "Are you alright?"

"Hgn~ yeah...peachy..."

"Hope it's not a migraine," said Lute. "That said, and don't take this the wrong way, but—"

Jacques looked up from his lap, still wincing from a sudden headache. "Won't, as long as yar not rude about it this time."

Lute flinched. "You know I already said I was sorry."

I looked between the two. "What's wrong?"

Jacques broke away from staring Lute down and cleared his throat. "N-No, sorry, don't worry. Anyway, my steed Avon continues to like his carrots and daily rides. Horse trainin' I'll leave to my former right-hand man, Leal Valen. Remember him from the days back in the Ridge Desert? Yeah. Also, I've been pullin' books from the royal library when there's time."

I smiled. "Let me know if there are stories you like." I turned to Lute. "And you?"

He set his napkin down. "I've been studying under Lord Quild's aunt, Doctor Balfor, between my helping at the hospital and here."

"She's the one with a long yellow braid, right?" Jacques asked. "Didn't the doctor once wrestle an ox to the ground?"

Lute snorted with a grin. "Pfft, heh, yes, the one and only. Her husband runs a farm. She's a kind woman, but she isn't shy from giving me plenty of books to study."

"Reading," Jared said before I made a peep. "There will always be matters and subjects to brush up on."

I just about threw my napkin. "Jeez, by all that I am, study, read, study, read. How *have* we become so boring?"

Jacques chuckled. "Like I said, growin' pains."

After parting ways, I went upstairs, changed into a nightgown, and went to the small balcony to gaze at the stars. The view was nice, but a hill interrupted the sky, and blocked the moon.

I miss Johari...I miss home...

"It's all changing," I sighed, left my balcony with its disappointing view, and crawled into bed to sleep.

KAYLA – 12 YEARS

"PARDON, YOUR MAJESTY?"

I did a double-take when I looked up from the Folk-kin as an individual appearing like Xenos showed up at the doorway.

"O-Oh, come in," I closed the diary and sat up straight, still in bed.

"Did I startle you?"

I shook my head. "N-No! Well. A little. It's just, seeing so many who dress and look alike in town are...um...."

"Jarring?"

"Yes, I suppose, when you don't understand why."

They nodded. "I see."

"I remember you're the same R.M.N. who checked up on me before the attack at the castle."

"Really?" They scratched an itch on their cheek. "That's astonishing."

I tilted my head to the side. "Is it? Between you and Xenos, you have different scars on your hands. Xenos doesn't—are you okay?"

They startled back, correcting their posture. "Y-Yes, miss."

"Did I upset you? You looked sad."

"Not intentionally, for you were not made aware we who look alike find happiness in being so, your majesty."

I blushed. "Ah, sorry. I'll be more mindful."

"There is no need to apologize, but thank you."

"Okay...Are you here to take me home?" I pushed back the bed covers.

They cleared their voice and recomposed themselves before taking a step forward. "H-Home? Ahem, no, your majesty, I was asked to check on you upon the hour. Sir Lute wanted to make sure you were rest—ah...ahem...."

One look from me, and they stopped.

I relaxed my deadpan into a smile. "Yeah, Lute means well, but I've been stuck in bed too much." I stood and walked to them. "Please take me to the castle."

They didn't budge from the doorway. "But—"

I folded my arms. "I'm starving. It's dinnertime, right?"

"Yes, but—"

"I'll go back, rest, and wait for food here instead *if* you tell me your name already."

"You know why I won't, your majesty."

"Officially calling shenanigans." I put my hands on my hips. "Everyone else introduced themselves when I first woke up. You can too."

With a short nod, the attendant cleared their throat. "Vaerin."

I smiled, ignoring the brief twinge in the back of my head. "Thank you. Can you please take me home?"

"Answer this first, your majesty. Do you know what the town looks like yet? As in, remember where your favorite pastry store is, for example?"

"Er, no?"

"Then I request, insist, you keep your head down as we ride home. For your safety."

"What? Why?"

"Spoilers. Introductions are one thing, but Jared made it quite clear to keep your remembering as sequential as possible."

I huffed a sigh. "Fine. Cover my head, and let's go."

Vaerin stepped away from my exit. "Very well. Your bedroom in the castle is still under the rubble, so I'll take you to the courtroom."

I snapped my fingers, transforming my hospital wear into a simple dress and boots as I walked past. "Yes, let's go, please."

KAYLA – 9 YEARS

A FAINT GLOW OF SUNLIGHT shone into my room when I woke up with a plan. I needed to get out. Fresh air, the sun, I **had** to get out.

Once dressed in a simple, light blue dress with long sleeves and a green cloak, I hurried, afraid Miss Wanda would come to my room any minute.

After I grabbed a leather pouch of coins, I materialized a rope tied to my balcony with a snap of my fingers and slid down.

My heart was pounding in my ears from the thrill. I put the large hood over my head as I rushed around the outside of the castle, picking up an unattended basket with plucked flowers along the way. A man and a woman at their posts dressed in light armor stood at the open front gates.

"On a trip, milady?" he asked.

I nodded yes, keeping my head low, intending to look shy. "Going to the hospital with these."

His partner stepped to the side. "Very good, milady, have fun."

That was easy...too easy.

Questions like "Can they tell who I am?" or "Did I not need permission to leave?" ran across my mind. Walking through the gate, I struggled keeping it cool and not sprint forward like a thief.

"Do send my regards to Sir Lute, milady!" a robust voice called after me.

I turned around and saw two plain faces with large smiles. Both guards waved at me like I had made their day already.

Oof...they do, don't they...well, let's see how long my freedom lasts.

I bashfully set the basket alongside the road as the two chuckled and skipped-ran toward the village, more than ready for fresh air.

Rows of small wooden homes stood on either side of the dirt road with blue-gray shingles and little windowsill gardens of all sorts of blossoms. The day had begun, yet the smell of freshly baked treats hanging in the air was already mouthwatering while the buzzing of chatter to the sawing of wood filled my ears.

I made my way among the townspeople, surrounded by all shapes and sizes. Women carried baskets of supplies, men with tools or wood in their hands, and kids laughed, played catch, or weaved between the adults and food carts in a game of tag.

"Hello, my lady!"

I stopped and waved. "Hello, how are you?"

A young woman with sparkling green eyes stood on her doorstep. She pushed a few of her many thin black braids off her shoulder before she pulled her beaded shawl around her. "I'm well, thank you. It's a lovely day."

I nodded. "Yes, it is—"

"Greetings, maladies!"

A round man with red triangles on his tan forearms and a bushy, maple-brown beard gave us a friendly smile, tipped his straw hat, and continued onward with a large sack of flour over his shoulder.

"Hello, sir—"

"Oh! My lady, how are you?" A young woman with freckles and dark honey hair waved from behind a cart of apples. "Would you like one?" she asked, holding up a big red one.

"Sure—"

"Greetings, milady!"

Wow...it's a lot to take in...

After the fifth or sixth hello, I pulled my hood down, waved goodbye to the lady on the doorstep, and continued my walk. While meeting others as I took in the sights, I blushed with excitement. Smiling, my fear of getting away with it shrunk to me regretting nothing.

"My lady, are you hungry?!"

A cheery woman with a clean apron over her clothes waved while standing under the wooden sign of our village tavern.

I smiled and walked toward her. "Starving. Do you have buttered rolls and milk?"

Her three bright purple lines rose with her eyebrows as she pulled out a chair to an outside table. "Absolutely."

I sat and offered a coin. "I'll take some, please."

"Right away, milady."

While I ate alone, a handful of kids ran around the village's small fountain in the middle of the square. Like the adults, they had different, colorful shapes on their necks, arms, or faces. The kids looked like they were playing tag. Once in a while, a kid stuck their hand into the falling streams and splashed their laughing playmates.

Eagerly scampering among them was one of the few dogs Jacques' band of former Outlaws—along with their horses and few cats—brought over from their abandoned camp in the Ridge Dessert. The playful, slobbering mutt with shaggy brown and white fur often barked, and the dog's tail thumped and wagged to all the pets and treats.

As I finished eating, a little boy about five waved at me. He jogged over with his smile, missing a front tooth. Once beside my table, a bright green swirl on his sweaty forehead peeked out from under his carroty bangs.

"Hello." He lifted his hand, opened it to reveal a small violet flower and offered it to me.

I smiled in return and took the blossom. "Thank you."

"Would you like to play with us?"

The kind boy and others behind him all smiled as they waved me on to come to take a splash. I grinned, took off my cloak, and got right in.

We all screamed, laughed, and carried on without a care. I was happy to make friends. However, the fun drew to an abrupt close when I recognized one of Jacques' recruits, going by in their warm gray uniform, was trying to get my attention from back across the square. I glanced at the sky—the sun was well past its highest point.

Oh, come on...I'm not ready to leave!

Looking away from the recruit to find a place to hide in the crowd, shouting and frantic neighing erupted behind me.

I whipped back around. The horrified squire's spooked horse galloped toward the fountain, ignoring its rider pulling its reins.

The other kids ran. I bolted to stand in front of the horse and held up my hands.

"YIELD!"

The steed reared back mere feet away, landed, and turned itself around in a circle, huffing and counting with its hoof.

I stepped forward and took hold of the horse's muzzle. "Easy! Easy...e~asy..." I stroked the horse's face. "Embarrassed too, I see, it's okay...."

"Y-Your highness!" the soldier declared and dismounted. "Is everyone alright?"

My continued petting of the horse helped calm my nerves, and shaky knees. "I-I think so. But please, *why* were you rushing?"

He bowed his head. "Many pardons, your highness. Pranksters from behind spooked my horse—"

"You're too loud," I hushed.

"S-Sorry, milady."

"No worries. Please, what's your name?"

He ruffled his wispy blond hair over his right ear and wrinkled his freckled nose. "F-Fletch, Fletch Kirst, milady."

"Okay, Fletch, why are you here?"

"I-It's Lady Wanda. She insisted we find you, your highness Saqui."

"I see."

I looked from side to side. People around us bowed their heads. "Everyone, please. It's just me."

Many looked up while others laughed, nervous. Eventually, all appeared to relax.

"Mil'dee, do you have to go already?" an eager girl asked. "Could you tell us a story about the Masana?"

The next thing I knew, the request encouraged the rest of the kids to beg for a story too.

I looked at the squire and shrugged. "Would Miss Wanda be upset, Fletch? Do I need to go right now?"

He fiddled with the reins. "D-Don't believe so."

I smiled and moved to sit on a bench. "Then, let's stay a bit."

Other kids soon sat around me, on the ground, or next to me while some adults stood behind them. At first a little shy, but I relaxed as I shared about the Masana Territory. I spoke of its culture and tried describing the shapeshifting appearances to those younger than me. Finally, I told how Basi and I became family.

It turned into a question-and-answer time rather than a storytime. The sky was dim, and I was hungry when Fletch and I walked with the kids to the palace gate.

"Thank you, mil'dee," they shouted, waving. "Goodbye!"

I waved back with a smile, entered the castle doors, and idled in the small foyer while the doors closed behind me.

Maybe...if I run really fast, I can reach my room unnoticed?

Upon the thought, however, Jacques came around the corner.

"There ya are."

I raised my hands in surrender. "Look, Jacques, don't blame Fletch. I needed to get out for a bit, okay?"

Jacques shrugged. "Wasn't gonna say anythin', but—"

"Oh, no..." I rolled my eyes, and my shoulders sank.

My captain pointed with his thumb over his shoulder. "She's waitin' in the throne room, ya know. Nice try, but ya shouldn't stall."

"Miss Wanda always expects me there whenever she wants," I groaned. "I don't want to be with her today."

Jacques folded his arms. "Better now than later. By this time, ya missed—"

"Nothing." I turned my back to the entrance to the throne room. "It's always the same boring stuff. How to eat, how to dress, and to talk," I hissed as I pointed in my tutor's direction. "She needs to drop it."

"Hey now, when it's all official, ya can walk the walk all ya like. But give her a break. She's got a lot on her plate to get ya lookin' and actin' the part."

I let my head drop forward and sighed. "Being royalty isn't new for me."

Jacques scratched his chin. "Uh~ don't think I need to tell ya Masana royalty has different conduct than Overland royalty."

I pursed my lips. "Oh? Care to explain?"

Jacques rolled his eyes. "Ya know what? Just go."

With a firm push from behind, I was in the throne room before I knew it. Miss Wanda was standing there before the empty, gilded chair as usual.

"And be nice," Jacques whispered before taking a sidestep to the right and exiting upstairs with a short wave goodbye.

Miss Wanda stepped forward the moment I was halfway there and curtsied. "Your highness, where have you been?"

I tucked my hair behind my ears. "Out. I had fun today and want to go out tomorrow. No, wait, I'll be busy."

She nodded. "Yes, you will be. We have a lot to learn."

I stopped beside her. "What exactly?"

My tutor rambled a long list of topics I'd never heard of before.

Okay. That's it...

"No."

"W-What?" Miss Wanda stuttered.

I took a deep breath. "Look. I tried. But I'm going crazy at your speed. And I don't like being treated like I'm slow."

My tutor knitted her brow. "Now see here—"

"*Please*! I'm fine with learning and getting ready for important parties and things, but this cheetah speed of yours needs to stop." I held out my arms. "I feel stupid because I can't keep up."

Miss Wanda took a step back. "Th-That was not my intention."

"I'll still be learning after I'm queen, right? It's too fast and too much." I pressed my hands together. "Please, slow down?"

She stared at me in silence for several moments before she nodded. "While your teacher, I have to meet your needs. As one of the Overland, I recognize you're upset and understand, my lady Saqui." She pulled back her shoulders. "I will work to slow down the pace."

I sighed. "Thank you...also, I'd like to sleep in tomorrow morning and not get up at a silly early hour."

"Like you did today?" Miss Wanda replied, raising an eyebrow.

"Yeah...wait, was that sarcasm?"

She shrugged with a small smile in reply, turned, and walked away.

KAYLA – 12 YEARS

"ARE YOU SERIOUS?!"

I halted my jumping jacks and slapped my hand over my heart. "Ah! Lute, you scared me."

He waved a dismissive hand and folded his arms. "First, you returned to the castle with Vaerin's help yesterday, and now you're back in the courtroom this morning rather than resting? Why won't you listen to me?"

"Meh, I'm restless, okay? I need to keep going, plus Jacques and Jared are still not back. Besides, I slept in already, no lie." I gestured to Miss Wanda to my right. "Since I can't sit still, she's been reading for me."

Lute looked at Amelia on his right. "You? You're okay with Kayla doing this?"

Miss Wanda folded her hands upon the table. "Her majesty wants to get healthy. Seeing her up and well is the best thing I've seen in a long time."

"Uh-huh," Lute deadpanned and returned to me. "I searched all over the castle, too, you know."

"Then you should know her majesty's bedroom is still under the rubble," Miss Wanda reminded.

Lute's head fell forward. "Crud, I forgot. Still, Kayla, it's been a week since you came back to us. Don't overdo it."

I began wall pushups by the door. "Fair, but I should keep going to help our friend. I don't believe Xenos took those pages to become our enemy."

"What makes you say that?" Lute asked.

"I told Miss Wanda about the pages, that Xenos turned feral, with no warning. Don't remember much, but we have to find out why."

"Okay, but—"

I stopped to stretch. "I felt useless in the last battle. Gotta start somewhere." I returned to my exercise.

"Sure, with rest—"

"Sir Lute?" Amelia asked.

"Yes?"

"Xenos took the blame for her majesty losing her memories from the start. So, why would our friend steal pages to stop her from remembering? Something is amiss, so her majesty wants to be as prepared as possible."

"Still, " said Lute. "Kayla isn't alone. It's not like Jared, Jacques, and I haven't been trying to figure out motives too."

"How is that going?" Miss Wanda asked.

"Hm, Jacques is out with a search party while Jared has taken off to Annika's place."

"Then, surely, your fellow Guardians will return with news when they have some," Miss Wanda continued. "Nothing can be done until Xenos is found, or Jacques returns with his report. So, for now, I will read for her majesty."

Lute shook his head. "Naw, Amelia, I'll take over, and we can take turns. No matter how we look at it, we're not safe yet."

I stopped and turned around, stretching my arms.

"Very well," said Miss Wanda, rising from her seat. "I will check on castle repairs."

Lute took her spot. "Sounds good, and thanks."

"Yes, thank you for reading," I said as she curtsied.

Miss Wanda brought her hands together before her stomach. "My pleasure. I will return with snacks later."

"Thank you," I looked at Lute while Miss Wanda left the room. "You okay?"

"What now?" he asked. "You expect me to read with sword clanging? I think not."

I shook my head. "No weapons, just exercise."

Lute sighed. "Annika likes leaving things to you often, huh?"

"Let's hope she's okay. Haven't seen her since the attack on the castle."

Lute knitted his brow and gave a steely sideways glance. "Still, Jared can easily heal most things."

I rolled my eyes. "She could *also* be looking into something about Xenos. Let's not be mean."

He picked up the diary left open on the table. "Sorry, I wasn't trying to be. It gets old."

KAYLA – 9 YEARS

"YOUR HIGHNESS, YOU have to meet with the dressmakers for your gown," said Miss Wanda.

Like I haven't been busy these past two weeks...

As the main event came closer, the more sleep I found myself losing. This morning, Miss Wanda practically dragged me out of bed. While I stood there, yawning, those around me all talked at once, holding up bolts of colorful cloth. I tried not to nod off, yet they never spoke to me until Sir Haley clapped his hands to get everybody's attention and be silent.

"What is your age?" he asked with a gentle smile.

"Nine," I yawned.

All gasped. Tall for my age, I looked older, I guess. The tailors raced around me, begging for new cloth while describing a new kind of lace, and kept holding up a cord to make knots to mark their measurements.

Seriously...I could whip this up faster myself. Why won't they let me?

The answer? They wanted to make it. What was I to do? I didn't want to be rude.

I wonder...if Basi hates to be fussed over, too?

By the end, we made most of the decisions for my outfit. What I chose from Sir Haley's provided options; my gown would be violet with—and I quote—"a scoop neckline, minimal beading, including a scalloped skirt hem."

Thankfully there wasn't anything crazy, and Emil was still thinking about the sleeves. Eventually, I insisted on straight sleeves to my elbows, no poof.

"I like it simple."

Finally given a break, I decided getting some fresh air and visit my horse Starlight. I left all the mad chatter about my dress and walked to the stables.

There, my white filly munched on feed and appeared freshly brushed. I reached to pet the side of Starlight's neck when familiar voices made noise out on the nearby training grounds. Following the clangs, knocks, and shouts, I discovered my three Guardians had begun sparring outside on the patchy field.

To my right, Tomas Valen, a burly man in a green tunic with rolled-up sleeves and gray trousers, walked by carrying spare swords in his thick hairy arms.

He saw me and stopped. "Yar highness, welcome. Are ya here to watch?"

"Hello, Quartermaster, I am," I greeted and pointed to Jacques. "He and Lute seem to be having fun."

"Fun ya say—*achoo*!" He turned right before sneezing and returned, wiggling his thick, black mustache under his large nose.

"Bless you."

Tomas sniffed. "Thank you and pardon, yar highness, but this is grand to hear. The Fates dealt the captain a tricky hand, ya see."

"A tricky hand?"

"Challenges. But, back at the Ridge Desert, he trained and worked hard to be happy with himself as well as his skills. I'm pleased to know a Volt is smilin' again."

"Was he not at home? Smiling, I mean."

Jacques parried with Lute's training sword, and the observing hazel-green eyes wrinkled, happy. "Not like today."

"You know." I tilted my head to the side. "The Ridge Desert. I'd like to learn more about how all of you started living there."

"Ah, well, our history is a long tale. In short, however, we weren't always branded as 'Bandits'. An age ago, we were sent away when we refused to help the Saqui before ya. Sent away and made to forget who we were and were a part of."

I almost let my jaw drop. "I see...but I'm glad Captain Jacques' village is here now."

"Likewise, miss."

"How is Leal?"

"Ah, my cousin is doin' well. He misses the desert oasis, as many us do, but we're settlin' here in town just nicely. Last I heard, the big man was off to gather lumber for some repairs."

"That's great." I looked at the weapons. "I've kept you. Can I help?"

"Oh, no. I'm good, miss. Thank you, but I better be off."

"Alright. See you later."

Tomas smiled and left for the armory.

"GO!" Jared shouted.

The exercise was two versus one. I leaned against the fence right when the wizard's personal shield around him vanished. Jacques charged from the opposite side of the yard with his practice longsword in hand. Lute rushed ahead, took out his quarterstaff from his leg holster, and whipped the magical weapon into its full length.

The boys leaped into the air, about to strike.

The shield respawned around the wizard in a blink of an eye and knocked both boys to the ground in their dirty, padded suits.

"Too slow," said Jared.

"Oi, then you're counting too fast." Lute sat up from the ground. "This is impossible."

Jacques rose to his feet and helped Lute up. "That's the point. Sharpens the reflexes." He looked my way. "Ah, let's take a break, guys."

Lute followed Jacques' pointing finger, and he waved to me.

I waved back and came forward. "Hello."

Jacques sheathed his blade while Lute tapped the end of his quarterstaff onto the ground three times. The magical weapon collapsed into a smaller cylinder, and Lute stored it in his leg holster.

Jared walked closer. "How was Sir Haley today?"

I shrugged and grinned. "He's the same as always. Happy to help and excited about the dress. We're on a break, too, but I have to go back soon."

"That reminds me," said Jacques. "We need to schedule yar practice, Kayla. Hate for yar skills to rust, as it were."

"If you want to help me convince Miss Wanda, that'd be great."

He chuckled. "Okay, I will."

Jared returned his sword to Jacques. "I recommend restarting after the Coronation. That said"—he looked at me—"what will your dress look like once finished?"

"Not too fancy, thankfully. And I hope I'm not wearing anything heavy on top."

ASHLEY SCHELLER

"You might, though," Jared warned. "Overheard Miss Wanda insist to Sir Haley it was a ceremonial tradition to wear a cloak."

I rolled my eyes. "Shoot."

The next day? Pretty much the same. There was no end to the decisions about my Coronation. Sir Haley's helpers came to me for tablecloth color, flowers, and vases to put the flowers in, followed by what kind of lanterns for the ballroom's great balcony, and so on.

That afternoon it was time for rehearsal in the great hall at the back of the castle. Practicing my speech with Miss Wanda, the eager team bustled around the ceremonial area. Some carried huge, glossy vases carved from wood and placed them at each corner of the gray stone room, ready for fresh bouquets. Some were hanging white and blue cloth streamers along the left and right sidewalls between the narrow, arched windows. Last but not least, others were pushing and dragging long wooden benches to create a long aisle for my procession.

"Clearer, your highness, and project more, please," Miss Wanda would say over and over.

On the opposite side of the great doors I entered, was a low-rise platform decorated with more vases. When the big day came, I would walk up the few steps onto the stage where a removable stone pedestal waited for me to place my Imogen-Kythe, the Folk-kin diary, onto it and give my *Speech of Intent*. Afterward, Lord Blackfrost would crown me to conclude the ceremony.

Even if it was a repetitive lesson, it was a speech. I could never have enough practice, the idea of being in front of a large group made me nervous.

Why...am I so scared?

I inwardly shook my head.

No, I can do this...

The night before the big day, I paced back and forth in my bedroom.

"I am fine...don't worry about it. I'm fine."

There was a knock on the door.

I ran my hands through my hair. "What is it?"

"Your brother and his wife are here, my lady," a guardsman informed.

I rushed to open my door, revealing Basi and Moli standing tall, healthy, and strong. Both dressed in gold and blue regalia, necklaces of golden chains and multi-colored beads hung around their necks with matching bracelets.

I squeezed Basi around his waist. "Brother, you made it!"

He gave a hearty chuckle, returning my hug. "Wouldn't miss it. Sir Gibe and Captain Volt say hello from downstairs. They had duties to get to."

"Good." My smile faultered. "But, I'm sorry I didn't greet you with them."

"Actually, I'm happy we got to surprise you," said Moli. "We miss you."

I stepped back and took Basi's paw in my left hand and took Moli's paw in my right. "I know we visited on your wedding day last month, but between all my lessons, it feels like it's been forever."

My brother pushed his blown-out mane by his ears and chuckled. "Well, you have been busy. I'm sure you were never bored."

I let my head fall forward. "No, but tired."

"Heh, then this news will cheer you up," said Basi.

"Oh?" I looked up right when he and Moli exchanged an endearing look.

My friend beamed and fiddled with the end of one of her many long braids. "It's good news, but let's keep this between us."

I leaned forward. "Do tell," I whispered.

She smiled and gently placed her free paw on her stomach. "I'm pregnant."

"O~h," I squealed and covered my mouth with my hands. "Ahem...Congratulations."

Moli's long whiskers twitched with her smile. "Te he, thank you, my friend."

"Of course. Since it's late, let me show you to your room."

"Is it outside?" Basi asked.

I winced. "Ah, I knew you would want that. Miss Wanda insisted royal guests have their quarters but...sorry."

"Now, now, none of that," said Basi. "What would you like to do?"

"Would you prefer the gardens?"

Both my brother and his wife nodded.

"Then that's what my family will have. Follow me."

We chatted up a storm as I led the way to where my family would rest. They were pleased and gave me the best of luck.

I rubbed the back of my neck. "Thanks! I'll need it."

"You'll do fine, Sis," Basi encouraged. "Our parents would be so proud of you."

"Thanks, and you too. Moli, may I have your help tomorrow? I'm still nervous and would love to have a friend with me as I get ready."

She smiled. "Of course."

—⧪⧪⧪—

THE CASTLE WAS FILLING up with guests ever since lunchtime the following day. I mumbled my speech to myself in my room while I dressed.

"This is lovely," said Moli, tying a golden rope around my waist.

Beaming, I touched my collar. "My favorite part is the beaded lace. Here, I'll help you tighten the knot."

I put on my golden lion pendant to finish my look while my friend placed a white rose in my hair.

"Perfect," said Miss Wanda as I gave a spin. "Now, I need to give Sir Haley the cue, so I'll meet you both at the staircase when ready, your majesties." She curtsied and headed out the door.

I turned around and gave Moli a hug. "Thank you."

"You're welcome, **Queen** Kayla," she giggled and hugged me back.

"Oh, call me Kayla, please?" I begged. "You didn't call me princess back then. This also goes for 'Your highness' or 'Saqui,' ugh, all this formal stuff makes it...weird? Ah~ I don't know."

Moli stepped back and smiled with a shrug. "Can't. Times have changed, so have our roles."

"Do you like being called 'Queen Moli' now?"

She raised her chin. "Yes."

There was a pause before we let out a giggle.

"C'mon," I said.

"You caught me"—she raised her hands in surrender—"as friends, we won't use titles."

I smiled, triumphant. "Yay."

Moli helped me fasten my long white cloak for the ceremony, but I stopped before the door.

"Kayla?"

I stepped back and sat on my bed. "No...."

"Are you all right?"

My knees went weak, and my heart was pounding. "No...I'm just nine."

Moli took a seat beside me, on my right. "Yes, you are." And she offered to hold my hand.

I took it. "T-There are kids like me, who are nine, too. They don't have to do this."

"What do you want to do?"

"I—"

The door creaked open, and Miss Wanda returned inside. "Your highness?"

"Kayla," said Moli. "It's perfectly okay. I got the jitters, too, when crowned."

I blushed.

My tutor walked over and sat on my left. "Your highness, not to inflate your ego, but this is a celebration." She held my other hand. "I encourage you to look at it this way. Do you feel you'll be alone? That you will rule alone?"

I shook my head.

"You may wear a crown, Queen Moli Roybishki may wear her crown, but what is on your head, or your duties, mean nothing without your people."

My friend nodded. "We wear it for the people."

I let go of both hands and gripped my skirt. "I'm scared and excited. I don't think I'm ready."

"Then trust and lean on those who think you are," said Miss Wanda. "We believe in you."

Moli smiled. "We both do. There's a lot to figure out, but your family, friends, we will be there and all help shape our future."

I took a deep breath and stood up when ready. "Okay."

"Miss Wanda, hold her train," said Moli. "I'll hold her hand, all right?"

I smiled. "Thank you."

After we three reached the great hall doors where everyone was waiting inside, I closed my eyes.

Don't pass out...breathe...you got this...

Despite the butterflies in my stomach, the Coronation and the party following went as smoothly as rehearsed. However, the nervous feeling wouldn't go away as many guests complimented my dress and speech while others asked about my first line of action. There were a ton of questions. Asked one after another before given a chance to answer the previous one.

The party music was pretty yet dull. I didn't feel like dancing and ended up sitting on the throne most of the time. As for my friends, well dressed in new attire, complete with black pants and embroidered tunics over white shirts? They looked great. According to his squires, the one and only inspiring Captain Jacques Volt insisted he be on duty Once in a while, I spotted his half cape over his shoulder as he took laps around the ballroom to discourage trouble. Lute, on the other hand, ate and talked with other nobles. What, I couldn't quite tell, but they laughed often.

Meanwhile, Jared's purple and silver-trimmed stole around his neck gleamed under the chandelier light. Now and again, the wizard casted a little spell, showing off to captivated lords amid their chat. My favorite was an orange-sized ball of light that danced in his hand before it disappeared into a bout of sparkles.

It was well into the night before I went onto the grand balcony. The air was warm and breezy and lightly smelled of grass and flowers from the rolling hills. I let out a long sigh and let my shoulders relax.

"I knew you'd be out here." Lute walked over and stood by the guardrail next to me. "Are you alright?"

"I think so." I looked at the stars. "Had to get out of there for a while. People were constantly in my face. It was driving me nuts."

He pulled on his high collar. "Heh, don't let your Court-to-be know."

"Talking with the noble Blackfrost, Shellfore, and Quild families are one thing. It's just, I didn't want anyone to notice or sense my nervousness, so I'm taking a break."

Lute nodded. "I think I understand. We were sort of thrown into all of this without much choice."

"Heh, does saving the world one day sound like a choice?" I asked.

"Pfft, that's my point, silly."

I huffed a laugh. "Yeah, well, why aren't all of you here?"

He shrugged. "I got the short straw—ow, heh, heh."

I had struck him on the arm but smiled. "Oh, stop, it wasn't that hard, heh. How are things at the hospital?"

"Strangely uneventful today, though if I'm not helping the nurses or hitting the books, I'm weeding the herb garden outback."

"How...fun?"

"Don't judge. Doctor Balfor believes books are great, but the tasks help teach faster."

"But, do you like it?"

"That's...hm~ you know? Yeah. I'm sore and tired often, but I like learning what I'd like to think my father knew."

"I see. If you didn't work for the doctor, what would you do instead?"

"Easy. Dance." With a grin, Lute straightened up and offered his arm. "Would you like to, your majesty Saqui?"

"Oi," I softly mocked, taking his arm. "Not you too."

We chuckled and returned to the party. Thanks to all the practice, I figured we knew the steps well enough to enjoy ourselves.

Miss Amelia Wanda, I owe you an apology...

"What are you sighing about?" Lute whispered as we made our way through the crowd.

"O-Oh, ah, sorry! I-It's nothing."

"Heh, get your head out of the clouds. Ready for some fun?"

I felt all eyes were on us, but nodded anyway.

The timing was perfect as a new music piece had begun when Lute and I reached the middle of the dance floor. Colorful skirts, clapping, smiles, and glee—any awkwardness before melted away after the first several measures. We glided, twirled, and I couldn't stop smiling by the middle of the song. Yet, the tune was over before I knew it. We curtsied, bowed in turn, and left the floor to get a drink.

Right when I took a cup, gasps of surprise rippled among the guests. I turned around. Lady Eider appeared in the middle of the ballroom in a steel gray dress with her silver-snowy hair was a mess of curls about her blue face, far from her usual glamor, but it didn't matter to me.

Smiling, I handed my drink to Lute and rushed forward before the surrounding guards could act. "Annika, I'm happy you made it!"

My mentor held out her blue hands, taking mine into hers. "Greetings and congratulations."

"Thank you. Will you be here for a while?"

Her fair smile melted away to a look of worry. "Sadly, I need to ask you to—"

"Is everything all right, Queen Kayla?" the Shellfore twins chorused.

"Oh"—I turned around—"yes, um, my Lords and Ladies and Honored Guests, this is Lady Annika Eider. I wouldn't be here without her. She's also Jared's teacher and is welcomed in the castle."

Applause erupted from the group. "Welcome, Lady Eider!"

I was happy, but she frowned. "My child, I did want to bring better tidings."

"What's going on?"

I followed her toward the throne as the music continued. There, Jared, Jacques, and Lute met with us.

"Why do I have the feelin' yar not here with glad tidin's?" Jacques asked.

With her back to the crowd, Annika waved her hands. The Folk-kin, though left in the great hall, appeared in my hands.

I jumped with a gasp and almost dropped the book. "Oh, no. No, no, no."

Splotches of bright lime green pulsed, staining the blue crystal cover.

My teacher didn't speak. Instead, she formed a triangle with her hands. A pinkish aura surrounded the book. She, next, waved the book over to float above her hands, suspending it in the air.

Lute leaned forward. "What in the world?"

Jared held his chin. "Something or somewhere is under attack."

I leaned toward the book then turned to Jared. "There's a strange, almost screaming coming from the covers." I stepped back.

"That's the Crystal itself," Annika whispered. "It's in pain."

Jacques looked over his shoulder. "Strange, I don't hear anythin'. Then again, not my book."

"Can we repair it?" Lute asked. "Save whoever or whatever is under attack?"

Jared shook his head. "Who knows? We can only save those we can."

"How long will the Folk-kin do that?" Jacques asked, turning to face the crowd.

Lady Annika shook her head. "There is no precedent, so I do not know. I will return when the Folk-kin is repaired or finished with this reaction."

With a twirl and a dusting of snow, she vanished.

My heart pounded in my chest. "I...I..."

The music stopped.

Chatter ceased.

I held my head and pinched my eyes shut.

What...do I do?

"Oi, we will take care of this together, Kayla," said Lute.

"Lords, Ladies, and Honored Guests," Jacques began, "we——"

A loud boom came through from the other side of the ballroom. I rocked around as the ground shook, following the thunderous ruckus. Lute tried to catch me, but we both landed on the floor. The rumbling of breaking stone, the smashing of pottery, and the screaming guests all made a deafening combination.

When the shaking eventually ceased, a blue light caught my attention. Mild winds blew from the orb of Jared's staff, which ushered all the smoke and dust out of the room. Forced to close my eyes, I turned my head away. After the spell finished, all the dust clouds were gone, but my vision was blurry.

"Kayla, are you all right?" Jared asked.

"Y-Yes." I coughed.

Lute took a brief look at me. "Aside from your watery, bloodshot eyes."

"Bet it's the same for you." I rubbed my eyes. "The stinging hurts."

"Oh, man." Jacques waved at us in a hurry. "H-Hey guys, ya need to see this."

I blinked until my vision cleared and looked over where a bizarre...

*What...**is** that thing?*

A large, swirling disk of blue and purple light—its size took up the hole it somehow created in the air.

Our small group and a few soldiers with drawn swords remained at the ready as all the guests fled the room, if not the castle.

"Do ya think it's the Leaf Turners?" Jacques asked.

Jared gave a rare shrug. "Your guess is as good as mine."

LUTE – 12 YEARS

A LOUD SUCKING NOISE emitted from the swirl of light before it rotated and condensed, reshaping itself with a ripple-wobble-like effect into a tall rectangle. In the middle of the new rectangle, what looked like pairs of purple hands were pushing outwards. The light bent and seemed to push back, stubborn. Next, there were frustrated, muffled cries before the light snapped like a twig. The torn rectangle flashed a blinding white before it vanished with an eerie whistle. Among the fading sound, a commotion of people had appeared.

The strangers were dirty, dressed in blue and black uniforms that had seen better days. A wave of burnt all-spice and smoke filled my nose. It wasn't foul but wasn't flowers. Stuffed bags of books, unusual tools, and metal devices were either still in their hands or clattered onto the ground. I struggled not to stare as the newcomers varied in height and size, but each had intense, large, dark blue eyes and stark white hair.

Wow...are they...Ack, focus! Doesn't matter.

One among the group of about twenty came forward. He? I guessed. He could've been as young as Sir Haley or as old Jared, for I couldn't tell. He was tall, had cropped white hair, like many, yet was one of the few in the group with pale as flour skin—which almost matched.

Jacques held out a protective arm in front of Kayla. "My name is Captain Jacques Volt. Yar in the castle of the Overland Territory. What business do ya have?"

The one standing stumbled a few steps more.

No, a she?

"We hail f-from Genecia. W-We mean...no harm," she replied, holding up an apple-sized tooth in her right hand. "There was little time to escape...with this."

A few newcomers rocked back and forth on the floor. "And so, it was true, and so it was true," they chanted.

"What makes that tooth so special?" Jacques asked.

Jared looked at him. "That is a carved Dragon fang."

Jacques shrugged. "How do ya know?"

"Dragons can go through other worlds. Our guests—these survivors—just did."

A chill ran down my spine. "And all you need is a tooth?"

"Are you okay?" Kayla asked the stranger. "Do you need help?"

Said stranger gripped the fang in his hand. "A-Apologies...but there's no time."

Kayla stepped forward. "But we——"

Blue eyes flashed a fire red. Marks resembling letters covered by the uniform lit up through the cloth around his neck and on the back of his hands. He crouched as did a few others around him. Then, with a gust of wind, the handful flew past us, sprinting at great speed toward the balcony.

"Wait!" Kayla cried, but they paid no mind, who made a mad dash in pursuit.

"They jumped off the balcony! Are they crazy?" Jacques cried.

"Look! There they go!" Kayla pointed.

The strangers' glowing pale blue symbols shone brightly in the night as their silhouettes traveled up the hillside.

"We must follow, Jared," Jacques demanded. "Transport us closer. Kayla, stay here——"

With an instantaneous costume change, she was gone. A flash of lion claws over the rail into the moonlight.

"KAYLA!" I shouted. "Get back here!"

I let out a deep sigh, letting my head fall forward. "Kamali powers or not, I'm gonna kill you," I grumbled, turned my head, and there was Jacques inside Jared's transport orb of sky blue light. "Hey, don't leave without me!"

"You have patients. Take care of them," Jacques ordered.

By all that I am...by myself? Oh, sure, grand plan, dingus!

I picked up the stole Jared left behind and walked back into the ballroom. The others remained, huddled in the middle of the floor. They looked at me and grew quiet like a group of timid fawns.

"My name is Lute Gibe," I said. "Not going to lie, I'm having a bit of trouble. You all look...similar?" I rubbed the back of my neck. "S-Sorry, I don't know how else to say it."

They smiled.

Oh, that's a compliment.

I returned my arm to my side. "Um, but, to be honest, I don't much care for how your friends stood and left, but mine are off to help if they can."

One with a long ponytail raised their hand. "We don't mean harm. Coniphur Yalene, the one with the fang, is trying to save more."

I stepped forward. "Save more?" I shook my head. "Listen, save your strength. My friends will see what they can do."

Silver blood? Oh boy...

"You're holding your injury with your other hand, and all of you need rest—"

"Do you need help, Sir Gibe?"

I looked over. A concerned Miss Wanda and Sir Haley were by the ballroom doors.

"Yes, please. The drama is over here, but I can't do this alone. Send word to Captain Jacques' unit of recruits to head west toward the hills. Queen Kayla is with him and Jared."

Emil turned to leave. "I'll do so at once and come back to help."

At the same time, Amelia hiked up her skirts. "I'll grab some bedding with the maids!"

By the time the two provided cots to our surprise guests in the ballroom, Doctor Balfor, her nurses, and I had wrapped all the wounds. It was all we could do. Though unsure if any ointments would do the trick, we needed to act fast.

"Everyone appears settled, Sir Gibe," Sir Haley reported.

I gave a tired grin. "Thank you and all who helped. Sadly, our party ended short, but we will make up for it, I'm sure."

The town doctor headed for the door. "This way, gentlefolk. Sleep for our patients will be best as soon as possible. They clearly have gone through a lot."

The rest of us quietly followed her out and kept walking until we reached the middle of the throne room.

Miss Wanda shook her head. "What a mess. What are we going to do?"

"First, where do we think they even came from?" I asked. "What was that purple thing anyway? Plus, there was this weird thing latched to all their left forearms. None wanted to take them off."

"Yes, I saw that, too," said Doctor Balfor and slid the strap of her bag over her shoulder. "The device had tiny lights, and no patient would let me look at it for long, protective. Do you think it has magic?"

I shrugged. "Don't know I—"

BAM!

I whipped around. Kayla entered through the foyer with Jacques and Jared close behind.

"What's going on?" I asked.

She choked back a sob, holding her head in her hands.

"Go to bed," Jacques insisted while he and Jared strode toward me. "I'll catch Lute up."

"That bad?" I whispered, witnessing Kayla leave with Miss Wanda up the stairs.

Jacques sucked air between his teeth and nodded. "Ya have no idea."

JACQUES – 16 YEARS

JARED TILTED HIS GOLDEN staff forward and drove his transport spell due west.

I kept my eyes on the muddy tracks lit by the spell's radiating light. "Veer left a little, ah, now to the right." I wiped my forehead. "This is ridiculous. Why wouldn't Kayla wait?"

"She was right to follow," said Jared. "She's the fastest out of all of us and could see where they were going."

I huffed a sigh. "I think she just wanted a chance at adventure. And now, we have strangers who are faster. We have no idea what these people are capable of."

"Would you have left Lute alone if they truly meant harm?"

"I see what ya mean."

"Exactly, do try something new. Trust," Jared replied.

"Now see here—ah!" I pointed. "There she is, stop."

Jared put a hand over his staff orb, and the spell vanished.

I landed on my feet and ran toward Kayla.

"Hey, by all that I am, what are ya do—"

There was an enormous tear down the hillside but a hundred paces away. The bright, jagged edges shone gold, but inside was a storm.

"They tore reality with the Dragon fang," Jared shouted over a gust of wind. "Their world is what we are seeing!"

"Or what is left...."

"I couldn't stop them in time," said Kayla, catching her breath. "Why didn't we see this kind of tear before?"

"Needed the space? Anyway, not important." I shook my head. "Others are comin' through, Jared. Set up a Vrastia shield. We don't need outsiders sprintin' off like rabbits. Contain this mess."

"Very well!" Jared slammed his staff's end to the ground, and the perimeter check sprawled in every direction, ballooning into a dome of light overhead.

I shivered. The air grew colder as the tear grew taller than oak trees. I barely saw anything beyond the crackle of lightning swirling in the torrential downpour. Then, in a wild stampede, others of white hair and frantic faces came through the ripped opening as strange bricks, stone, and metal pipes flew into view and away again with the high winds.

Kayla's eyes flashed gold. "Their leader's hurt. His hand is burning, holding that glowing fang."

Jared waved his hand over his staff. The orb turned sunset-orange. "Fang bearer, let go"—he threw his voice over the crowd for all to listen—"or your disaster will pass through to here if you don't!"

A blistering roar blended with the rage of the storm came through from the other side.

Kayla gripped my sleeve as the feline traits of her Kamali form retreated and disappeared.

"Let go of the Dragon fang," Jared repeated.

Hands of the surrounding, desperate masses reached out to us. "No! Others have yet to make—"

The sounds from the other world went quiet. The nightmarish view through the tear froze. In the eerie silence, the tear broke apart like glass—shattering into pieces that blinked away.

I looked at Jared. "The tooth?"

'*NO!*'

The word carried the devastating woes across the others' wailing. Some fell to their knees, others cried out in anguish.

"It's gone!" a voice cried. "Why did the fang break apart?!"

The orange light from Jared's staff faded. "I saw the fang dissolve into blue-lit ash in the bearer's hands."

I looked at Kayla and whispered, "What did ya do?"

She looked at me, trembling as tears rolled down her face. "I-I had to do something."

She snapped her fingers...

I opened my arms, and she hugged me. "It was a difficult choice, your majesty."

Kayla pulled back from my arms. "How many are there?"

"At least fifty more." I turned to the sound of hooves. Past Jared's shield, silhouettes of squires upon their horses lit under the flickers of torchlight rode toward us. "Jared, can ya let our people through the barrier?"

"Yes, but allow me to lower it now the commotion is over."

"Fair." I nodded. "Go ahead."

Squire Fletch Kirst rode up to our side and raised his hand, holding it flat. "Captain Volt! Here to report as ordered."

"Did Sir Lute send ya?" I asked.

"Yes, sir."

"Fantastic. Stay put, Squire Kirst, give me your torch, and have the unit spread out to keep the Genecians here." I turned back around. "Jared, keep Kayla company. I'm off to speak with this fang person."

Kayla gave no protest, and no one stopped me making my way toward the broken individual on their knees, cradling their blackened hand.

"My name is Captain Jacques Volt. Ya have two choices. Stay here or come with us to the castle to rejoin the others."

The fang bearer remained despondent.

To their right, a trim Genecian with a pale, square face streaked with ash and shaggy white hair cut just above their shoulders stepped forward instead. "My name is Sephur Vaerin D'Lana."

"Sephur?" I asked.

"A title of achievement, no more, no less. I am a Researcher of Metaphysics and Neo-laws."

"Er, sorry. A what?"

"R.M.N. is fine." They brushed back their disheveled locks with their nicked hands and gestured to fellow refugees. "That aside, we would like to stay and mean no trouble. We will grieve, and if this land isn't too much, we would like to not move from here."

"There are trees and fields here, but nothing more beyond a cave or two," I replied. "Do you even have the means to take residence? We have shelter in the castle."

Sephur D'Lana nodded. "We have the means for shelter if kindness can extend to some rations."

"Very well. Do understand ya cannot move beyond here. My men will watch and inform ya of any other rules. I will return to follow up on this invite on behalf of Queen Kayla Roybishki. Please come with yar Fang Bearer to the castle in a couple days. We have those ya came with. Rest assured, all are bein' treated well, but her majesty, her people, and our allies will need to know why yar here."

The R.M.N. bowed their head. "Of course. By the Designs, I thank you."

KAYLA – 9 YEARS

"AND MY NAME IS CONIPHUR Xenos Yalene." Sunken eyes looked around the room. "Now that introductions and—" They paused, looking left at a transformed Moli sitting in her chair with Tula standing beside her. Then the tired eyes turned back to me as I sat in the great hall. "—formalities are out of the way this morning, Gentlefolk of the room, what do you want to know?"

All eyes, human and cat alike, within the hall looked at me.

I sat up straighter. My palms were sweaty as I stifled a yawn. "Um...Coniphur Yalene, how is your hand?"

Bandaged, he let his hand flop back and forth. "It's adequate...your majesty. Next?"

I swallowed. "I-I would like to know how you got the fang."

He sighed, a bit frustrated. "I found it...and?"

I glanced at Jared and rubbed my right arm. "I-I—"

"You're new to this, aren't you?"

I cleared my throat and raised my hand. "Yes. And, one, you crashed my party. Two, ran through my castle and, three, brought—how many, Captain Jacques?"

"One-hundred-thirty-seven Genecians—"

Sephur D'Lana stepped forward. "Jen-neh-shens, not Gee-nee-seens."

Jacques forced a smile. "Yes, thanks, now can we **please** get some answers?"

Coniphur Yalene shrugged. "Why must you know more? We have no place to go. All we can do is look to you for help."

I hit the right arm of my chair. "Because it can happen here."

Blue eyes flashed red.

"O-Oi, you two okay?" Lute asked.

"J-Just startled, we're fine." Coniphur Yalene dragged his hand down his face as his partner took a small step forward.

"W-What do you mean it can happen here?"

I looked to Jared for answers, who said, "From what I saw, a force destroyed your home, or you would not have acted so rashly to save as many as you could. I fear said force may attack our home one day."

Both Genecians glanced at each other and looked back at Jared.

Jacques folded his arms. "As I said two nights ago, our queen, her court, and our allies of the neighborin' Masana Territory will want to know what happened, to understand in order to move forward, if not take measures. There is no reason to keep secrets."

Coniphur Yalene ran his free hand through his hair. "Very well...to start, my day job. I'm an archaeologist and historian."

"Sorry, an archer-what now?" Jacques asked.

"A scientist," said Sephur D'Lana.

Silence fell across the room.

"Explorer?" the R.M.N. tried again.

Lute pointed to his head. "Now that, I understand."

Said explorer put his head in his hands. "Oh, great, we've ended up in a stone age."

"And you're alive," said Lute. "I'm still stuck on why you call yourself a 'Coniphur,' though."

"And we thank you for that." He folded to the floor and sighed. "I'd rather save the lesson in titles for another day, though. We're still in the middle of setting up camp, thus exhausted."

The researcher took a knee beside his partner. "We've made it this far. Honestly, they have been accommodating. We should tell them as much as we can. It'll be a great weight off your shoulders."

"Look," said Jacques. "Yes, it's a lot, and ya hurtin' too, but we're here, wantin' to understand."

"Please," said Jared. "Take it slow. Share what you are able."

"Very well...first things first." The historian pointed to the mysterious object latched on his forearm. "I've been told, Sir Lute Gibe, you were curious about our *Gieci* while treating some of our injuries. I'd like to not overlook this and inform everyone it is a device we need, one we should not lose. Plain and simple. It keeps information, which helps us with communications and other tasks. I assure you it's harmless."Plain and simple. It keeps information, which helps us with communications and other tasks. I assure you it's harmless."

"Can we at least remove it next time, now that it's known the doctors and I mean you no harm?" Lute asked.

Sephur D'Lana nodded and shrugged. "Don't see why not."

"Good," I said. "Now, what about the tooth?"

Coniphur Yalene stood back up with his comrade's help. "I had that fang in my hand because that was the only way to escape. None knew it'd lead here. I've come with my team of colleagues and families, now the last of Genecian culture."

"I...have so many questions," said Jacques.

The historian pursed his lips. "Very well. It's not like I can lie. As I've said, I am an archaeologist, and our story begins with a book."

I grinned. "Most do."

"Ah...okay," he snorted. "I'll give you that, your majesty." He shook his head. "Jokes aside. A year ago, D'Lana and our team excavated and explored recently discovered dilapidated castle ruins. In a run-down room, we discovered this volume in a chest. The book had a cracked cover and plenty of missing pages."

"Did this book have a crystal cover?" I asked.

Our guests glanced at each other.

"Y-Yes, smooth to the touch," Coniphur Yalene stammered in surprise. "Do you have something like that?"

I shrugged a shoulder. "Maybe. I would like to compare, but my book is with my teacher for now."

I still hope Annika was able to fix the Folk-kin...

"Was yours black?" Sephur D'Lana asked.

I shook my head.

"So, ya went diggin' and found the tooth?" Jacques redirected. "Because a book told ya so, or am I missin' somethin'?"

The R.M.N. waved his hands. "No, we weren't spurred to hunt bones. The fang was discovered two months later, once our team could make our way underground. There, we unearthed the fang and put two-and-two together. If we had more time, who knows what else could've been found, but the site was barely excavated."

"Fail to see how the fang is connected to the book," Moli wondered aloud, prompting others to nod in agreement.

Sephur D'Lana turned to her and the Lords and Ladies behind him. "The book's surviving pages were all written in glyphs, pictures. We found it contained skills we'd only dreamed of rediscovering."

"One of the insights was how to perform Journey Arcana," Coniphur Yalene added. "At least, that's the literal translation."

Lute raised a hand. "So, you found a book, and then you found the bones below these ruins?" He lowered it. "That's convenient."

"Do you have this volume with you?" Jared asked.

The historian nodded with vigor. "Absolutely. A prize like that, where we just scratched the surface? Yes, we have it at our camp." He looked at Lute. "And, yes, it was convenient. When we discovered the fang, we hypothesized someone had it out to test on creatures long ago."

"That's horrible," Moli gasped.

Sephur D'Lana frowned. "History often is."

"So, you've never seen a Dragon before?" Lute asked. "And had no idea you were testing on Dragon remains?"

"By the Designs, help me understand," Coniphur Yalene exhaled, pinching his eyes shut for a moment.

Designs...?

The R.M.N. turned to Lute. "Correct. At first, we didn't."

Coniphur Yalene folded his arms. "Listen, we will never know if the rest of the skeleton was elsewhere." He looked at me. "You want to know how I got here, your majesty? I took a chip of the tooth to study it and"—he held up two fingers—"with rune carvings, copied from the text, I had gone between two points"—he pointed to the gap between his fingers—"I traveled in a blink. I went across the lab, five feet in seconds."

"But, Coniphur Yalene, the piece you carried was larger and heavily carved," Jared pointed out.

"Also was the final result after many tests," said Sephur D'Lana. "Such tests included flashes here, short distances there."

Jacques huffed a sigh. "Disregardin' possible danger, by the sound of it."

"There will always be critics," the historian dismissed with a wave of his unwrapped hand. "I followed the text because the experiment required it. That said. Attempt forty-five was, somehow, destroyed the other night, though I'm thankful it was successful in saving people."

"You should be proud of yourselves," said Jared.

"Proud?" Coniphur Yalene looked to the side and frowned. "Reports of a tremendous disaster striking our cities amidst our research came out of nowhere. There's no pride over the loss."

"And we are sorry for your loss," I said. "If I may, what are cities?"

"Home to thousands," Sephur D'Lana replied. "There were buildings taller than your hills."

My heart dropped. "I'm sorry."

The historian let out a labored sigh. "Three weeks ago...we watched the destruction of the capitol: Mauro. We may have been miles away, but could receive the transmissions. Uh...." He exhaled a sharp sigh and grumbled before he pressed some buttons on his Gieci. "Here." Images leaped from the Gieci into the air, and everyone in the hall gasped or cried in surprise. Terrifying scenes of a great storm swirling in the clouded sky played out. People were screaming. A terrible roar filled the hall.

I covered my ears. "We get it!"

The projected images disappeared. My heart still raced as murmurs and whispers continued among the Lords and Ladies. Finally, my eyes fell to Moli on my left. She raised her paws up and down, breathing in and out, and never broke eye contact with me until I nodded.

Right...breathe...

"Kayla?" Lute asked. "You look pale." He nudged my shoulder. "You, okay?"

"W-What? O-Oh, yes, I'm fine."

"You sure? You look fright—"

"S-So, Sephur D'Lana, what did you do?" I interrupted.

The researcher stepped forward. "Every day, more of the sky fell away into an abyss, like growing cancer or illness. Our people couldn't do much of anything to combat it. So, my partner, here, and I sought to complete the means to reach another plane or dimension, as interpreted from the text."

Lute tilted his head to the side. "You didn't see a big, scaly creature with wings attack you before coming here?"

Both became still, then looked at the ground.

"So, within that storm, you saw your first Dragon"—Jared glanced at me with a solemn look—"evident by the tremendous roar we heard."

"Plus, you came in hot and hurt through the connection the fang made. Why?" Lute asked. "You did tests."

Coniphur Yalene frowned. "Distance, maybe? Not sure why the Arcana lashed at us."

"You do not have scales, nor did you come through with at least an energy shield, is my guess," said Jared. "Fortunately, none of you were terribly injured in crossing over."

I gestured to the historian. "Lute, can we let him take his people from the ballroom back to the western hills?"

Sephur D'Lana raised a hand to his mouth. "O-Oh, shoot...um, Yalene, nor I am a 'him.'"

I bit my bottom lip for a moment.

Oh no, I messed up... What would Miss Wanda do? Would 'they' work? Now what?

Lute cleared his throat. "Uh, what now?"

My face grew warm. "I-I'm sorry. I didn't mean to make things awkward."

Sephur D'Lana blushed ash-gray, looking to the side as their lips stretched out, revealing teeth gritted together. "Oops." They relaxed their jaw. "Not to worry, your majesty, it's our fault. It never occurred to us to explain we Genecians are a 'ze' not a 'he.'"

The room went quiet.

Coniphur Yalene's head fell forward. "Your eye-blinking silence tells me you've more questions."

"Yep," Lute deadpanned.

"Forgive us. This is very new," said Jared.

The R.M.N. cleared their throat. "To clarify, we study and conduct our society under *'Arinamo's Great Alchemic Designs.'* We live according to this philosophy and strive to uphold our Unity. Ze, zem, zir, and zirs are what we use. It has always been. We can respect yours, but please respect ours."

"I'm fine with what's easier for you," I said. "Who is Arinamo?"

"To us, Arinamo was the first—the original teacher and crafter to perform amazing feats," Sephur D'Lana explained. "The founder of our Order and the practice of Arcane and Neo-law."

Lute scratched his head. "So...you're an it—"

I glared at him. "Don't."

"H-Hey!" Lute blushed. "I just don't understand."

"Ze, zem, zir, and zirs for plural. Period. What is there to 'get'? My word," Jared remarked, pinching the bridge of his nose.

"O~i." Beet red, Lute slid his hand over his face.

The researcher gave a light chuckle. "If your 'it' means neither one nor the other, in *Kelnys Code of Civility* thirty-seven-point-two: 'As is based in the upheld Doctrine, as WE are neither one nor the other, referring to the other's *Varkal* would be a compliment among—'"

At the same time, Lute gestured to Sephur D'Lana with an open palm, looking at Jacques. "See?" He paused and then looked back at the researcher. "What does 'Varkal' mean?"

"'Among friends,'" D'Lana finished in Yalene's stead. "Varkal means to look as one, to be part of the one. Unity is treasured."

"Again, I didn't understand." Lute shook his head.

Lord Blackfrost raised his hand above his hand. "I could use some assistance with this as well."

"Let's use my partner, Xenos, as an example," said Sephur D'Lana. "'Ze gave zir book to"—they pointed to themselves with their thumb—"zem, a friend.'"

"They gave their book to them, a friend." Jared followed.

Lute pursed his lips. "That's...still gonna take me a hot minute."

Coniphur Yalene put zir hands behind zir back. "Understandable, cultural clashes are expected."

"Yes," said Jared. "A learning curve may happen, but I think it is safe to say we are amiable and can respect your preferences."

Jacques lifted his hand for a moment. "If I may, however, somethin' still does not add up. Dragons attackin' innocents who have no power of their own, or in this case...zirs?"

The R.M.N. nodded.

"Right. Or, is yar rune magic just for show?"

Sephur D'Lana tilted zir head to the side. "Not sure we can talk about that today. We have others to answer first."

I raised my hand, leaving my elbow on my chair arm. "That's fine. We should talk about food and shelter anyway."

"True," said Jared, gesturing to our guests as I put my hands in my lap. "One last comment on the matter, and forgive me if this is blunt. This testing of powers you did not understand no doubt fed whatever attacked Genecia."

The historian folded zir arms. "My discovery of the tooth and our abilities are not correlated."

Jared pressed his lips into a fine line. "Yes, they are."

"I am not a simpleton."

"Dragons feed off magic." The wizard tapped the end of his staff on the floor. "This Dragon attacked because it was hungry. So, I will ask the captain's question again, are your rune abilities for show?"

"Don't do it," Sephur D'Lana warned zir companion, soft and worried. "You don't have to do this."

"He may have a point, though," Coniphur Yalene replied, turning to look back at me, and held out zir right hand.

Next, much like we saw in the ballroom the night before, small blue lettering glowed around zir neck and back of zir hands.

ᛋᛏᛗᛚᛚᚠᚹᛗᛏᚾᛋ

A BALL OF WHITE FLAME shone in Coniphur Yalene's palm. "My *Ryna Blessing* is the star-wind. This is strong but doesn't work well to push back an incoming storm, nor do the other rune-state types among us." Ze rapidly shook out zir hand, snuffing the light as the symbols disappeared. "Now my turn. Within the text my team discovered, it described a person who could do much destruction or creation. Do these notions describe you?"

A hand rose.

"Lord Quild?" I asked.

The noble stood from his seat. "Ahem, pardon, but it should be noted her majesty would need to see this black book before any can know who or what our guests are truly talking about."

"I agree," said Jared.

The historian held out zir hands. "But do you have power, too, Queen Kayla?"

I looked at Jared, who gave the nod, and turned back to both of zirs. "Yes." I squeezed my hands in my lap. "I've seen things ruined and seen things grow. But, my teacher who has my book has told me I still have a lot to learn."

"Yet, your teacher knew to trust you," said Coniphur Yalene. "Trust we know how to handle our gifts."

Jacques raised his hand for a moment. "Trust is earned, but we're willin' to try."

Sephur D'Lana nodded and turned around in place, addressing the crowd. "Earlier today, it was said what happened to us can happen here." Zir eyes fell on me once ze completed a full circle. "Now we know the danger is a Dragon. What's stopping it?"

"Other Dragons, I suppose," I said.

The R.M.N.'s jaw dropped. "There are good ones?"

"The remainin' Elemental Dragons," Jacques added. "Yes."

Sephur D'Lana shook zir head. "I...find that hard to believe. Plus, we will need more assurance than simply words."

"Sure." I rose from my chair and stepped forward. "I'm curious if your book had these symbols?"

I turned sideways and showed the symbols Annika made appear on my arm. Coniphur Yalene knelt to look, but shook zir head. "No, I have not seen these before." Ze rose to zir feet. "What do they mean?"

"I am the Saqui." I snapped my fingers.

Sapling branches erupted from the stone floor. Both Genecians retreated several steps and watched, speechless, as the tree grew taller. Wood cracked and popped. In moments, a rushed flurry of fresh leaves sprouted from the limbs right before peaches grew, fresh and pink.

I plucked two peaches as fast as I could. "These are for you. Please, Dragons or not, I don't want anyone to get hurt."

Orange leaves from the dying tree fluttered around us—the price of my magic upon living things. With red eyes fading back to blue, our stunned guests' pale hands trembled to each take fruit from me.

"Are we going to be okay?" I asked.

Each Genecian nodded. I turned and walked back to my seat. The withered tree soon retreated into the ground and the split stones tumbled back to their spots like nothing happened.

"Very good," said Jared. "Though there is more to learn about each other, I do suggest discussing what to do for accommodations as coexisting is unavoidable."

Moli raised her paw. "My biggest concern is about hunting."

The R.M.N. turned on zir heels. "We've been informed on what, or who, to avoid. Plus, we've no intention of crossing the border without invitation. One day, I would like to ask you about your culture and, forgive me, but are those cat whiskers?"

Johari's queen smiled. "Yes, and my husband, the king, would be happy to receive you one day."

After a pause, Lord Blackfrost rose to his feet. "At the moment, grains, fruit, and other resources are being shared. I do fear if we don't grow more as soon as possible, we will be asking for a shortage later."

Again, I felt all eyes on me. Problem was, I had no words.

"Teamwork, sir," said Lute.

"Agreed," said Sephur D'Lana. "Not all of us are historians, but soldiers, teachers, children, and those who can work the land."

I brought my hands together with a clap. "Good. Then we can figure out more tomorrow?"

A big 'Uh~' might as well have been said by all.

"Er...or after lunch?" I asked.

From the corner of my eye, the twin Ladies of Shellfore nodded together.

Yep. It's going to be a long day...

JACQUES – 18 YEARS

MY BOOTS NEVER FELT heavier when Jared and I walked into the courtroom, passing by Miss Wanda leaving with an empty tray that afternoon.

"Kayla? Are ya in here?"

She stopped her shadow boxing and wiped her brow. "Hey! It's been two days. How are you?"

Lute looked up from the Folk-kin, saw my face, and frowned. "Shoot. No luck?"

I shook my head. "No, we couldn't find Xenos, but I brought company."

"Moli!" Kayla rushed forward with her arms wide.

The Lioness queen embraced Kayla with a laugh. "My goodness! Didn't think I'd see you working out so soon."

Kayla pulled back first and nodded. "A little, at least. Been taking plenty of breaks. What brings you here?"

"To see you, silly." Queen Moli smiled, letting her friend go. "We could spar, just like old times, if you're up for it."

Her eyes lit up. "Ooo~ please. I've read about my Kamali and would like to reach that again."

"Ambitious as always," the Lioness giggled.

Lute rose from his seat. "Spar? Inside?"

Queen Moli turned to him. "Too windy."

I raised a finger. "Can attest." I looked at Kayla. "Not to dash yar hopes, but it's only been a few days—"

"That's what I've been trying to tell her," Lute interrupted.

"We could move to the armory's training hall if we need to," Kayla suggested. "But Lute and I stayed here so others could find us."

I cleared my throat. "Thank you. Anyway, here's my report. Jared and I didn't have to go all the way to Johari as we found the royal family on a stroll. In short, his majesty, King Basi, is aware and told me he would have the Samaria Troops keep an eye out.

Kayla nodded. "Good to hear"—she looked at Jared—"Xenos. Is there anything we can do to find zem?"

She...read that far already?

I shifted my weight to my right and the wizard answered her question with a yes. "Ya know 'bout Genecia now, eh?"

She gave a little shrug. "Just introduced, but what happened out there?"

I rubbed the back of my neck. "We lost the trail earlier this morning. It's as if Xenos vanished. I've conferred with the Lords and Ladies of the Overland and Vaerin. We've all agreed to not let the rest know about yar missin' pages, as it would do nothin' but stir up a commotion or scandal."

"Happy to hear that," said Kayla.

I looked at Lute. "Ya still good in helpin' her read the Folk-kin? I mean, I figured that's what was goin' on."

Lute shook his head. "I need to get back to the hospital and see if Neo-Gen could use some help."

I pointed at him. "Perfect. Our allies are still recoverin' from our battle with Zar three days ago."

Jared stepped forward. "Then I will take over reading. My feet could use a break. And, if Kayla is going to train, I can help monitor that, too."

He and Lute traded spots, and Lute pointed to Kayla as he left. "Don't push it, promise me."

"I won't."

"In the meantime, goin' to increase patrols," I said. "If someone spots Xenos, I wanna know about it."

Kayla sighed, scratching an itch her forearm. "Okay, but don't let anyone hurt zem."

"Of course." I pivoted on my heel and headed out.

We will try...

KAYLA – 9 YEARS

SEPHUR D'LANA STEPPED forward to shake Jacques' hand. "Welcome to *Neo-Gen*. It's a beautiful day, isn't it?"

Jacques dismounted his horse Avon and shook zir hand. "Agreed. It's good to see the sun out."

Wow...so much has changed...

I remained in my saddle and watched survivors enter and leave these silvery crystal tubes half jutted out from the grassy dirt on the right as others tended to fields and trees on the left.

I took in a long breath of the fresh flowery air. "This is amazing. Neo-Gen is a great name."

Lute dismounted his horse alongside Doctor Balfor. "As it's been three weeks since you've arrived"—he grabbed his satchel—"we'd like to follow up with those who got hurt."

The R.M.N. stepped to the side and gestured to Lute to follow zem. "Right this way."

"Since those three are off, I want to say thank you for this meal," said Xenos—peering over to the loaded cart a few of Jacques' soldiers had towed with their horses.

Jacques stroked Avon's black neck. "Of course, the new fields of vegetables and replanted trees will take their time growin'. Until ya see the fruits of yar labor, her majesty and I will bring yar weekly rations, as agreed."

I nodded. "Also, wondering if we can visit for a while?"

Coniphur Yalene shrugged. "I don't think there's a single individual here who wouldn't allow your visits, your majesty."

I dismounted, walked up to zem, and held out my hand. "I'm happy to hear that."

The historian shook my hand. Zir fingers were cold to the touch, despite the warm weather.

Hope ze is okay...

Ze let go. "If I may be bold? How old are you again?"

"Um, nine, almost ten."

Ze grinned and looked at Jacques. "Weeks later, and I am still impressed." Ze turned back to me. "I mean, at your majesty's age, my nose was stuck in large books in school, and here you're leading and helping people."

"Friends and family help. It's not all me," I said.

"But, ya can say our 'Order and practice' depends on a younger mindset," Jacques added.

Coniphur Yalene folded zir arms. "Huh. Interesting."

I giggled. "Ah, you mean 'odd.'"

Ze surrendered, raising zir hands. "You said it, not me." Ze lowered zir arms. "But, no, to be honest, it is interesting. By the way, I am surprised your advisor, Jared, isn't here."

"Yeah...he had a cough and wasn't feeling great, sorry," I replied.

"Oh?" Coniphur Yalene snapped zir fingers. "Darn, I hoped to speak with him too. Please send my regards for a quick recovery."

"I will."

From the corner of my right eye, a resident took a small, metal tube in one hand and a shiny blue stone in the other. Ze put the two together, and a bright light shone from zir hands.

I pointed. "What is ze doing?"

The historian looked over zir shoulder. "Ah, good, you're about to witness an example of our transmutation ability. Ze is about to create another housing structure."

The caster separated zir hands, pivoted to face the hillside, and pushed zir hands forward to fire the material into the dirt, thrusting another silvery tube into place.

I jumped at the sound of the blast of dirt and rock, raising my fists to my chest. "Whoa!"

Jacques came forward with a large basket from the cart. "Alright, spill. That was incredible."

"Yeah! I'm glad I got to see—" I gasped. "O-Oh, almost forgot. Miss Wanda packed berry tarts to share with the other kids if zirs want."

"Sounds delicious," ze said and followed Jacques' lead by taking another package from the cart and handing it to another Neo-Gen resident for distribution. "We use blue opal to create all sorts of things and, as you can see, refracts speckled colors under the sun. We'd mine it in our surrounding mountains. We've utilized transmutation for generations, creating everything from lights to weapons to our Gieci."

"We still use candles and lamps," Jacques noted.

"We'd upgrade you, if willing, but as you can figure, it'd be limited. We don't have much of this opal at our disposal anymore. A few bags from my excavation site at best."

The tenth child gave me a bright smile with a few missing teeth. "Thank you, your majesty."

I paused from handing out the tarts, turning around. "Coniphur Yalene, if we find any opal here, we can help you."

"And that's kind, but let's not raise hopes," ze said. "Please, keep in mind, our society's entire foundation is about the equal exchange, and the Overland has provided us a great deal."

I handed out another tart and looked back over to zem. "About that, I—"

Jacques tapped the historian on the shoulder. "Does this opal have anythin' to do with yar powers? The scars on yar skin?"

My captain glanced over to me, slightly shaking his head as ze spoke.

Not yet...

Coniphur Yalene nodded as other happy kids arrived to try the pastries. "Yes. It even creates the means to bestow our Ryna abilities." I looked over my shoulder. Ze had raised zir hands to show scarred etching of symbols. "To follow our path by Alchemic Designs, one from three possible abilities was chosen and blessed to me at three."

My eyes grew wide, and I turned on my heels back around. "Three? I didn't learn of my powers until I was six."

"Mmhm," Ze hummed in agreement, passing me to take out another crate from the cart. "We underwent training very young too."

Jacques raised his hand to signal the soldiers to head back to town. "I remember, ya said somethin' about Unity? Is that why ya wear the same clothes?"

The historian grinned. "Yes. Each of us was raised to strive to help, enhance, and improve the knowledge of our unified community."

"I was curious, how ya know what is needed? Which ability should be given to a toddler?" Jacques continued. "Trial and error?"

"Ah, I knew you'd ask, Captain Volt, and to that, we have those who problem solve this. Gazers study the Alchemic patterns and figure this out. This is zirs Ryna Blessing, though viewed as more a form of science, really. Sadly, it's not a common one and takes years to master."

"Wow," I replied. "Heh, sounds complicated."

Ze chuckled. "Yes."

"Wouldn't Sephur D'Lana be one? Ze researches, right?" Jacques asked.

"Ah, no. My friend is a Researcher of Metaphysics and Neo-laws as an area of study only. At the end of the day, our mission in our community is the same. A uniform helps us express this. Now, as a small group of survivors, we have but a few weavers. Our general look may shift to something simpler—"

I hung my emptied bag on my saddle hook. "I can help."

Coniphur Yalene shook zir head and shrugged. "Clothes change. Food was one thing, your majesty, but, with all due respect, if everything came to us as easily as a snap of your fingers, hard work would become meaningless."

"Yes, but we can't make sheep grow faster," I said.

"Your majesty, do give us credit. We found the creek to wash our clothes. Plus, patches and mending aren't going to be a problem when our weavers"—ze pointed to zirs left—"can do that."

A Genecian in the distance was repairing a shirt, radiating runes of zir own. I couldn't read them from where I stood. However, the tattered shirt floating in the air between zir hands was mending with no needle or thread.

"That's amazing," I gasped.

Ze nodded. "Anything once transmuted can be repaired by our weavers at no additional cost in supplies, like tangible patches. Zirs can also perform transmutation, but duplicating items require opal. It's zirs Ryna Blessing."

"O-Okay, wow, uh...."

I looked at Jacques, who waved his hand near his throat, signaling to stop.

In short, help, but don't push it. Got it...

"I'm glad you're going to be okay then."

Coniphur Yalene smiled. "Thank you—"

"My olie?"

The historian looked to zir right as a person shorter than zem with rosy cheeks and a loosely braided hairdo walked up to us. "What is it, my alie?"

The two whispered amongst zirselves before Coniphur Yalene pulled away and nodded. "I understand."

"What's goin' on?" Jacques asked.

Xenos dragged zir hand through zir hair. "Hate to ruin this outing, but that was my alie, my sibling, Dissapha Xyphir."

"But, sorry, didn't your sibling call you 'olie'?" I asked.

"Yes, because I am the older one. My alie stopped by because it would appear friends are preparing for our *Darifim*, and zirs need my help."

I raised a hand to my lips. "Oh, I see. Everything okay?"

Coniphur Yalene shrugged. "It would appear we lost track of time, is all. Earlier today, my people decided we would like to honor those we lost. Among several things, we put this off long enough, so we are having it tonight."

My knees locked from a pang of guilt as I lowered my hand to my side. "O-Oh! Sure, not a problem. W-We can leave—"

"Oi~!" Lute waved, walking over to our horses. "All good, and Sephur D'Lana sends zir regards as ze got tied up. How did the distribution go?"

"Went well, but we need to head out," Jacques replied.

The historian bowed zir head. "Thank you for understanding."

"Uh, what's going on?" Lute asked.

"A ceremony is being held tonight," said Jacques. "For those who were lost."

Lute's smile disappeared as the wind picked up. "Ah, a private thing. No problem, we can head out now. Everyone is healthy."

I stepped forward. "I do want to say I'm very sorry, Coniphur Yalene."

"Me too," said Jacques. "Do ya have any more family here?"

My heart sank as ze shook zir head. "My parents Xilo and Nifor, then my siblings Cyr and Vette." Ze paused, struggling for control of zir breathing. "None traveled through the tear, save Xyphir and me. We were both at the dig site." Ze wiped the corner of zir left eye with zir thumb.

"I'm sorry," I repeated. "I've lost family too."

Lute nodded. "Same. Both of my parents are gone."

Jacques rested his hand on the hilt of his sword on his hip. "Yar not alone, and we're willin' to listen if ya like."

Ze cleared zir throat. "Thank you, I'm content I've found those who can understand. Be forewarned, harmless lights will rise in honor, so don't be alarmed."

We said our goodbyes, and my friends and I headed home. It was a silent trip back. I almost missed Lute and Doctor Balfor saying goodbye before they headed for the hospital. I missed those who greeted me as I walked inside the castle.

"Ka...?"

I snapped back to listen. "Y-Yes?"

"Kayla, ya alright?" Jacques asked. "Been in a daze."

I handed my summer hat to Miss Wanda and looked at Jacques. "You know I was the reason the fang was lost."

My friend took a moment and rubbed the back of his neck. "Yeah...I see where this is goin'. Ya feel guilty."

I bowed my head. "Yes, and I don't know if I should say anything."

"In yar shoes, I would, eventually. Ya had yar people to think of, and Xenos would've lost zir hand if ya did nothin'. I can see zem understandin'."

I looked at him. "All of zem lost so much though...."

Jacques held out his hand. "When the time is right, it will be yar call."

After a small dinner, I turned in early to catch up on my studies in my bedroom. Later, the night sky grew a bit brighter from my desk. I moved to the balcony. I pulled my robe around me as the night wind tossed my hair and watched the release of flickering, mellow blue lights rise from the western hills and disappeared among the stars. There I stayed until sleep called for me to go to bed.

KAYLA – 12 YEARS

I DUCKED AND SLID TO the right across the stone floor. "So, you're saying I didn't tell zem anything?" I blocked another punch with my left arm.

"Cannot skip ahead in the story, remember?" said Jared. "Please stop asking."

"Focus," Moli insisted.

"Ack!" I bent backward right before her sidekick grazed over me. I hobbled a few steps, shook my head, and wiped my brow with my forearm before I raised my fists close to my chin.

Jared coughed. "Please take it easy, Queen Moli. Hurt her, and I feel it too."

"I'm fine," I cried, dodging side to side. "Don't close the Folk—"

I fell to my knees. Dizzy.

My friend shook out her left paw. "Kayla, you okay?"

I wrapped my arms around my stomach. "Y-Yes," I squeaked. "S-Sorry."

She offered her right paw and helped me up. "You sure?"

"I-I'm fine, honest."

"Take five, at least," Jared encouraged. "You are picking it back up faster than you are giving yourself credit."

"Agreed," said Moli.

I held up a finger as I paced. "Fine, but I'm embarrassed, Jared. Why didn't anyone inform me about Neo-Gen's pronouns or culture, like yesterday or sooner? Also, don't get me started about Jacques or learning about any of you. I feel shady."

Jared hummed, knitting his brow. "Shady?" He shook his head. "We knew the diary would explain it better. Also, we could not take the risk of you going out of order. Do, please, sit."

I shrugged. "Highly doubt I'd get backlash from the Folk-kin for knowing a bit more than names sooner. Sheesh, I even pestered Vaerin to tell me zir name." I continued to pace in the courtroom. "Plus, I feel more anxious the more we stand around, so why sit? We have yet to find a real clue as to where to even look for Xenos."

"True, but I insist." Moli took me by the shoulders, spun me around, and guided me to a chair. "Sit."

I rolled my eyes and plopped into my seat. "Besides. What's the risk? Oooo~ what? Massive headaches?"

Jared sighed. "Understatement if you would prefer the feel of a dagger between your temples, but no use discussing a precaution."

I flinched, as did Moli, who took a seat across from me. "Yeesh...okay, so either I feel like dirt or *really* feel like dirt. Lovely."

Jared nodded. "Lady Eider warned me to make sure you dared not skip *any* of the Folk-kin's pages. It would have felt like ravens screeching in your ears."

But speak spoilers and I get headaches?

"Er, got it," I scratched my head over my left ear. "Ahem, u-understood." I poured Moli a cup of water on the table beside us and passed it to her. "What about Xenos? Why do you think ze took the pages?"

"What do you mean?" Jared asked.

I poured myself a cup. "There had to have been clues. Xenos' eyes went fully red in the hospital before running away."

Jared stroked his chin. "If indeed there are hints from the past, said hints will prove useful. I am positive they will turn up."

"Hope so"—I shrugged—"but don't you have any idea where ze would go? You have some sort of tracking spell, don't you?"

"Yes, I do. Believe me, I tried using—"

I covered my ears. "Oh, wait. Better not get too descriptive, or I may blow my mind." I ducked and looked around, pretending to be scared. "Oh, deary me~"

"Ha. Ha," Jared deadpanned.

Moli snorted and smirked. "Your queen has a point."

"Yes, but knowing this spell will not be a problem."

"What did you try it on?"

"Queen Moli, the spell requires and works best with items with special attachments. Most of Xenos' belongings are shared among zir people due to zirs belief in Unity."

"Ah, so, we need a 'last gift' or something." My friend took a sip and set her cup down. "And zir uniform won't work?"

"Yes to the first, no to the second. Xenos left zir Gieci back at the hospital. That said, it did not work."

"What, why?" I asked.

"Sometimes I miss. We must use something symbolizing the person, not the role. If I had to find Jacques, his blade would have a higher chance than his jacket. What makes Xenos' Gieci unique to zem has to be missing."

I tucked a piece of hair behind my ear. "Hm~ what about a hair or something?"

"No, not stable enough."

"Oof. Not even zir hairbrush?" I slouched in defeat.

The wizard shook his head. "Apologies, but those are the facts."

I took my cup with me and walked over to Jared. "Well, I've yet to fully remember Xenos. We must have forgotten something or haven't seen it."

"Are you going to read on?" Moli asked. "Might be nice for you to rest for now."

I switched spots with Jared but remained standing. "Yes, I have to."

She set her cup down and rose from her chair. "Of course. I take my leave anyway. I need to check in with the cubs and see how they're doing."

"Oh, okay." I gave her a hug. "Thank you for coming. Tell Basi hello for me, please."

"Will do and stay safe."

"Very good," said Jared with a tap of his staff. "Queen Moli, I will escort you to the castle door."

JACQUES – 16 YEARS

I STOOD FROM MY BED. I took a deep breath as I stretched and exhaled. The scent of lavender hung in the air. I walked over to my right and pulled apart the velvety curtains of my window. The sun had yet to break the horizon.

Peace...

I walked across the wooden floor and faced my mirror on the wall. From the training last week, scattered bruises along my right side, across my chest, and down my arms had faded to a patchy yellow-red. Many were still tender, but I wasn't a stranger to injuries. I'd live to see another day, left the mirror, grabbed a laundered wrap with some clothes from my drawers next to my bed, and dressed.

When I want to ignore the pain, my mind drifts. Today it was about family. I felt sorry for the Genecians and those zirs were missing. Loss was never easy.

[Ya desire to be a boy, now ten?]

"Father..." I mumbled and slipped my shirt over my binding.

[Very well, Jamie is gone...]

"Dead gone," I grabbed my trousers with a sigh. "Why am I rememberin' this—"

[Here, wear this if it makes ya feel true to yarself...]

I buttoned and looked out the window. "And you called me son," I whispered and glanced at my two swords leaning against my desk. "Ya and mother would've liked my friends. I miss ya both."

Even if Lute and I had a terrible start, to his credit, he improved. Put simply, the brat was confused about me, and I was a hothead.

Not like I should have to talk about it, though...

I frowned at my reflection while tucking in my shirt. "Maybe I should get my hair cut or somethin'?" I pulled back my long hair with a leather tie. "No.

I'm fine." I breathed in and out and balled my hands at my sides. "I am who I am...I am me, and I have good friends."

After a few moments, I turned away from my mirror, sat on the edge of my bed, and grabbed my shoes nearby.

I am fine...

I stood, having tied my boots, and clapped my hands to focus. My candle clock displayed on the left wall, near my door, showed I had a solid two hours of peace before the first formation with the troops. I walked over to my oak desk, sat, and picked up my quill.

Time for practice...

'I look forward to reading <u>The Winged Rider</u> later today.'

I loaded my quill with chestnut ink.

'Today, I train with the Genecian's. They have powers I've yet to understand, but their willingness to—

I loaded it again.

—help around town, picking up jobs, will be an appreciated asset I will not ignore.'

I squinted at the weird 'g' but kept going.

'It is my hope the weather will be good again today.'

I set the quill down and leaned back in my chair. "Shoot! Still gettin' splotches on the parchment."

At least it's just practice...

There was a knock at my door.

"Ya've gotta be kiddin'," I grumbled.

I rose from my desk, opened the door to peek around the edge of it, then opened it all the way. "Lute?"

"Hey, man."

I tilted my head to the side. "Yar never up this early. Did Doctor Balfor call ya in?"

He rubbed his shoulder. "Nah, couldn't sleep. It's been crazy, and I'd like to talk to you before the day gets nuts again."

I stepped to the side and let him into my bedroom. "Okay...shoot."

Lute came in and turned around, passing his fingers through his auburn hair over his ear before he let out a sharp exhale. "Ok, I...wanted to apologize."

I closed the door. "Er, okay." I leaned against the wall to my right and folded my arms. "For?"

"For taking away your choice."

"My...choice?"

"Or, like, insisting about stuff when you weren't ready. I want to say I'm sorry."

I glanced at the floor. "I see...I think."

"Should've let you be you, man." He rubbed the back of his neck. "I know I've said sorry before, but with the Genecians and all"—he clapped his cheek with his right hand and shook his head—"No. I was a rude idiot, and I'm sorry."

My eyes widened for a moment. "Oh, this again." I looked to the side. "Yeah, I mean, back then ya had to mend my injuries when ya found out." I shrugged. "Plus, to yar credit, it's not like ya ever dropped my regard as male." I breathed out my nose. "But...as fights are a two-way ordeal, I was a hothead. Should've been clear how yar actions hurt."

Lute nodded but remained quiet.

I clapped a hand on his shoulder. "Listen, we can move on. I forgive ya, bud. Seriously."

He gave a weak smile. "Thanks, man. I'll do better."

"What, do ya want to hug it out?" I joked.

My friend shook his head with a grin. "N-No, no, I'm good. Um, do you want to grab breakfast early?"

I pushed myself off the wall and reached for the doorknob. "Sure." I closed the door after us. "Do ya know if Kayla has any meetin's today?"

He hummed a short note. "Hm~ most likely. I'll be in the hospital all day—apprentice stuff—but you know Jared has it handled."

True...

JARED – UNKNOWN

STANDING IN MY SPOT beside the throne, Kayla took her seat. Her young majesty was my charge as both a Guardian and her advisor. That said, although a little over a month into her new reign, it had been a whirlwind thus far.

Coniphur Yalene bowed from zir waist. "Thank you for receiving me this morning, your majesty."

"I'm glad you're here," she said. "It's been a week since your Darifim."

Our guest pulled back zir shoulders. "Indeed."

"I hope everyone is in good health?" I asked. "Surprised Sephur D'Lana isn't here."

Zir blue eyes crinkled with zir smile. "Yes, we are well, and even though ze may be my attendant and colleague, my friend had other duties today."

Kayla smiled. "I understand"—she put her hands on her lap—"what brings you?"

Ze patted the side of zir brown carrier bag on zir hip. "Today, this meeting isn't about survival but knowledge. Today, I requested to see, your majesty, about the research I've conducted as of late and believe you will want to see this."

"Would you like to move this discussion to the castle library?" I asked.

Coniphur Yalene's eyes flashed with excitement. "Yes!" ze almost squeaked and right away cleared zir throat as a blush of gray tint zir nose. "Y-Yes. I would. I-I think that will be wise due to what I have to share."

Kayla nodded. "Heh, good. I think you'll like it."

"Though I reason it will be humble, in size, from what you are used to," I added.

Our guest adjusted the strap of zir bag over zir shoulder. "New place, new information. A gold mine for one such as myself. I hope to borrow books one day."

"One day?" Kayla tilted her head to the side.

I swallowed. "Ahem, we have yet to make any allied agreements."

Coniphur Yalene shook zir head. "If I may be bold, I can tell where this is going. Given what your kingdom has supplied so far, your majesty, I wouldn't worry. I believe what I have in my bag is a means to compensate. At least to some extent."

"I see." Kayla then rose from her seat. "Okay, then, let's move to the library."

"I assume Captain Jacques Volt and the hospital's apprentice, Sir Lute Gibe, will be joining us?" ze asked.

She shook her head and walked down the few steps. "No, my friends, like Sephur D'Lana, had other duties."

"Ah, very good then."

Our guest and I followed her majesty's lead from the throne room to the library of the east wing. Past great walnut doors with iron handles, polished golden oak shelves of dusted books rose from the matching floor to the pale gray, fan-vaulted ceiling.

A gentleman dressed in muted violet and silver on our right turned on his heel and promptly bowed. "Your majesty."

"Lord Calistor Quild," I greeted. "How are you?"

He finger-combed his short beard. "I am well this morning, Jared, thank you. Queen Kayla, how are you?"

She smiled. "I'm good, thank you. Did you pick out new books?"

Lord Quild bobbed his head as his green eyes sparkled. "Y-Yes, I finished my latest, so I figured I'd pick a couple more while my wife is at her tea party."

"How is your aunt?" Kayla asked.

"Ah, well, she speaks of Sir Lute every day. He is a fast learner."

"Fantastic." I stepped forward. "Do tell your wife Almea hello for us, will you?"

Lord Quild bowed his head with a smile. "Of course, excuse me, everyone. Your majesty."

While the noble left with his volumes in hand, we moved toward the back of the library. Kayla's skirts swished and my staff's end echoed. Simple melodies of the robin and sparrow trilled beyond the tall stained-glass windows between the towering bookcases.

"This is incredible," ze finally whispered. "Does the public have access or just nobles, Jared? Is there a theme to your catalog, like magic only? Or are all of these general collections?"

"The castle residents and nobility primarily use this one, but the public does have access to another, limited library in town," I replied. "It would be highly inconvenient for all to access one spot, no? That said, we have a general collection circulating between here and there. We have fictional works to history to recorded spells. The last subject is for reference and has 'restricted access.'"

"Are they on loan? Are there other towns or kingdoms aside from the Masana Territory?"

"No. Speaking of sharing, however, visitors such as Lady Tula have told stories to the children in town." I stopped beside a long cedar table. "As for the spell books, I, simply, do not have enough space between my chambers and study."

"Ah," Coniphur Yalene replied. Ze set zir bag on the table, took out a plain cloth, and wiped down zir hands. "Well then, let's begin our meeting."

I took a seat on the historian's right. "You wanted to speak to us about your Journey Arcana?"

"Not quite," ze replied, and took out an onyx artifact, a thick book, and set it on the table. "Here we are. Though titleless, we identify this as 'AO-17.'"

"It is in a rather good condition," I commended.

"Thank you. As you can see, however, the parchment is thin and faded, so please allow me to handle the pages."

Kayla scooted her chair closer to the table on zir left. "It smells old—if that makes sense, heh."

Our guest chuckled. "Yes. From this, my colleagues, my team, hope to learn more about rites lost to our culture over time. Others have also hypothesized—guessed—it may contain more insights into our history rather than be a 'how-to' textbook, per se."

I shrugged. "It has been my experience that books of facts often have history. In short, my guess lies in it having both."

Ze nodded and opened the book covers. "Agreed, which is why I've continued my research—"

"Wait," Kayla interrupted. "Sorry, but, Jared, do you remember Lute's journal from his father?"

I raised an eyebrow. "Yes, how is that related?"

"I remember it was weird. I could read those poems inside it when no one else could, but these, I can't."

Okay...yes, that is odd...

"Don't know about that, but for this artifact, we are fortunate to have this."

Coniphur Yalene took out a small magenta disc with crosshairs etched into its center. A thick, swirled blue opal and gold band encircled this disc with runes engraved around the outside.

ᚲᛖᚱᛉᛁ� ᚠᛖᚱᛒᚠ

I ABOUT JUMPED IN MY seat. "An *Atsain*? Y-You have a working Atsain?"

The historian stopped, hovering the device over the page. "We didn't have a name for this. We only knew this thing helped us read this old language."

I cleared my throat. "Well, I do my share of research too. Acquiring knowledge is what these old bones do to pass the time."

Ze grinned. "Ah, a like-minded goal. I respect that."

"May I see it?" Kayla asked.

"Of course. Here."

Her raised her eyebrows, weighing the item in her flat palm. "Oh, it's lighter than it looks."

"Indeed, Sephur D'Lana identified this device was made with resin," ze said.

I extended my left hand. "May I see it, too?"

Her majesty was correct. No heavier than a fig or a date.

"Atsains are said to be 'Dragon eyes,'" I said, passing it back to zem. "Not literal ones, but the creatures themselves are said to know all languages."

Our guest placed the unique disc on a random glyph. The runes lit blue, the crosshairs gleamed gold, and the dark resin rippled into translucence.

Coniphur Yalene took a step back. "If you peer into the center, you'll see the picture has flipped—"

Her majesty leaned over first. "It says 'turning.'" She looked up at zem. "Sorry, but how did Jared know what this is, and you didn't?"

The historian picked up the Atsain and flipped to the next page. "Or why was it at those ruins? Or, how come, until your Coronation, did my team not see a live Dragon at all?"

"Fair points," I sighed.

Kayla rested both of her elbows on the table. "It's weird. Sad and interesting. But weird."

Ze shrugged. "Heh, if you think that's weird, try answering this question—why would an old book have this image?"

My eyes grew wide as I leaned forward. "By all that I am," I whispered.

Coniphur Yalene folded zir arms. "Yep, don't need a mythic translator for that."

A faded, black-and-white illustration of four symbols was in the corner of the page. The collection of was too close for my comfort. In a way identical to her majesty's, a fierce canine replaced her lion while battle axes replaced the sword.

"I THOUGHT THE SWORD on my arm was the Sword of Elaiobus," said Kayla. "Why an axe—oh no." she gasped and looked at me. "Genecia's people used to be part of a Folk-kin story, weren't they?"

"A what now?" Coniphur Yalene looked between us.

I drummed my fingers on the table for a moment. "Much like the former residents of the Ridge Desert. But, unlike them who were wrongfully outlawed by the former Saqui, perhaps Genecia was isolated altogether at some point."

"Desert? Again, what is a Folk-kin?"

"My book," Kayla replied. "It's special."

I whipped out my handkerchief and coughed. "U-Understatement."

"Oh no, Jared, I thought you were better," she said.

I coughed again and cleared my throat. "I am fine. I-It has been stubborn is all, but no worries."

"Is it a cold?" ze wondered aloud.

I tucked my handkerchief away in my cloak pocket. "I believed so, but allergies, I am afraid. However, I have managed to reduce the symptoms, thanks to Doctor Balfor."

"May I come in?" a familiar voice rang.

The historian almost dropped zir device. "B-By the Designs! W-Who are—"

"Annika!" Kayla greeted her with a big smile before she rose from her seat and walked over with open arms.

Dressed in earthy silks, Lady Eider smiled. "My dear, it is good to see you." She let her pupil go and waved her hands in a circle to make the Folk-kin appear. "Here, I cannot say I did much, but the diary's affliction settled itself within the Realm 'Of Never and Ever After'."

Her majesty took the book. "Thank you, I'm glad to hear it."

Our guest raised a finger. "W-What's this about sick books, your majesty? And who...?"

My Saqui looked over her shoulder. "O-Oh, heh, I'll explain later but, Annika, this is Coniphur Xenos Yalene. Coniphur Yalene? This is my mentor in magic, Lady Annika Eider. She lives in the north, so she travels here to visit."

"Portal Arcana?" the historian muttered before ze cleared zir throat and extended zir hand. "Pleasure. I must say, I've never met anybody like you before."

Lady Eider smiled, taking zir hand to hold for a moment. "And I, you and likewise."

Our guest let go. "A-Are you cold milady?"

She shook her head. "Oh no, I am fine, really. Have you been able to make yourself at home?"

Coniphur Yalene lowered zir hand to zir side as ze nodded. "Yes, but I regret not saving more."

The sorceress looked at me. "What happened?"

"Genecia was attacked and is assumed destroyed," I said.

"We think a Dragon did it," Kayla added.

Lady Eider frowned and took a seat across from zem at our table. "Would it...be the Dragon Zar, perhaps?"

"Who?" Coniphur Yalene asked.

"There is but one Dragon in recent history who despises others with have magical powers," Lady Eider replied. "Who I can see attacking those splintered into other lands."

"So, we weren't separated once?" Kayla asked.

Lady Eider brought her hands together before her upon the table. "No, child, once upon a time we weren't. There was a time when the prosperity of Dragon kind and great stories kept this world whole."

"This 'Folk-kin' is vital then," the historian concluded.

"Yes." I nodded.

My queen placed the diary on the table and rested her hand on the blue cover. "It records my story by itself. I hope the Folk-kin can catch up, now that its color has returned to normal."

"By itself?" Coniphur Yalene raised zir eyebrows only to shake zir head. "Actually, after everything today, I shouldn't be surprised. Now, sick books. What do you mean by 'back to normal'?"

Kayla ducked a bit with an awkward glance. "Right. Um, we might as well start from the top."

Of course, Coniphur Yalene proved to be a quick learner. However, the sunlight had long passed the stained-glass windows once the retelling was done.

"The Folk-kin is now better," Lady Eider finished.

Kayla's stomach growled, and she blushed. "A-Anyone ready for a late lunch?"

Our guest ran zir right hand through zir hair. "Yes, but...let's recap." Ze leaned back in zir seat and pointed at me. "You, Sir Gibe, and Sir Volt are these destined Guardians? Plus, there may be more?"

"Yes," I said.

Ze gestured to Kayla with an open hand. "You protect her majesty and help wherever needed?"

"Naturally."

Coniphur Yalene leaned forward and rested zir elbows on the table. "And—if I'm getting this right—your majesty, you're using this Folk-kin, a diary, known as the Crystal of Elaiobus, to mend this mysterious force of yours while utilizing it?"

"Yes," said Kayla.

The historian rested zir head on the table. "My poor brain."

Kayla giggled. "It's a lot, yeah." She rose from her seat. "I'm going to have the guards outside go ask for a snack."

Ze sat up in zir seat, following her leave for a moment with zir eyes before looking at Lady Eider. "Shouldn't zirs already know? Three magic users and none of you 'create' food?"

I grinned. "Well, none of us are mind readers."

"Right...."

"Ah, this may help," I added. "The Ones of Reflection, or any who reside in the Overland Territory who aren't Guardians, are connected to Kayla's experiences."

Our guest took a deep breath, exhaling with a shake of zir head. "Your explanation *really* doesn't. Are you saying they're empathic? What, she'll fall in love, and suddenly everyone will?"

"I...huh," I looked at Lady Eider, who brought a hand to her smiling lips, holding back a laugh. I blinked and shook my head. "I-I do not think it will ever work like that. Instead, if she is well, healthy, so are they. It is not a one-for-one exchange like you are used to."

The historian guzzled zir water. "Ah~ you know, some days I miss wine." Ze shook zir head. "Anyway, would you say we were once these Reflectors, too? In another life—ah, too many questions."

Lady Eider waved her hands. "No, no, I have to believe you have deviated from this destiny, having separated. In short, between the Folk-kin and their Saqui, the Ones of Reflection thrive and help create the unfolding story. Elaiobus thrives on stories. Much like a lantern and its oil."

Coniphur Yalene shook zir head in disbelief. "Stars, if an official alliance were to be called, what would I be signing up for? How am I going to explain your ways to my people?"

"Strength in numbers and continued peace and safety," I replied, resting my hand on the table. "And in time, as you see fit, I assume."

"Here we go!"

Her majesty had returned with a bread and cheese tray as guards carried pitchers and cups behind her.

"Looks tasty," ze said, standing from zir chair. "Here, let me move the books...."

Once the guards left after laying out the meal, Kayla took a slice. "What were we talking about?"

Coniphur Yalene poured a cup of water. "Politics. We don't know if the Dragon, Zar, will come here one day."

Lady Eider raised her hand. "To that end, I do not believe the Dragon Zar can come here." She gestured to Kayla. "Because we have a Saqui. Genecia didn't."

"With all dues respect—" ze set the pitcher down with a loud clunk "—you mean a Calph—a child—was the reason I lost my home?"

"No, I am saying a *Saqui* was the reason the Dragon could not have the strength. He laid trapped in a dormant state for a long time—"

Blue eyes flashed red. "And was set *free*? How?"

Kayla sharply lifted her shoulders to her ears as zir voice echoed among the bookcases.

Coniphur Yalene took one look at her and flinched. Ze blinked away the red and took a long breath through zir nose. "A-Apologies. I was loud."

"As I was saying," said Lady Eider, "Zar is said to be quite a tempest. Our Saqui has two unique Imogen-Kythes, under her control: a special diary, the Folk-kin, and a talisman of Elaiobus in the form of a sword." She put her hands together on the table. "From what I know now, my standing theory Zar is too weak to come here. But I can only picture the horror you experienced. For that, I am sorry."

The historian scowled. "A lot of people have said sorry." Ze looked at zir food. "How do we stop this monster?" Ze looked at Kayla. "When might it become strong enough? Knocking at our—oh wait—non-existing gate around your lands?"

Her majesty tore off another piece of her bread. "We fight, as my brother would say, together."

"You'll need to build a wall around your home at the very least," Coniphur Yalene advised. "Don't know or care how isolated this kingdom is. If that nightmare can come here, I don't think I need to tell you protection is necessary."

I set down my cup. "Agreed, magic aside, much is in the works for as small a kingdom as this. When the time comes, we will need each other."

Our guest brought zir hands to zir lap. "True. I will run it by my people." Yalene looked at Kayla. "I have to ask. Do you focus, picture it, and materialize your desires, creating whatever you want?"

"Not exactly." Kayla hummed and bit her bottom lip. "Hm~...only if it's right. Living things die almost right away. Also, I get tired. So, I can't snap my fingers without care."

Coniphur Yalene tilted zir head to the side. "So, you have better control over non-living things, then?"

Her majesty nodded. "Also, what about your ability? I am curious. Why can't you make more opal?"

Ze raised an eyebrow. "As in transmute?"

"Yes." Kayla leaned forward. "I'd like to see if I can replicate it."

The historian threw back zir head and laughed. "No, no, no, that's impossible. Heh, if duplicating raw materials were that easy, nothing would be finite. Endless resources. Our top Distiphurs would generate *water* from—"

Lady Eider and Kayla held balls of water mid-air in seconds.

Coniphur Yalene deliberately blinked. "No way..." Ze grabbed zir bag, threw it open, pulled out a fragment of opal, and handed it to Kayla. "H-Here."

However, Lady Eider promptly whisked the stone away from her pupil. "No."

Kayla slapped her hands on the table. "Wait, what?"

Her mentor shook her head and held the piece over the Folk-kin. The cover lightly glowed with the fragment in tandem.

Our guest's jaw dropped.

"Water is one thing. When refined and processed in a special way, this opal is the same blue crystalline material used to create the diary."

"So, it already exists here?" Coniphur Yalene asked.

Lady Eider returned the piece to zem. "Yes, thus duplicating this stone is not needed."

Ze gestured to zir artifact. "What about this? Can we confirm this isn't another Folk-kin?"

Lady Eider glanced at the glyphs and shook her head. "I cannot read those."

Kayla gasped. "You, too?" She picked up the Atsain and showed it to her. "We had to use this."

"Show her the page of the illustration," I said.

She leaned forward but shook her head. "....interesting, but no. This is not a diary. A journal perhaps, but not a Folk-kin."

Kayla looked between her and me. "Why didn't you say anything before? The opal, I mean."

I pursed my lips. "I, frankly, had no idea."

"Yet," said Lady Eider with a smile, "you still are my apprentice, after all."

"Then, you know how to process the stone?" Coniphur Yalene asked.

My teacher sat back in her chair. "In one specific way. It is a special duty. Such performed between one Saqui leaving and the next arriving. However, I am not a blacksmith or a transmuter such as yourself. Plus, such a task is forbidden for me to explain. If everyone knew, we could very well have fake diaries running amok."

Her majesty scratched her head. "Ah. Fair...sorry."

"If this world has the stone Neo-Gen needs...." our guest wondered aloud only to shake zir head. "Nope, that's a whole other discussion."

"Exactly," I agreed and looked at Lady Eider. "My lady, are you planning to stay here for a while?"

"Sadly, no. I came only to return the Folk-kin." Lady Eider rose from her seat. "I best be off."

"Ah," Kayla sat up straight. "It was great to see you, Coniphur Yalene." She looked at me. "I better go too. Miss Wanda's lessons start soon."

Ze nodded. "Of course, thank you for visiting with me. I will return to Neo-Gen short—wow, Eider just blinks away, huh?"

"Oh, heh, yeah, it's a habit," said Kayla, leaving her seat with ze and I rising in turn. "But have a safe trip home. Jared?"

"Of course. I will escort Coniphur Yalene to the gate soon."

"Thank you."

I returned to my seat the moment Kayla was gone and sighed.

The historian remained standing. "Shouldn't we go?"

I waved a dismissive hand. "Yes, but there are a few questions of my own to answer. That is, if you do not mind?"

Ze took a seat. "Yes? I-I mean, I don't."

"Good. In brevity, would you please enlighten me about these ranks of yours? Never heard of 'Coniphur' in my long life."

"I-I'm afraid that will take longer than ten minutes."

I leaned back in my chair. "Then make it twenty."

"Sir?"

"Try me."

LUTE – 12 YEARS

"LUTE?"

I looked up from my armful of sticks. "What's up?"

"Ya sure D'Lana and Yalene aren't goin' to take forever in gettin' here?" Jacques asked, looking south.

I shook my head. "Naw, Jared is with zirs and Kayla, and it's a clear, sunny day. They'll get to Johari soon, I'm sure."

"Curious why did ya invite—wait, ya were countin' on zirs to ask questions?"

I stood upright with another twig in hand. "And give us time to set things up, yes."

Jacques grinned. "Smart man."

I flashed a smile and wiggled my eyebrows. "Devious, I say, heh, heh."

"Pfft~ right, right."

I rolled my eyes and chuckled. "Is the banner ready?"

Jacques pointed over his shoulder with his thumb. "Yeah, up and nearby the cave's entrance as planned. The members of Johari, his majesty King Basi, and Baobi all looked to be pacin'—high ready to start."

I turned north with my friend by my side. "I'm ready too. Books in and books out have been exhausting." We walked toward the fire pit. "Sure, I'd still like to know what the shapeshifters are thinkin' about, but it is what it is. That said, you should've seen Vaerin, man. Ze was raring at the very *idea* of coming to the Masana." I glanced at him from the corner of my eye. "You look nervous."

"Oh, I'm fine." Jacques shrugged. "More...pensive than anything. It's not like I don't trust zirs. It's just...has me thinkin' about the bigger picture lately." He rested his hand on the hilt of his sword. "But I'm sure yar plan today is goin' to pay off, and we all needed this break."

"Heh, heh, I hope so. Took us two weeks to get the time off while hiding things from Kayla—"

Jacques let out a sharp exhale. "Oof, true. I mean, I know how to dodge, but to get away with this better not be the highlight of my career."

I cackled as I dumped the sticks, got on my knees, and started to put them under the logs. "I promise it won't. You're too stubborn for that. By the way, how is your story coming along?"

"Good. Slow, but I've about forty pages. I write about a page or so a week these days."

"Really?"

"Meh, what can I say? Lately, it's been turnin' into more like journalin' for now, but it's been helpful."

I got up and dusted off my pants. "Ah, I've never tried calligraphy, so how's that going?"

"It's tricky, but between all the trainin', it's been nice to take a load off, y'know?"

"I hear you. Everything okay?"

Jacques brought his head back but nodded. "Yeah, man. It's not like I don't get to catch up with the old desert crew in the town square now and again, so no worries."

"Right, how is Leal doing?"

"Good, good. Enjoyin' a simple life with his new family."

I raised my brow. "The big man is married?"

"Yup, recent too. How are yar studies?"

"Took a test on medicinal herbs the other day, actually."

"Aced it?"

I smiled with pride and chuckled. "Ya got that right, pal."

Jacques gave a thumbs up. "Congrats. How's life beyond studies?"

"Ha!" I rubbed the back of my neck. "I have as much of a life as your squires do when they're not training."

"Fair, but everyone needs a hobby."

I held my arms out. "And it's this. This, right here."

"Puttin' together parties is technically Emil's job," he teased.

"What? No." I let my arms fall with a slap. "Not the party exactly. Hanging out, being with people."

Jacques raised an eyebrow with a grin. "That's a hobby?"

"Ha!" I barked. "Hardy har."

Tula Lilac de Rollers of the Bird Tribe swooped down and colorfully transformed into her Beakless form beside us, dressed in woven yellows and greens.

"They are getting close," she said. "I can't wait."

"Perfect," I replied with two thumbs up. "The sun is setting."

"Nice," said Jacques. "Let's hide."

Tula twirled around and hustled off to hide in Johari's cave with the others. I looked west. The orange sky glimmered with yellow and red streaks as it lost its fight against the coming stars. A low chuff caught my attention. Looking to my right, King Basi walked past.

"Ya think he's off to greet her?"

I nodded. "Yup, we better hide."

3...

2...

1...

"SURPRISE!"

"Oh gosh!"

My stomach hurt from laughing. Kayla screamed and jumped, nearly losing the bouquet of wildflowers she carried. Eyes sparkled, giant smiles gleamed, and hands reached out to welcome Kayla back home. I gave Jared a high five—well, I held up his hand and gave him one as Lionesses, Baobi, Tula, family, and friends transformed as they rushed out of the cave.

"It's been so long since your last visit! We **had** to celebrate your tenth birthday," his majesty laughed.

"Ha, which means you're one year older too, Brother," Kayla laughed as several pulled her into one hug after another. "T-Thank you! Oh my gosh! Hi! Ack! Thank you! H-Hello!"

Meanwhile, Vaerin and Xenos stood still, if not stunned, from the scene of those shapeshifting.

Oops...I hope zirs aren't in shock...

"Oi? You, okay?" I asked.

"If only my Gieci was recording," Vaerin muttered.

I raised an eyebrow. "Er, what?"

Ze shook zir head. "Ah, n-nothing. Ahem, thank you for letting us come."

I looked between Xenos and zem. "Sure...you two going to be okay?"

D'Lana cleared zir throat. "Y-Yes...does...weren't they...not animals before?"

I turned and gestured to the crowd. "Certain groups of the Masana Territory are unique. According to Jared, a world-magic outside Kayla's control required her to be nearby for them to access their transforming ability. After finding the Saqui's Folk-kin, they're able to do it more so on their own. Kayla was raised in these parts, by the way."

"How did you two meet?" Xenos asked.

"She was escaping tragedy. Not my story to tell."

"Ah, I'm sorry about her misfortune and hope I didn't put you in an awkward spot."

"It's fine. The point is, these days, shapeshifting is as you saw it. I can't explain it. But I do know Kayla has never controlled anyone's transformed appearances. Magic was blocked, she arrived, and now it's back."

"Heh, put in simple terms," Xenos remarked.

I put my hands on my hips. "Yup. I didn't make the rules."

"But, before the magic was realized or found"—D'Lana knitted zir brow—"what if she didn't want to talk to them because, let's say, one happened to be upset?"

I shrugged. "They didn't. Two sides to every talk, right?"

Vaerin nodded. "Well, more importantly, they look happy. I'm glad and look forward to getting to know others."

"Heh, I'll be sure to pass the message." I waved for zem to follow me. "Come, you're going to want to watch this—oi, Kayla, we have a fire to start, or dinner can't be put on!"

She gave her brother and his wife big hugs then came over.

I gestured to the readied pile of wood. "Excited?"

"Absolutely."

With an infamous snap of her fingers, the wood whooshed into flame. The event guests cheered and whistled.

I clapped. "Awesome!" I turned to the crowd and raised my hands. "Let's begin!"

There was dancing around the fire, eating, and singing. Kayla received fresh kiwano melons from Baobi and bouquets from several Lionesses. When the moon was high overhead, their majesties gave her a deep purple stone discovered on the banks of Sky Lake. To use for jewelry, I figured.

Kayla clutched the stone in her hand and almost cried. "Th-Thank you, everyone, for being here. I've missed you, and this party has been fantastic."

All of us applauded.

"Hear, hear!"

"Huzzah!"

"Happy birthday!"

Queen Moli stepped forward with her newborn cub on her hip and gestured to Jacques, Jared, and me. "We couldn't pull off your surprise, Kayla, without their help." She turned to Yalene and D'Lana. "Honored guests, we do hope you have enjoyed your visit."

Zirs both bowed zirs heads with a smile.

"Yes, your majesty," said Vaerin and looked up. "It has been more than memorable. May we also congratulate you on your baby."

King Basi moved to his wife's side. "Thank you. We had his naming ceremony with Baobi two suns ago"◇Queen Moli held up her cub to the crowd—"therefore, allow me to formally introduce Prince Tori Roybishki."

"To Prince Tori!" Kayla cheered.

"To Prince Tori!" the crowd replied with applause.

The party lasted well into the night, and it was nearly dawn when we arrived at the outskirts of Neo-Gen. A cool breeze passed through. Each crystal home appeared lit from within like a giant lantern which gave off a light violet-blue at its brightest points.

Jared yawned and released his transport spell right after Jacques and I halted our horses.

"Thank you for letting us come," said Xenos.

Vaerin yawned, too. "Yes, we will never forget it."

Kayla waved. "See you soon."

Jacques dismounted. "Hey, lemme help ya up onto Avon's saddle, Jared, yar beat. I'll walk us from here."

I offered a hand to Kayla. "Want to ride with me?"

"Yes, thanks."

Onwards to the stables, Jacques yawned. "Yup, by all that I am, I couldn't be more tired."

Jared rubbed his eyes. "Yes, I am off to bed."

"Yeah, sleep for the day, you mean," I yawned. "That's what I'm doing."

Kayla laughed, sitting in front of me. "I had so much fun, though! Tori was so cute and—"

"Yes, again, we *know*," I interrupted with a tired laugh.

"Oops...Whole trip?"

"Whole trip," Jacques and I chorused.

"You've talked non-stop all the way back," I added.

Kayla giggled. "Still, though—oh!" She looked at me over her shoulder. "Did Miss Wanda know about this surprise?"

Both Jacques and I nodded.

"Couldn't exactly *not* tell her,'" Jacques replied.

She hummed. "Hm~ okay, that's fair...so, how did you put this together without making a fuss?"

Jacques and I groaned.

"Long story?" Kayla giggled. "Okay, no rush."

———————

...AH, SHOOT...

The following morning in the throne room, I was about ready to take my leave from the castle with my medical texts in my bag but was in time to catch Miss Wanda confronting Kayla.

"Your majesty Saqui, it would've been grand to know about your birthday," said Amelia. "I request we celebrate during the *Summer Harvest Solstice* in two weeks."

"I don't see why we need to," said Kayla from her chair. "I mean, the festival isn't about me."

Miss Wanda stood fast. "It will add a new purpose, true, but, your majesty, forgive me, but I insist. It would lend us a great opportunity to open the gates. An evening event marking the end of the big day's festivities in the courtyard."

Kayla opened her mouth to protest. However, Amelia kept going.

"And it's not as though Sir Haley was going to ask for your participation in the parade."

Kayla leaned forward. "There's a what?"

Miss Wanda raised an eyebrow. "Do we need to go over chapter fifteen in Custom—"

"No, sorry, but no. I-I'll be there."

"Very good, your majesty Saqui. I'll help organize the cooks as well as the decorations with Sir Haley."

"Thank you."

"Of course." Amelia curtsied and headed toward the dining hall doors.

"I guess we must listen to Sir Haley again, huh?" Jared asked, who had seen everything.

"Guess so," Kayla sighed.

An eager Sir Haley busted through the same doors. "What wonderful news! Just heard we're to include your birthday celebration in the Solstice festival, your majesty." He bowed from the waist.

Kayla bobbed her head. "A-Ah, o-of course—"

Emil stood upright, putting his hands behind his back. "The event will be added to the town announcements at once. I will have dress designs and fabrics for you to choose from tomorrow."

"Thank you, I-I'm sure it'll be great."

"I'll be at my shop if you have a request." The planner bowed again with a flourish and hustled out of the room.

The door shut, and I let out a low whistle.

Kayla's shoulders slumped. "Wow," she sighed again.

"Troubled?" said Jared.

Frowning, she stood from her throne. "Is that a joke—and, Lute, you could've said something. I see you there. I did hope to relax during this event."

"And not be the center of attention?" I chuckled and shrugged. "Oi, don't girls love to have two parties?"

Kayla rolled her eyes. "Lute, come on. One was enough."

I held out my hands. "C'mon, let Emil have this. He still feels bad the Coronation became a bust."

"But it wasn't his fault." She looked around the room. "Will *anyone* tell me why I have to?"

I raised a finger. "Ah~ but why not?"

Kayla opened her mouth to speak but stopped to tuck a piece of hair behind her ear instead. "Alright. Guess it won't be *too* bad."

"There." I lowered my arms with a smile. "You see? You'll have fun."

"Still though...."

"What was that?" Jared asked.

She shook her head. "N-Nothing."

"What is it?" I insisted.

Kayla looked off to the side. "What if something goes wrong?"

Jared leaned on his staff. "Then we will fix it. But, for now, live and have fun."

"Right...right, okay."

KAYLA – 10 YEARS

MY PALMS WERE SWEATY, and my throat was dry when I tried on my party dress the following weeks.

A round, freckled woman tucked her thin hair behind her ear, lowering a large pincushion to her lap. "Aw, are you alright, your maj—"

"Yes, Miss Kirst, I-I am," I fibbed and looked at Sir Haley with a forced smile. "H-How does it look?"

He stepped back and looked up and down. "Yes, I think we're finished with your alterations. Do you like it? I'm sensing nervousness."

My knees buckled. "S-Sorry. I do like the dress. You and Wryn—er, Miss Kirst—both did great. Honest."

Emil smiled, pulling out his leather pouch to put his piece of tailor's chalk inside. "I know it's been a quick turnaround putting this additional party together, but this sunny yellow suits you nicely—"

I'm not nervous about the dress...

"—and I think the bow in the middle of the scoop neckline is a nice touch. But like you told me, I'll shorten the puff sleeves."

I stepped down from the stool with a nod and headed for the privacy curtain with the tailor close behind. "Great. Thank you. I'll change."

"Of course, your majesty, I will be out in the hallway."

"Thank you, Sir Haley."

I heard my bedroom door shut and let out a sigh as clicks of heels came closer.

"Not to worry, miss, lemme help you with the buttons."

"Yes, please."

Don't worry, relax...You'll have f—ah, shoot lessons!

I rushed to change from my party gown to a grass green dress, left the privacy curtain, and handed the outfit to Wryn.

"All is well, milady?" she asked.

I spun around. "Need help with buttons again, pretty please."

"A-Ah, of course, sure thing."

Once ready, the kind tailor and I hurried out of my bedroom.

Emil beamed. "Good to go, your majes—"

I turned on my heel and walked ahead. "Yep," I squeaked. "What's next? Are-the-booths-in-town-almost-ready?"

"Ho, now, wait for us, sweetheart," Wryn called after. "I can only go so fast."

Sir Haley hustled by my side, keeping with my pace. Even if impatient, I forced myself to go slower.

"Is my brother coming, Sir Haley?" I asked.

"Uh, busy, unfortunately. The baby."

"Not a problem." I put my hand around the starting peg of the staircase banister and made a sharp right turn. "Neo-Gen?"

"I've heard plans on sending their—zirs—usual delegates."

I skipped down the last couple of stairs and spun on my heels toward Emil. "Coniphur Yalene and Sephur D'Lana then?"

"A-And possibly a few more—"

"And Lady Annika?"

"Ahem, *she* sends her regards."

I froze. Then turned and saw a disappointed Jared looking at me from across the throne room near the dining hall.

He stepped forward. "Now, if you are quite done raising everyone's heart rate, I would hope you can blow off this extra energy on a walk or something."

I huffed a sigh, closed my eyes, and inhaled.

1...2...3...

I exhaled and turned back around where Wryn was still coming down the stairs. "Sorry for rushing, Sir Haley and Miss Kirst. I was late for lessons and didn't want to forget anything."

The tailor dabbed her brow. "N-Not to worry, miss."

Sir Haley smiled. "Exactly, but thank you."

I rubbed my forehead and blushed. "Still, between everything, I just...."

"You have a right ol' lot on your mind. Miles a second, it seems." Wryn gave the dress to Emil. "I've a boy who gets flustered too." She opened her arms. "Crown or no, could you use a hug?"

I looked at the ceiling and let out a big sigh. "Yes, please."

Miss Kirst wrapped her stout arms around me and pulled me in for a firm hug.

"Thank you," I mumbled after a couple of moments.

She let me go and bobbed a curtsy. "Of course, happy to help."

Emil smiled and gestured toward the foyer. "Now, if it's all right with Sir Jared, before your majesty leaves with him for lessons this afternoon, can I show you how the party space out front is coming along? Maybe that can put you at ease."

"Agreed," said Jared.

Wryn took my hand into hers with a smile. "I think it will too, miss. It'll be one less thing to worry about and would do you right good."

Sir Haley grinned at his assistant, then at us all. "Come, everyone, follow me."

I nodded as Jared reached my side. "Lead the way."

Despite the cloudy sky, I gasped at the beautiful transformation of the cobblestone courtyard.

Sir Haley turned around and stood before me as Wryn stood to his right. "Your majesty, as you can see, we have decked out the space with hanging lanterns and streamers. Wildflower bouquets and garlands will be stationed around and hung closer to the event tomorrow. To the right, the wide rectangle stage is for the musicians, and this space will be for dancing. Over there"—he pointed left—"the long tables decked out in pink are now ready for punch and platters of food."

"Well done," said Jared.

I couldn't stop smiling, looking around in complete delight. "Yes, this looks pretty already. What about games?"

"Ah, yes, can't forget the entertainment," Emil replied. "There are tables for cards while there will be hopscotch and ring toss for you and your friends in town."

"Perfect, thank you very much. I hope you have fun celebrating tomorrow, and I'll see you again soon."

He bowed as Wryn curtsied before I turned to go back inside with Jared.

LUTE – 12 YEARS

BEFORE THE ROOSTER'S crow, there was cheer in the air. Scrambled eggs and flapjacks sizzled before being piled onto plates. Barrels rolled out of the pub and sellers pushed carts of strawberries to pickled food around.

Four lads in dark gray knickers and white shirts, each with a leather flagon in hand, jumped onto the edge of the stone fountain in the square.

"Hear ye! Hear ye! The morning breeze be fine and dandy!"

"Rise and shine, both young and old!"

"Come, be merry with good fortune!"

"Let the Summer Harvest Solstice commence!"

The four ran off, each in a cardinal direction.

"That will be two coins, Sir Gibe."

I took my money and handed it to the baker in exchange for a tart. "Where are they off to?"

The stout man with a full mustache grinned. "The day starts young. 'If yer still at home, be sure ye have yer boots on,' they say."

I stepped to the side for the next one in line. "Ah, so no rest then."

The cook spoke between orders. "No rest today, young sir. Are you going to peruse before your demonstration with Captain Jacques later?"

I swallowed my first bite. "Intend to. That's after the parade, so I've plenty of time."

"We will be cheering for you," a girl cried from the middle of the line.

I waved. "Thank you."

Peruse I did, indeed. Under the streamers, drummers to fiddlers to pan flutists played merry tunes as several booths and stores were open.

In the northeast quarter of town, there was a booth selling palm readings and a stall with leatherwork, including side-laced shoes.

In the northwest quarter, a lady dressed as a colorful, cartwheeling jester passed out favors in her bag strapped to her back—trinkets in the form of

95

cheap necklaces, bracelets, and rings. The performer would give one to every person who asked. She gave me a ring of copper and tiny stones before she twirled away to entertain a small group of children. From there, I wandered among a few stores and picked up a new, silver stemmed goblet. I couldn't help it among so many shiny wares.

In the southwest quarter, girls, boys, and zirs alike lined up at a large tent for hair braiding with optional flowers as artists painted small dragons on customers' faces.

Last but not least, the *food*! Taking up every inch of the perimeter of the town square, fresh produce from berries to rhubarb to a variety of veggies stacked high on the farmers' displays.

I was taking a break on a bench, eating lunch, watching and listening to a bard nearby when the same four lads from before jumped onto the edge of the decorated fountain once again.

"Hear ye! Hear ye! The high sun be bright and warm!"

"Come hither, both young and old!"

"Her majesty Saqui and Lords and Ladies approach!"

"Come, be merry with good fortune!"

I coughed and dumped out the last few sips of water in my mug. I was late, yet the eager crowds already filled the square. I could hardly move.

Castle flags and banners of the noble houses waved as the festive Lords and Ladies rode their speckled and chocolate brown horses side by side in sets of two. Our queen rode her white horse, Starlight, alongside Jacques as Jared rode behind them.

Kayla spotted me and waved me over.

I waved back, and the crowds parted, allowing me to come forward and take her reins. "How are you doing?"

She smiled with a shrug.

"Happy Birthday!"

"Hello, Queen Saqui!"

She smiled at the crowd and continued waving.

"You're late," Jacques declared over the applause and cheering.

"Long live the Queen!"

I lead Starlight around the fountain behind the Quilds' horses. "I'll give you a free strike at the demonstration. How about that?"

"Ha! Make it two, and we'll be even," said Jacques. "This chest plate is unbearable in this heat. Tardiness shouldn't mean missin' out on wearin' parade armor."

I sniggered. "Fine, it's a deal."

———— ‡‡‡\‡‡‡ ————

"NO DEAL! NO DEAL! ACK!"

Right on the back of my shoulder...

I spun around with a practice staff in hand. "Take it easy!"

Jacques grinned, took a side stance, and raised his dull sword. "Then don't make this easy."

"I'm trying." I pulled at the collar of my padded suit.

Lit by the torchlights surrounding the narrow stage, the half-tipsy and elated audience applauded.

"Two points to one," Fletch declared from the right corner of the platform. "My fellows of the Overland, dear friends of Neo-Gen, can we get a cheer?"

"Huzzah!"

I ducked, swiped, ducked, and missed.

Jacques swiped, dodged, swiped, and dodged again.

"This stage isn't big enough for the both of us," said Jacques.

I swiped for his feet from behind.

He fell over my staff onto his rump.

"Two to two points!"

"Huzzah!" the crowd laughed.

Jacques rolled over and lunged.

I dodged but his blade poked my right side.

"Three to two," Fletch cried. "Captain Volt is the winner!"

"Huzzah! Huzzah to Sir Jacques Volt!"

"To our contender," he followed with a sweep of his arm.

"Good show! Good show, Sir Lute Gibe!"

From across the stage, the four lads stepped onto the edge of the fountain once more.

I tapped Jacques' shoulder with the back of my hand. "We better go."

"Hear ye! Hear ye! The orange-red sun bares low!"

Jacques and I handed Fletch our blunt weapons.

"Come by torchlight to the castle, both young and old!"

Quartermaster Valen and a few assistants helped us ditch our padded wear.

"For celebration, there are glad tidings still!"

We scrambled onto our awaiting horses.

"Come, be merry with good fortune!"

I waved. "See you there, everyone!"

KAYLA – 10 YEARS

THE NIGHT SKY WAS CLEAR with a light breeze carrying the smell of flowers into the warm air. The courtyard shined and gleamed as musicians played.

Having changed into my new gown with a wreath of white flowers on my head, Jacques escorted me to the right side of the front gate near an empty table.

"You up for this?"

"Next time, there should be breaks," Jacques whispered. "But I'm fine."

Sir Haley clapped his hands. "Lovely, Queen Kayla. Captain, your half-cape has a flower on—there you go. Yes, looks perfect—oh, the entertainment has arrived! Your majesty Saqui, I have someone who would like to meet you."

"Yes, sorry, we are running a bit behind." I looked at the guards. "Please open the gate and let them in."

A slender woman strode through the gate with confidence, dressed head to toe in deep purple and green with a high-to-low skirt paired with black leggings, polished boots, and elbow-length, fingerless gloves with golden nails. Her thick, red hair was wildly curly, decorated with ribbons and shiny hairpins. She also wore a black lace over satin rose-pink mask that hid her eyes and covered her nose, leaving us with her bright smile.

"Fear not, for Poppy has arrived!"

Before I said a word, she swept her arms wide open and curtsied. "Happy Birthday, Queen Kayla Roybishki."

"Eccentric and lovely, isn't she?" Emil commended and kissed Poppy's hand. "She goes by *Poppy the Illusionist*. She auditioned earlier this week and will, later, perform some tricks for the guests."

Said Illusionist set her bag down and swept forward. A red rose appeared out of thin air with a twist of her wrist, and she presented it to me.

"A pretty gift for a pretty queen."

"I-It's lovely." I took the flower. Thank you, Poppy, for coming."

Jacques raised his hand. "Uh, I'm sorry, I don't believe we've met."

The performer tilted her head to the side. "Captain Volt, your honorable reputation precedes you." She looked at me as Sir Haley passed her a party favor basket full of trinket jewelry. "However, your majesty, I will take my position and hope you have a wonderful evening."

Sir Haley clicked his heels. "Yes, I'd hate to keep the rest of the guests waiting."

The dreaded butterflies in my stomach came back. "R-Right. Go ahead."

"Happy Birthday, Queen Kayla," Lord Blackfrost cheered as his lady presented me with a bouquet of flowers.

I forced a smile, ignoring the pit in my stomach. "Thank you for your gift," I replied and handed the present to Jacques to lay on the table near us. "Please, Tyford, Carmen, enjoy the party."

"Happy Birthday!"

A new, woven scarf from Ada and Akilah Shellfore.

"Thank you," I said. "I love how soft it is."

"Happy Birthday!"

New stationery from Calistor and Almea Quild.

"Thank you," I said. "I will use it well."

"Good year to you, Queen Kayla."

I had passed the Quilds' gift to Jacques when Coniphur Yalene came through the gate. Sephur D'Lana walked beside zem as five more followed after. All seven came dressed in zirs repaired black and blue uniforms, hair flawless, moved in sync with arms at zir sides.

"Coniphur Xenos Yalene and Sephur Vaerin D'Lana, welcome," Jacques greeted.

I smiled. "Hello and welcome."

"Good year to you, your majesty," Sephur D'Lana repeated, taking out a pouch. "From Neo-Gen, this is for you."

My heart twisted at the gift of an oval stone upon a silver band. Happy or sad, I couldn't quite tell where I stood as the R.M.N. presented me with blue opal jewelry.

"This is **very** generous," said Jacques.

"Y-Yes, it is beautiful." I took the gift and slipped the piece over my wrist. I looked back up with as much of a smile I could muster. "Thank you so much. I will treasure it."

Coniphur Yalene rested zir hand over zir heart. "We are also here to inform you Neo-Gen would like to enter official talks of an alliance. Of course, at a later date."

"Fantastic," said Jacques. "Let's toast to that later."

The historian grinned. "Absolutely."

I nodded. "Great, thank you again. Please, enjoy the party."

Members of Neo-Gen smiled in turn and left to mingle.

I let my face relax.

"Ya okay?" Jacques asked.

I breathed in and out and glanced at the guests entertaining themselves. "My cheeks hurt," I whispered.

"A~nd, there isn't more to it?"

I kept looking ahead. "I've yet to tell them about the Dragon Fang. That I snapped it away."

I don't deserve this...

"I'm sure ya will. Eyes up," Jacques encouraged as more guests filed in.

In time, many of the commonwealth and their families arrived for some fun. The dance floor filled with couples and laughter filled the air. Soon, the gift table was brimming with baskets and packages when I figured it was okay for me to go. I let out a deep sigh, let my worry fall away—if only a little—and joined the party.

JARED – UNKNOWN

'PLEASE GIVE KAYLA MY regards. I do not want my absence to worry her. The immense pressure from The Realm weighs on my mind, thus needs my attention. Tell her I'm sorry, but I cannot attend.'

Lady Eider's words rolled in my head when I spotted Kayla watching Poppy the Illusionist with other children.

But you should be here...

But she could not—The Realm 'Of Never and Ever After' required lengthy meditations on her part.

Whereas I stood near the castle's front door, the festive magician was off in a corner of the courtyard with a fair-sized audience. Her majesty sat in a chair up front. Those around her appeared entranced, oo-ing and aw-ing at the performance.

This has Sir Haley written all over it...

The Illusionist juggled scarves. Additional scarves would appear out of thin air, growing her collection all the more colorful. She went on and on, tossing the silky pieces of fabric around.

"The redhead magician isn't half-bad, eh, Jared?" Lute asked with his mouth full.

I frowned in disgust and stepped away from him a little. "Eat or speak. You could at least show some decorum."

Lute swallowed and wiped his mouth with the back of his arm before wiggling the fingers of his left hand. "Check out my new bling I got from town. Where's your party favor?"

I rolled my eyes. "I am good, thank you, but, yes, this one is excellent at sleight of hand."

With ten or so scarves tossing in a circle, the magician stopped juggling. She stood back, and the scarves continued without her.

"Whatever you say, man," Lute teased and continued to stuff his face with dessert in hand.

A few moments later, the scarves individually fluttered away and reformed as a long scarf. The magician clapped once, and the fabric softly fell onto Kayla's head.

*Okay... **impressive...***

I stepped forward to study her tricks.

"Now, Poppy the Illusionist will perform a disappearing act!" the show woman declared, and the audience clapped in anticipation. "First, I will need a volunteer."

Kayla innocently wrapped the long scarf around her neck and bounced onstage. Poppy curtsied before both smiled at the cheering audience.

"Now, I want all of you to count to three, and I'll make our birthday girl, our beloved Saqui, disappear and reappear elsewhere!"

"What was that about sleight of hand?" Lute teased.

"Quiet," I hissed.

"One!"

The magician covered Kayla with her long cloak.

"Two!"

Poppy waved her right hand about while lifting her mask to reveal...

One glowing purple eye...

"Something isn't right." I moved toward the stage.

"Three!" the audience cried.

A tall bout of thick, green smoke billowed around Kayla and the magician. If I had blinked, I would have missed the blip of light within the cloud.

"What did you see?" Lute asked.

As the smoke wisped and floated away, the audience gasped. Her majesty and Poppy had ***both vanished***.

Lute and I rushed to the front of the stage, yet nothing was there but a small note.

'THANK YOU & GOOD NIGHT!'

Lute hit my arm with the back of his hand. "Oi, I thought you said magicians—"

"They do not," I interrupted and retrieved the note. "This 'Poppy'...she must be."

"A. *What*?"

"Think 'evil me'," I summarized in haste.

"Oh...aw, man!" Lute ruffled his hair. "Seriously?"

"Captain," I called over to my right. "Captain Jacques, quickly, call off the party!"

"Can any celebration go without interruption?" Sir Haley cried as the guests left. "Her majesty worried this whole time something would happen, and, guess what, none of us did our job and—"

Coniphur Yalene clamped zir hands on the planner's shoulders. "Noted, sir, but pull yourself together and help us." Ze turned to us by the stage. "Honestly, did anybody do background checks?"

Lute pointed to the captain with a straight face.

"H-Hey!" Jacques squawked, hustling to join us.

Sephur D'Lana rushed over next and put zir hands on zir knees. "I-I've sent my colleagues home," ze said, breathless. "How can I help?"

"Do you or anyone know anything more about the magician?" Jacques asked.

Sir Haley came forward.

He blew his nose and raised a trembling hand. "'Poppy' was a stage name. Her real name is Renjor."

Why does that ring a bell?

"And what made her trustworthy to ya?" Jacques asked.

"She came in costume to my shop," Sir Haley sniffed. "She presented me with the crest of the Blackfrost house."

"Outrageous!"

Lord Blackfrost, red in the face, joined us at the stage with his wife at his side.

"B-But true!" The planner clapped his hips. "I keep credentials"—he dug through his right pouch—"for all my vendors."

I held out my hand once he took it out. "May I see it?"

"Here—"

"A fake, surely," said Lord Blackfrost, folding his arms.

His wife took the crook of his right elbow. "Are you accusing him, hun?"

I unrolled the small parchment. Pressed into a burgundy wax seal in the right corner was the Blackfrost crest—a bear's head in front of a sun setting from the top meeting a half moon rising from the bottom.

"Interesting."

"N-No! No. Carmen, it's just...."

Lute looked over my shoulder. "Interesting?" he muttered between us. "C'mon."

"No one is standin' to be accused," Jacques added. "We're all just frustrated."

"I must apologize, though," said Sir Haley. "Should've been more care—"

"Renjor slipped under all our suspicions," I interrupted, then looked at Lord Blackfrost. "I'll have to test this."

"Bettin' on forgery," said Jacques. "A magic-made fake."

"Stands to reason," I agreed, tilted my staff forward, and passed the orb over the scroll.

In moments, the item turned into a small feather between my fingers.

"A noble house crest from a chicken?" Lady Blackfrost gasped, raising a hand to her cheek. "By all that I am."

"Now the illusion is broken," I said. "However, again, we all have been duped." I tucked the feather away and looked among my companions. "We need to move."

Lady Blackfrost pursed her lips and nodded, playing with the beads of her trinket necklace. "Agreed." She looked at Jacques. "Not all attended tonight. I recommend a town-wide roll call, Captain Volt."

"On it." Jacques pointed to nearby guards. "Send for the order, and you there, gather a party together to search the castle too!" He looked at Sir Haley. "Go help them with Miss Wanda."

"Very good, sir, on it," said Sir Haley and he turned to head inside the castle.

In a couple of hours, messenger birds flew to the Masana Territory to keep an eye out. Every noble household went to account for the townspeople and returned to the throne room when finished.

"Guardians," the Shellfore sisters hailed. "We've returned."

Jacques met the nobility halfway in front of the throne steps. "Lady Ada, Lady Akilah, anyone missin'?"

Both shook their heads.

"All accounted for in our district," said Lady Akilah, pushing her copper-black twists in front of her right shoulder. "Fortunately, the panic was minimal, and everyone was compliant."

Our captain folded his arms. "Hmm, the same went for the others."

"We can't be stuck," said Lord Blackfrost. "There has to be somewhere—"

Lady Quild slapped a hand over her chest and cried in agony.

Her husband rushed toward her. "Darling, you alright?"

She pushed Lord Quild away hard. She slapped to cover her face and whipped violently back into an arch. Her fingers parted and bent into claws.

In front of the great hall doors, Coniphur Yalene and Sephur D'Lana took on zirs rune-state, fire in hand.

"Stand down," Jacques cried. "Ya can't burn the woman."

"Sister!"

Lady Akilah's body twisted to the right; her arms flailed to the left as Lady Ada, held her own head in her hands.

"It hurts," she wailed and fell to her knees.

On my right, near the Quilds, Lute withdrew his quarterstaff from his leg holster and sliced the air to fling it into full size. "Yeah, but she might burn us!"

"Husband!"

Across the room in front of me, Lord Blackfrost fell to his knees. Shadowy vines erupted from the trinket on his wrist before he lifted his head to reveal glowing green eyes. "No more lies~" he hissed, with a voice unlike his own.

"The party favors," Jacques cried, removing his bracelet. "Ditch them now!"

Thrown rings and beads clattered to the ground.

Lady Quild charged at me. "No more lies!"

"We will win!" Lady Akilah declared and followed suit with Lord Blackfrost not far behind.

"Jared, move," Lute shouted.

I stayed put and raised my right hand. "*Nao-fa-kish!*"

Unleashing an invisible concussive force, I knocked only those possessed onto their backs with a thud and cries.

Lute flinched on their impact. "Ack, jeez. Careful."

"Watch," I insisted and brought my staff in front of me.

Lady Quild coughed and laughed unlike her own before a shadowy, green spirit poured out around her body.

Is this a clue...

Formless entities save for piercing eyes slithered away from their victims. "No more lies~ No more lies~"

I held out my staff. "Begone."

All trinkets shattered and went up in tufts of smoke. Twisted cackles echoed throughout the room as the spirits phased out of sight.

Lute downsized his weapon and tucked it back in his leg holster. "Ghosts? Fan-flipping-tastic."

"H-How in the **blazes**?!" Sephur D'Lana exclaimed and pointed at me. "How about you start with that next time?"

"I was trying to gather information."

"About. What?" Lady Ada demanded.

Lord Quild rushed to his pale wife's side as the other Ladies attended their other halves. "Darling! Hey, hey, wake up."

I stepped toward him. "My Lord, Ladies, they will awaken in time. Possessions are not terminal."

"We hadn't seen one like that since we got here," Sephur D'Lana reported in hushed frustration.

Jacques looked from across the room. "What are ya two on about over there?"

Coniphur Yalene patted zir companion's shoulder and took a step closer to the captain. "We've...seen spirits like these. Within Genecia's great storm."

Sephur D'Lana folded zir arms. "We thought this was another Dragon trick, so we didn't say anything."

"It's the first for any of us," said Lute.

Lady Wanda walked out of the dining hall doors. "Heard a loud commotion"—she gasped and turned right around—"my word, I-I'll send for help."

"Yes," Jacques called out after her. "These three need to go to the hospital."

"Tell us," Lord Quild demanded, holding his unconscious wife's head on his lap. "Sir Jared, have you heard of this Renjor? The foul creature sent these spirits, didn't she?"

"And somehow cursed these objects," Lady Blackfrost wept at her husband's side.

I moved to the second step of the short staircase to the throne and rested my left hand upon the orb of my staff.

"Have you?" Lute folded his arms. "I'm curious too."

Here goes nothing...

"My Lords, Ladies, and representatives of Neo-Gen, I understand you're frightened. This Renjor, her eye flashed purple before she kidnapped our queen. I fear her magic is much like mine, but her actions, these trapped spirits we saw tonight, could all be the start of something much, much worse."

"Is there a name for one like her? If not 'wizard' like you?" Lady Blackfrost asked.

I shook my head. "Hard to say with these unusual feats from her tonight, but I intend to treat her as such."

"Agreed," said Jacques. "Does anyone have an idea where else to look?"

Lady Ada knelt by her sister, held her twin's hand, and raised her left. "I might."

"Only one place I can think of," the twins chorused.

Lute gestured between the two. "Okay, how do you do that?"

"S-Sorry...it's a habit," Lady Akilah rasped.

He raised an eyebrow. "What?"

The siblings pointed to their left temples. "We know."

Lute's eyes grew big. "Oh."

"Er, what?" Sephur D'Lana asked.

"Psychic." Lute gave two thumbs up in zir direction. "Apparently, we're learning all kinds of fun things tonight." He looked back at the twins. "Have to admit, it would've been nice to know from day one, though."

"Fair," said Lady Ada. "But it's a special link my sister and I have shared since birth."

Lute rubbed the back of his neck. "Oh, I see."

She gave him a kind smile and looked to address the room. "As we were about to say, our guess is the Dead Mountains. Many rumors have settled around that place."

"That doesn't sound ominous," said Coniphur Yalene and ze looked back at me. "Can you confirm?"

I stepped forward. "Yes. We have the Folk-kin. I can perform a tracking spell to locate her. I must warn, I do not know much about these mountains myself other than avoid them."

"So, we ambush and run," said Jacques. He joined my side and looked among the crowd. "I know it's askin' a lot, but the town will need leadership. When we're done here, I'll have soldiers help ya take yar family to the hospital. From there, help the people."

Lady Blackfrost stood and placed her hands together before her. "We will do our best. We will also need to quarantine the gifts for Jared to inspect when possible."

"And orchestrate fetching the other party favors," said Lady Ada. "Who knows who else may have a trap around their neck."

"Toss them in fire," I said.

"And if a ghost springs forth?" Lord Quild asked.

Silence fell across the room.

"Surely Jared isn't the sole person who can dispel these possessions," said Sephur D'Lana.

Lady Ada cleared her throat. "That is, I would reason Sir Jared's spell was much like a punch in the gut"—she looked at me—"correct?"

I shook my head. "I honestly do not know. However, should the situation call for it either try or run."

"Renjor...she's forcin' our hand, that witch," said Jacques. "Until we collect and destroy the corrupted favors—"

"Kayla is going to have to wait," said Lute.

Coniphur Yalene stepped forward. "I insist on staying."

Sephur D'Lana shook zir head. "What?"

"You need to go to Neo-Gen. Tell the others to destroy these favors."

The R.M.N. hesitated but walked. "Very well. I'm off."

"Ya sure, ya shouldn't go, too?" Jacques asked.

Our volunteer shook zir head. "This Renjor sounds dangerous, but Neo-Gen can't afford to lose another home." Ze held out zir left hand. "I'd like to offer an assist with my Ryna Blessing."

"Do ya even have combat trainin'?" Jacques asked.

Coniphur Yalene folded zir arms. "Star-wind users were required by law to go through a regimen as it's the one out of the three Blessings suitable for battle. Not that war was common in a peaceful society, but a preparation nonetheless. Plus, your nobles are otherwise preoccupied from going with you on a rescue."

"We all are," said Lute. "Until the trinkets are taken care of, it's gonna to be a long night."

KAYLA – 10 YEARS

POPPY TWIRLED ON HER left foot. "Ta da~!"

I turned in a full circle as soft chime-like music whispered around us. "Where am I?"

"Welcome to your afterparty." Poppy curtsied.

I touched a smooth stalagmite. "In a cave?"

She clasped her hands together. "Sir Haley asked your friends to put together a fun surprise, isn't that fun?"

I looked around. "But, where are they? How did you get us to this cavern?"

Poppy giggled. "So funny. Your majesty asking me to reveal my secrets?" She sighed. "Are you warm enough? I could light more torches." She brought a finger to her chin. "Or make another bonfire."

I shook my head. "I'm fine, but where is everyone?"

She waved her hands before her. "Oh, trust me, they are on their way."

"Really? Hope they get here soon."

"Sure, but look around. It's not like you ever took a real break from the constant lessons, the stress...the guilt."

My shoulders slowly fell. "You know?"

She came forward. "Why, yes, your majesty, we all do."

I had no words.

"Come now." She turned me toward bowls of sugary treats. "We can tell how it's eating at you. So young, you deserve a break. Let loose without the boring tasks for a change."

I turned back around. "I don't need the candy. I want to know how we got here so fast."

Poppy's pursed lips fell back to a smile. "Oh, well, Jared lent me a spell." She pointed to the decorated tables surrounding us. "Miss Wanda set up the toys and treats earlier today. Sir Haley provided the music."

"Right, the music"—I looked around—"where is that coming from?"

She gestured to me to follow her to the right. "Oh, over here. You'll like this."

A blue opal and silver box was left open upon another table. It's sweet, light music—I smiled as I walked closer.

"Sephur D'Lana lent this special box from Neo-Gen. Isn't it pretty?"

I picked it up. "It's not heavy, but I'm glad it wasn't broken from zirs escape."

"Relaxing, isn't it?" Poppy nodded. "Listening to it, I felt peace, too. Maybe it's a lullaby?"

The worry in my chest lifted but a little. "And my friends all did this for me?" I set the music box down.

"Now, now, I did say your friends were coming." Poppy swept to the right and walked on ahead. "Come o~n. I saved the best for last. Your one and only mentor has a mega surprise over here."

I closed the music box lid and followed her until she stopped before a large object.

A stone chest?

"Can't tell if this is a long crate or a coffin," I said.

Sudden iron chains erupted from the ground and crossed in complete disorder over the stone and metal lid. As though painted by an invisible hand, one by one, three swirled, round markings I couldn't recognize revealed themselves in the air and glowed purple.

ᛟᛈᚾᚠᛏᛁᛁᚼᛦᚾᛁᛗᛏᚾᚼᛟ

"GUESS WE ARE CLOSE enough now," said Poppy.

"What is this? Tell me."

She waved a dismissive hand. "Don't let those seals or clunky chains scare you, your majesty. That's part of the game."

I put my hand on my hip. "A game?"

"Well, more of a test, but tests sound scary." Poppy said, whispering the last few words, then winked. "You pass, and you win something extraordinary."

"I'm not getting near that." I folded my arms. "I'm waiting for Jared. "

"Wha~t a bummer."

"But, I don't like this. What's inside?"

"Another weapon."

I jumped. "What?"

"You earned the Sword of Elaiobus, did you not?"

I glanced to the side before shaking my head. "W-Wait. How did you—Lady Eider told you of my sword?"

"Queen Kayla Roybishiki, sister to great King Enzi of the Masana Territory. There's not a single person who doesn't know of your Folk-kin and the Sword."

I looked at the chest and back to her. "What's in this?"

"Come, come now," Poppy urged with excitement in her voice. "I've always wanted to see my Saqui in action. Maybe snapping your fingers will dispel the seals."

I walked closer, passed her, and approached the stone chest. "Poppy...what if I don't want to?"

She frowned. "Aw, then what will I tell Lady Eider?"

"Why today—"

"Why not today?" Poppy clasped her hands together and put them under her cheek. "Wouldn't it be *grand* to show what you unlocked? All by yourself?" She lowered her arms. "Another prize to protect the people?"

"It...would be nice." I slowly raised my hand. "I haven't been able to help with my magic in a long time."

"Do it, your majesty," she cheered. "Lady Eider is sure to be so proud."

Snap.

The seal on my left went up in smoke, and a faint green light shone from the crack under the lid.

"That's it. Only the worthy can—"

Snap.

The seal on my right vanished next, along with three chains sliding and clanking back.

Lies~

I stopped. A chill ran down my spine as haunted voices slithered and hissed. "What...?"

Lies~

"Where are those voices coming from?" I backed away from the crate—I was stuck. A brown-gray anklet with glowing gold runes had locked around my ankle. It had short chain attached through the cracked floor.

ᛗᚲᛁᚲᛋᚠᛏᚾᚱᛁᛏ ᛟᚱᛝᛁᛏᛗ

MY KNEES LOCKED. I looked at Poppy while pointing to my foot. "W-What is this?"

She smirked and put her hands on her hips. "They couldn't stay quiet. Figures."

Lies~

The music stopped.

Poppy tapped her left heel on the ground three times.

I gasped and held onto my elbows. A cold wind from nowhere blew through from behind. The dim cave rushed to light by revealed scattered pools of gurgling liquid fire bubbling and spewing. My throat went dry as the smell of smoke filled the air. The festive tables, torches, and even the bonfire all vanished. The toys and candy broke out into various rocks, and the music box crumbled into a pile of sand.

Poppy brought her elbows back and cracked her neck. "Ah~ that's better."

A magic user?

"Who are you?"

She sighed. "Well, I wouldn't snap if I were you."

I coughed as smoke wafted from the pools. "No more games, Poppy."

"Oh, yes, my friends call me 'Poppy'"—she gave me a big smile—"but you can call me 'Renjor, the Last *Kizin*.'"

She raised her left hand and removed her mask to reveal a flushed face. One eye shone purple while the other was scarred shut.

"Y-Your face," I gasped. "Did *you* do that?"

She posed with her right hand around her cheek. "Aw~ weese widdle tallies too scary, little girl?"

I balled my hands at my sides. "W-What's a 'Kizin'? W-Who are you, and why did you do this?"

My kidnapper threw her head back, tossing her mask to the side. "So many questions! How *do* your Guardians stand you?"

"What do you—"

"First up." Renjor twirled on her toes and took out a dagger with a curved blade. "Let's get rid of this stupid costume." She tapped the large purple marble held in the mouth of a metal wolf sculpted around the handle end onto her right shoulder. Within moments, her glittered costume illusion fell away, replaced with a dark tunic, pants, and boots.

She struck a pose, hand on her hip and the other behind her head, showing off a revealed crimson brooch around her neck. "What do you think?"

I could only cough again.

Renjor let her gloved hands return to her sides with a slap. "Hmph, no fun here—oh, wait, I didn't introduce you." She turned her back to me and raised her hands into the air.

My surroundings radiated purple and green. From the pools, the light reflected and bounced off the walls.

"Ah~ listen...isn't it beautiful?" Renjor let loose and spun around without care with wide arms.

Lies~

Lies~

I shook my head hard. "Arg, who keeps whispering?"

Lies~ He lied to us~

The Kizin laughed as I cringed. "Your presence stirs those who turn," she teased with a hiss and a wide, twisted smile. "With you here, I have to wonder what it's gonna take for you to break the last seal."

"You're crazy, why—"

I flinched when a dagger whipped into view, placed but a few inches in front of my cheek.

"It's amazing what one can do with a Dragon patron." She grinned. "Getting you here was still a challenge, though, my dear."

"I-Is that dagger—you brought us here with that."

"Oh, bravo, child," Renjor sneered. "You put something together at last."

"Let me go, or I will put my fist together with your nose."

The Kizin took back her dagger and cupped her free hand to her ear. "With what Kamali? Heh, rumors fly around town, you know."

I closed my eyes and visualized claws springing from my fingers, yet didn't feel the growth or any change.

I looked at my bare hands. "It's not...."

"Pfft, see? Blue opal gives power." Renjor pushed her red curls aside and pointed to the anklet and chain below. "*Smokey quartz*, well, it's quite special." She tapped her brooch. "Regardless, lucky me, I don't have to worry about it. So. You're not going anywhere until you fulfill a contract written in the runes." She pointed to the coffin. "Your freedom, for theirs." She patted my head once. "Understand? Can't have you a snappin' it away and makin' my life a chore until you fulfill the bargain."

I growled. "What did you do with my friends?"

She gave a wicked smile and bent at the waist. "Go ahead and try, Saqui-sweetie. You've already set a world on fire with your snappity, snap, snap. What's one more?"

I stomped my foot. "I'll get rid of the tomb then."

Renjor held up the opal bracelet she slipped from my wrist and dangled it before me. "Are you slow?" She threw the jewelry. "Smokey. Quartz. Powerless before the contract. Capiche?"

"No~!" I cried as the gift fell into one of the boiling pools. "No..." I bowed my head.

The crooked woman cackled. "How cute—" she slapped hand over chest once the brooch flickered and glowed. "Dearie me, it would appear we are out of time."

I lurched forward, and the chains shook. "Come back!"

"Oh, not to worry, dear, I'll come for you later. After all, you have a *high* role to fulfill."

"Come back. Why are you doing this?"

She shrugged her right shoulder. "What good is a goody-two-shoes without a bad guy? Till then, I'm famished." With a flick of her wrist, smoke swirled around her. "Ta!" Renjor vanished.

The whispers, the drips from the ceiling, the smoke. I fell to my knees. Numb as I shook, I leaned against the broadside of the crypt. My heart thudded in my head. I shook harder, and my hands balled into fists. I struck the cold ground and released a frustrated scream.

JACQUES – 16 YEARS

"ARE YA SURE YA WANT to do this?" I asked.

Coniphur Yalene nodded. "Yes. Thank you for your concern, Captain Volt, but Advisor Jared debriefed me about Queen Kayla's importance weeks ago. Thus, Neo-Gen can't afford to lose zirs newfound security."

Lute continued to poke the embers of our small campfire. "Oi, Jared. When we met, you took us to Annika's castle, no problem. Since we left our horses at home this afternoon, why are we pit-stopping here at Johari? We already took a day to prepare."

The wizard sat down on a log and placed his staff near him on the ground. "I understand your urgency all too well, Lute. However, if you want my backup later, I cannot go great distances all at once. Transporting takes a lot of strength."

Lute set his poker stick to the side. "Ah. So, you'd be about as helpful as a wet noodle."

"Yes."

Coniphur Yalene scratched zir cheek. "Still trying to wrap my head around the whole Leaf Turners' resting spot. 'The vengeful dead' thing." Ze sighed and shook zir head. "Sounds best to be left alone and forgotten, but here we are."

"Correct," said Jared. "Legend says the place is cursed. I had no reason to speak of a place I have never been."

"We get it," Lute groaned, then pointed his thumb over his shoulder at the looming mountains west of Johari's plains. "Can we not talk about that right now? Gives me the creeps."

I picked up my waterskin. "Sheesh, someone's grumpy."

Lute tsked and threw in another stick. "Listen. We have done nothing but play catch-up. First, if Kayla's hurt, then Jared or I heal her. Now, she's kidnapped. Aren't we supposed to prevent this?" He folded his arms. "What even is Renjor's goal?"

I gulped my drink and sighed. "We can do better, true. I'm still kickin' myself for not askin' 'Poppy' to lift her mask."

"We cannot afford to dwell on shortcomings given the circumstances," said Jared.

I pointed at him. "True." I rested my elbows on my knees. "Renjor slipped under all of our noses. We are going to have to work together to become stronger."

Coniphur Yalene raised zir hand. "Uh, no sense second-guessing now. I assumed the queen's Guardians would have a plan."

Lute scoffed. "Sure! We didn't twiddle our thumbs all day, exorcising twisted ghosts from dozens of people, no thanks to the haunted trinkets. But yeah, I'm sure we can take Renjor on with no other idea than a full surprise charge...." He shrugged.

I rolled my eyes. "Quit with the snark. We'll be fine."

The historian tilted zir head to the side as ze lowered zir arm. "Are you sure, Sir Gibe, these feelings aren't stemming from something else?"

Lute took a moment and rapidly shook his head. "Oh no, she's like a sister to me. Just saying we could've stopped this."

"Hm~" Coniphur Yalene hummed a short note. "Fair, you do look a bit young to have a crush."

Lute pointed at zem. "Listen, mister—Y-Yalene, sorry, but since you've been here the shortest, Kayla is like *family* to me." He pointed to me next. "Don't make it weird."

"Yeah, yeah. Of course not." I chuckled, tossing a stick into the flames. "That meant—"

"Nothing. Purely an accident. Drop it."

"What's this?" ze asked.

Lute threw his head back. "*Nothing*," he groaned. "We tumbled out of a mirror. It was just a peck."

"I assume magic was involved in this mirror," Coniphur Yalene chuckled. "Heh, somehow reminds me how Sephur D'Lana first denied kissing my alie, Xyphir. It was quite funny, heh."

I swallowed my bite of bread. "Sort of remember that name. Had zir hair up, right? How is ze?"

"Well, thank you."

"How long have you three been together?" Jared asked.

Ze smiled. "We met years ago, in school. Been together ever since. However, those two have been living together in courtship for two years now."

Lute rubbed his chin. "I forget, is 'Dissapha' above or below your rank?"

"Below, but it's not a race. It's a personal journey to reach higher levels of Arinamo's Alchemic Designs."

"Um, why would one want to?" I asked. "Advance, I mean, I'm curious."

Ze took an apple and a small knife out from zir bag. "That's fair. I suppose, from the outside looking in, it can appear we're striving for a sort of glory. But I assure you it's more of a way of life in aiming to understand ourselves, our world, and each other." Coniphur picked up a slice from zir lap. "My title reflects my level of understanding. I hope that helps."

"It does, thanks."

Jared wiped his brow. "Sounds nice—Lute? If you do not stop eying me, I will start to think I am not trusted."

"What now?" I asked.

"Sorry," said Lute. "I'm still confused."

"Okay, what is it?"

Lute shrugged. "You usually have theories. Who is Renjor? What do you think she is?"

Jared took a sip of water. "Well, how else would you explain her sudden exit?" He lowered his waterskin to his lap. "I thought Lady Eider, myself, and Kayla to be the only ones who can use magic. That said, I can confirm Renjor used magic, not tricks."

"Speakin' of her, ya also looked confused when ya heard her name." I stirred the embers of the fire.

Jared looked off to the distance. "True, the name rings a bell, but I cannot put my finger on why."

"But what separates you two?" Lute asked. "Y'know, your magic from hers?"

Our wizard nodded and looked at him. "I am a *Lukene*. If my theory is correct, her actions would make her a Kizin."

"Why haven't you told us your full title?"

Jared shook his head. "It's a long, hard story to share, Lute. 'Lukene' is not a title I like to share, to be honest."

"Are you...the last one, Jared?" Coniphur Yalene inquired.

"As far as I know. And, from history, Kizins are corrupted magic users who strayed from the enlightened path to follow the will of Zar. Supposedly, fanatics in pursuit of chaos."

Ze bristled with a flash of red in zir eyes. "If so. We now know this person has an association with Zar. And, by the way, I claim the first punch on that creature's snout."

I wiped my mouth with my sleeve. "Not when we're about to

head into battle, it's not. We could use the insight."

Coniphur Yalene raised zir hand. "I feel we are fine with what we have. Let's not open old wounds before the said battle."

"I agree," said Lute.

Jared remained silent.

Fine, later then...

KAYLA – 10 YEARS

I'M GOING TO BE SICK...

The smell of flesh cooking and loud chewing made my stomach churn.

"Hungry?" Renjor asked.

A bone hit my forehead.

"Did the voices keep you up all night? You look awful."

Lies~

Another bone hit my shoulder.

"Leave me alone," I coughed.

"Is that a glare I see—dang, this bird is delicious."

I gagged and hobbled to my feet. "Stop it."

"What? Eating? A girl's gotta eat." Renjor flicked another bone at me. "I love my curves, and these feathered buggers are tiny."

"I said stop," I ordered.

"Or what"—the Kizin swallowed—"you'll hit me?"

"Or my brother can rip your throat out. Wanna ask him?"

"Hm~ a lion's head would do wonders for the décor." She took another bite as she flung a decapitated bird head at me.

I caught it.

It's not Tula, at least...

"Ooo~ nice reflexes."

My arms and hands trembled. "You...wolf!"

The cave walls echoed with her laughter. "Oh, do grow up, sweetie. I'm a *witch*. Recognize."

I stomped my foot. "I won't break that seal. Let me out of here."

Renjor wiped her mouth with her sleeve and stood from her fire spit to walk closer to me. "You can't go without water forever, and the one way you're getting out of here is breaking what you say you won't—ah, ah, ah~."

I brought my head up from trying to knock my forehead against hers. "Stay away from me. You already said my friends were coming, or was that a lie, too?"

"Coming or going? Who cares? What good are friends if you lie to them?"

"But, I haven't lied—"

The Kizin gave me a bent, wry smile. "You don't think I know? About the fang?" She whistled. "Dearie me, I wonder what your guests will think of you."

"I had to protect my friends."

"That sounds so simple, yet here we are." Renjor shrugged.

"I-I will tell zem," I argued with a cough. "Ack, this smoke."

Renjor manipulated the smoke with her left hand, sweeping it to the side. "Oh? When? Before or after you tell your buddies about your grand mistake?"

I shivered. "It. It wasn't...my fault."

"Tch, no one has hated you before, have they?"

"I-I d-don't know what I did to you—" I coughed hard.

"Ha! Plenty. And that's the justice, you'll never know—"

Renjor was flat on her back, knocked from behind her knees.

"Oi~ shut up." Lute stood above her with his quarterstaff raised in front of him.

"I said move out on three, ya idiot." Jacques held his sword over his shoulder while Jared and Coniphur Yalene moved beside him.

"Oo~ company," the Kizin squealed and leaped to her feet. "Happy day!"

"Her dagger," I warned. "It's Dragon bone. She teleported us here and tricked—"

"So many to play with, so little time." The Kizin spun on her right foot, stopped sideways, and pointed to zem. "You...I think I know you."

Coniphur Yalene held up zir hands as zir rune-state charged. "Back away from Queen Kayla."

"Um..." Renjor twirled her curved dagger in hand. "No."

A blast of dark purple energy shot from the handle.

Lute hit the deck. Jacques dodged, pushing Yalene out of the way. Jared—fell to the ground on his knees. His staff clattered to his side.

"Jared! Jared, ya alright?" Jacques asked.

Lute stood with his quarterstaff. "He couldn't get a shield up in time. The orb shined, but the rocks around us sapped blue energy away."

The wizard held onto his shoulder as blood oozed down his left side.

The anklet's chain pulled fast when I rushed forward. "Jared, try to heal. Please."

The Kizin forced Lute to retreat to Jacques with another blast. "Now, I know a Lukene's staff when I see one"—she paced back and forth in front me—"but—and listen closely—why couldn't you deflect that?"

"Shut up!" Lute shouted, charging forward.

"Is it A: you're an idiot?" She fired her dagger again and forced Lute and Jacques to dodge further away. "Or, B: you forgot to look at the ***ground***?"

Coniphur Yalene looked about, yet on guard with zir fists raised by zir chin. "All I see is pebbles, dust, and...quartz?"

Renjor sliced the air with her dagger's blade. She slipped through the glowing silvery-green scar and vanished.

I jumped. "Watch out—"

The scar close to me disappeared to reappear next to zem. "Ding-a-ling!" Renjor popped out and dodged zir punch, spun on her heels, popped up, and rested her hand upon zir chest. "And we have a winner."

Coniphur Yalene flew several yards to the right, hit zir back against a stalagmite, and slid to the ground.

"Xenos," we cried.

Ze groaned and coughed downward.

The witch shook out her hand. "Oo~ that had to hurt, and all I did was a love tap."

I pulled on my chain. "Stop it."

"Oh, I would, my dear, but it's so much fun."

Jared lowered his staff. "Leave her alone."

"Humph." Renjor turned toward Jared and stepped forward. "A Lukene. Haven't seen one of you in ages, yet one would think you'd remember why this range is the 'Dead Mountains.' Are you senile?"

Jared shuddered in pain. "Yalene...your powers."

"No. I'd just incinerate her foot." Ze coughed as ze sat up. "I don't recognize the golden runes either."

Jared swayed, fighting to stand on his feet. I cringed seeing him in so much pain.

"I'd stay down, pal." Renjor put her free hand on her hip, playing with her dagger. "Did you think we'd duel like in the old days?" The purple light of her good eye flared. "How quaint."

A groan, followed by creaks and whispers, echoed from the crypt. Bone chips plinked as green smoke slipped and spilled out onto the ground. The chips glowed as they rose into the air. The smoke warped and took on the shape of disfigured creatures with terrifying large sockets of purple light. At first it was one, then three, then five.

Lies~

Lies~

"No—" Coniphur Yalene coughed. "—those like these specters were there when the Dragon ruined Genecia."

The witch clapped twice. "Ah, so you recognize them. Leaf Turner Crypts like these were almost in every world I found myself passing through."

"You couldn't open this one though, could you," said Lute.

Renjor shrugged. "No. But you have a Saqui. And Guardians, for that matter. Besides, Elaiobus is strong here."

Ze scowled. "Bully for you. Why did Genecia deserve destruction?"

"It didn't, darling." Renjor balanced the tip of the dagger on her pointer finger. "I'm just releasing the army he requires."

"He?" I whispered.

"In exchange? Power." The Kizin tossed the blade up and caught the handle. "Beautifully simple."

I balled my hands into fists, unsure of what to do. "N-No, these creatures must be an illusion. It's how she tricked me."

"Be assured. Though basic puppets, for now, they're real," Renjor insisted, and tattoos identical to the remaining seal transcribed over the back of her hands. "Not as strong as I would've liked, but they're at my call all the same." She pointed to me. "Y'all can thank her for them." The witch smirked. "Pfft~ or rather I should."

"Kayla, what did ya do?"

I looked left. Lute and Jacques appeared shocked and confused as they came forward with their weapons held out on guard.

My hands trembled at my sides. "I didn't mean—"

"Dea Guardians, your Saqui blessed by the Dragons has two choices," Renjor declared. "Her majesty can"—she rolled the dagger handle in her left hand—"watch me have fun or release my ghostly companions from their crypt."

"Kayla wouldn't do that," said Lute.

Renjor made a sharp right turn and blocked Lute's quarterstaff with a sidekick. "Then let's play."

Lute dodged to the right of another bolt.

Jacques rushed her with his sword.

She flowed around the captain's movements and blocked his weapon with her dagger when needed. "This is fun, but a promise to my benefactor is a promise."

Jacques spun to the right and missed. His diagonal slice with his magic sword cut through a stalactite. "I cut through trainin' blades with Lady Eider's gift back home. Why no yar dagger?"

"Irritating, isn't it?" Renjor sliced the air with her short blade and sidestepped to disappear into the cut.

Jacques looked around. "Where are—" Kicked in the back, he fell forward.

"Hardly time"—she turned to Lute's charge and punched him in the gut—"for the simple pleasures. But I will get my due."

The Kizin stepped on Jacques' hand and kicked his sword away. "Go fetch." She spun around and headed in my direction.

Lute slid between Renjor and me. He held his quarterstaff out at a diagonal. "We're not done—"

She blipped out of existence, reappeared behind Lute, and sent him to kiss the dirt with a roundhouse kick. "And the doctor is out."

I threw rocks at her as she came closer. "S-Stay away!"

"Your friends or the seal." She grabbed my hair and pulled forward. "Snap and be free."

"No!"

"Do it!" The witch yanked again. "Only my Heralded One *will* sit on the thr—"

She was ready to carve into the lion face of my arm tattoo when she viper-deflected a bolt of energy from the side.

"Again. Get away from Queen Kayla," Coniphur Yalene demanded.

"Oo~ another challenger"—she ducked—"rude!"

Ze took no chances and fired a shot of white flames from zir hands, followed by another.

The witch dodged, sprinted to the right, and threw a punch.

Ze ducked, and with a burst of speed, Coniphur Yalene threw a fist of flames but missed.

Jacques patted out his singed cape. "Careful!"

"Sorry!"

Renjor laughed and charged ahead. "I like you."

Coniphur Yalene blocked her punch with zir right forearm. "Shut it."

She pushed against it. "Genecian, right? Such a tragedy."

Ze pushed back. "I said shut it."

"Shame you're quite in the dark." Renjor sliced the air behind her and fell backward into the cut.

"Don't you go in—grah!" Coniphur Yalene didn't bother to look around. "Your majesty, duck!" Ze shot a blaze at the creatures.

I turned away and covered my head, left to hear gurgled, awful cries.

"Queen Kayla, zirs are gone—"

"Wow, the best of the group."

Where...is her voice coming from?

"Such a shame. You'd be fantastic as Zar's right hand."

Coniphur Yalene's eyes flared red. "Silence!"

"Oi, come out!"

"Your head is bleeding, Lute," I said.

My friend sniffed, his eyes bloodshot from the smoke. "Tis but a flesh wound. I'm fine." He stood in front of me and held out his quarterstaff again. "I said come out, hag!"

Renjor blipped up from the ground and slapped Lute across the face. "Rude." She looked at the historian and blew zem a kiss.

No star-wind came from zem.

"We outta breath, hotshot?" The Kizin put her hand on her hip.

Coniphur Yalene's hands were redder than a sunburn.

Out of ammo...

Jacques raised his sword. "I'm not—"

Renjor looked at her nails. "Save it, dear captain. Jared will get beheaded at this rate."

Silence fell.

Lies~

Lies~

The Kizin let out a long sigh. "I must say, Saqui, your Guardians could use some serious outside playtime. Out on the grass, on a tall mountain, y'know, train up a bit. Or, should I paint a picture for ya with them dead?" She came forward. "Now then. How about a little cooperation, or do we need to watch your wizard bleed out without medical attention?" Her brooch pulsed between red and white. She looked down. "Oh my, out of time." Renjor looked about. "Well, I've done enough anyway."

Coniphur Yalene came forward. "I will kill Zar for what it has done."

"Oh, I don't doubt you will try." Renjor looked up and down at zem and bowed with a flourish. "And he will be waiting." She slipped through another crack in the air and was no more.

"T'léyna~!" ze cried, kicking the dirt.

Lute made his way to Jared. "He isn't looking good—oi, Yalene, help me here."

Jacques made his way to me. "It's what we get for goin' in blind. Four versus one? Shows what I know."

"Don't be so hard on yourself," I said.

Jacques softly bopped me on the head with the side of his fist. "Goes for ya, too." He lowered his arm. "Can ya seriously not break out of this?"

I shook my head and coughed. "No. This smokey quartz stuff. Lady Eider never told me about magic draining rocks."

"Neither did Coniphur Yalene, and I bet Jared didn't know either," said Jacques. "Plus, Annika never shows up to help."

I frowned. "What are you saying—"

Jacques looked over to our friends. "We are goin' to need to run." He looked back at me. "Releasin' the bad guys is the last thing we need, but we have no choice."

I raised my hand. "One snap, we bolt."

Jacques nodded. "One snap, we bolt. Questions later."

"Three...two...one."

Snap.

The stone lid busted, punched apart. My anklet shattered and dissolved—the shards cut my skin.

HE LIED TO US~!

Jacques hoisted me over his shoulder, and we ran as fast as possible. We evaded the bubbling pools. I covered my ears to the screams of those long dead. The mountain shook, and the smoke shifted to thick green fog growing thicker by the second. Seemingly determined to seal us in and choke us.

We didn't look back. We didn't watch the mountain cave fall into itself or stop to catch our breath until we reached the mountain pass entrance.

Jacques set me down and fell onto the ground next to me. Lute and Coniphur Yalene also took to the grass while Jared leaned against a rock. I watched the green smoke furl into the sky, trying to catch my breath. I jolted in my seat the instant a beam of green light shot into a cluster of red clouds. All the smoke cleared with the light as though it had never existed.

"That can't be good," Jacques muttered.

Jared coughed. "Foreboding indeed." He tapped his staff's orb and brought his lit pointer to his shoulder.

Lute waved a dismissive hand. "Debrief later, guys. I need to check Kayla." He shook his head when I coughed again. "Jared, do your thing. All I see is inflammation and soot." He looked at my foot. "Fix this too, please. It's swollen."

Jared tapped the orb and came forward. Healing my throat was no problem, but nothing happened around my bleeding ankle. "Check closer."

"Ah, I need a towel or something."

Jacques came forward with his knapsack. "Good news, the supplies we dropped off are still here. Gimme a sec, I'll grab yars, Lute."

"Thanks." Lute took out a cloth and dabbed my foot.

"Ah, I feel a poke," I said.

"I see it. A bit of brown rock."

"It is the smokey quartz. Get rid of it," said Jared.

"On it. Kayla, it's gonna sting."

Once Lute removed the sliver with a pair of tweezers, he chucked the fragment as far as he could.

"I could have studied that," Jared sighed, tapped his staff's orb again, and brought his finger near my injury. "...Better?"

"Much, thanks." I borrowed Lute's waterskin and took a drink.

"Perfect." Jacques pointed with his thumb over his shoulder. "Load up when ready."

Lute offered a hand and helped me to my feet. "Let's head out."

The evening sky had fallen over the Masana when I jumped into the cool water of the Sky Lake, clothes and all.

"Careful, yar dress may bog ya down," said Jacques.

"Will do."

Meanwhile, Lute washed his face at the shore and picked up sticks as Coniphur Yalene worked to clear grass for a campfire. Jared? Was silent. Unmoving, sitting on a log with this staff at his side.

Little spoken among us, and later I set the woodpile aflame.

"Are ya sure yar okay?" Jacques asked me.

I shrugged and gave a tired smile. "Yeah." I pulled my blanket around my shoulders and looked at the stars. "We lived anyway." I looked at Jared across from me. "Are you okay?"

"Yes. I will be." He took a bite of bread.

I folded my arms onto my lap as the wind blew. "Y'know what's sad? I felt troubled all night during the party." I clicked my tongue. "Figures."

"You weren't the only one tricked," said Lute, taking a seat on my left. "We all were. It's not your fault." He took a sip of water.

Jared tilted his head to the side. "Hope you know you can come to one of us about anything going forward."

"Sure." I smiled and drank some water too.

On my right, Jacques turned to me. "Kayla, did ya learn anythin' about Renjor?"

I sighed. "Not much but, Jared, I saw how she looked at you. Do you know her?"

"I think so," he replied. "However, I do not want to worry anybody. I have to remember on my own."

"Okay." I shifted in my seat. "Um, about the quartz?"

Jared stared into the fire. "Apologies...I have no excuse but was not aware of its properties."

Coniphur Yalene tossed another stick into the fire and sat next to Jared. "Regret is the first normal thing I've heard all day. Not that hard to believe, to be honest."

"But gettin' prepared before our rescue attack?" Jacques asked. "That strange quartz should've been a known constraint."

I rubbed my wrist. "I feel bad, though. Renjor stole the opal bracelet." I bowed my head. "I'm sorry, Coniphur Yalene."

"Oh, no. N-No worries, it's alright. I'm sorry to hear it's lost, but, more importantly, I'm glad you're okay."

"Thank you."

"Same here"—Lute tapped his knees with his palms—"and, here's something that's not hard to believe. The usual never arrived."

"Who?" Yalene asked. "What?"

"Lady Eider," we chorused, save for Jared.

Ze laughed. "That's easy."

"What?" Lute asked. "What is easy?"

"Lady Eider, coming in to save the day?" Ze snorted. "How? Is she a fighter? Isn't she a magic user? What good would she have done?"

Lute shrugged. "Uh, give Jared a refresher? Come to the castle to warn that busting in wasn't going to work?"

"Oh~ so Lady Eider is a military expert and should've told you?" Coniphur Yalene unwrapped zir portion of beef jerky. "Also, it's a student's job to remember what they've learned, not the teacher's."

"I promise Lady Eider never told me of the stuff," I said.

"Then again, none of us saw ya havin' a reason to go there," said Jacques. "She was countin' on us." He looked at Jared. "However, ya knew nothin'?"

"No. When it is the badlands, you stay away." The wizard sighed through his nose. "In hindsight, I would have reached Lady Eider, first. However, per our last contact, she was unavailable thus why she was not at the party."

Jacques tossed a rock aside. "It's just. I feel we could've sent soldiers to guard the place if we knew a crypt was in there. Meh, I don't know."

Lute picked up his bread. "Okay, speaking of magic, how did yours work?"

"Oh~ no you don't. You're not deflecting this conversation back to me. Stay on topic."

Lute started to say something else but sighed in defeat. "Fine. Lady Annika couldn't be useful." He pointed to Coniphur Yalene. "Rune-state abilities did work, though."

Ze nodded. "Yes, I'm confused by that."

"I was surrounded by smokey quartz," said Jared. "Kayla was tied down with cursed chains of it."

"What are ya gettin' at?" Jacques asked.

"In the past, powerful Dragons were chained, too. My power is channeled externally. The Coniphur's and Kayla's are not."

"And I wasn't chained," ze reasoned. "Odd."

I fought back a yawn. "I agree. But, when Renjor said her Heralded One should sit on the throne, she wanted to hurt me."

"She spoke of a benefactor, Zar, too," said Coniphur Yalene. "Between that and those spirits." Blue eyes flashed red. "The beast is trying to break in."

"Then we should begin buildin' defenses," said Jacques.

"What's stopping them from coming tomorrow?" Lute asked.

"Far as I can tell, Kayla was bound because our enemies are scared," said Jared. "If she was not tricked like the rest of us, our Saqui would have pushed back. Also, Renjor is arrogant." He looked at Coniphur Yalene. "You saved her from being harmed and gave us all a chance. I, for one, am grateful."

"Not like we all didn't try," Lute muttered. "Thanks for the lack of a heal on my pride, by the way."

Jacques snorted but caught it. "Oops. Sorry, man, didn't mean to laugh."

Lute rubbed his neck. "Yeah, I'm gonna be sore for days."

"You're welcome, Jared," ze said. "Can you please explain what vendetta the crypt spirits have?"

"The Leaf Turners are restless," said Jacques. "They are former Ones of Reflection who went down the wrong path and revolted against their Saqui. We seem to have found the root of our problem, havin' possibly found their grave."

"Or *a* grave," said Lute. "If Genecia had one too, it would explain why Zar was there."

"Buildin' an army?" Jacques asked.

"Yes. Renjor spoke of other worlds." I slumped, tired. "Are we sure the crypt inside the Dead Mountains is gone?"

"It would explain the beam of light," said Jared.

"So, maybe, the Heralded One is real," I said

"How do you figure?" Lute asked and took a bite of jerky.

"Don't know," I yawned. "But I don't want to face Renjor again."

"None of us do," said Jared. "We may not have a choice."

Lute gasped. "Wait, wait, wait," he cried in rapid-fire.

"What is it?" I asked.

He pointed at me and looked at our friends. "What person or entity do you know has the power to relocate things or terraform?"

Jacques pointed at me.

"This 'Heralded One'...think about it," said Lute.

"Your theory...you believe this 'One' is a former Saqui?" Coniphur Yalene asked.

"Yeah, but it doesn't make any sense," I said. "We saw Leaf Turners. Why would they go off to help a Saqui they hated?"

"Zar is more likely who they're aidin'," Jacques added. "Although Renjor was adamant, maybe the Heralded One is someone separate."

"Look, I don't know," said Lute, scratching his head. "These are all guesses anyway. Remember the hyenas—"

"Don't." I shuddered and buried my head in my hands.

"Hyenas?" ze asked.

"Er, never mind," said Lute. "Sorry, Kayla."

I sat back up. "It's...it's okay. I'll be fine."

Jared turned to Lute. "If you think the witch was behind the hyena's turning"—he shook his head—"a Kizin cannot change creatures since I cannot."

"A Kizin may not follow your code of ethics either," said Jacques. "Who can do what will have to wait. For now, we are lucky to have escaped." He pointed over his shoulder with his thumb. "Once dinner is over, let's go home?"

I shook my head. "Sorry, but I'd like to see my brother first. To rest with my family sounds nice."

"Of course, not a problem." Jacques nodded. "I'm sure King Basi wouldn't mind the visit."

BASI – Appears 31 When Furless

I FOUND KAYLA SITTING on Johari's ledge, staring at the dry season's stars.

"You're still up?"

Under a blanket, she turned from looking. "Hello, Basi."

"I'm glad I found you. Jacques told me of your unfortunate adventures. I'm sorry I wasn't able to help."

She returned to stargazing. "I don't think my Guardians wanted to risk my family. We're fine now, but some got hurt."

"I suppose magic fixes everything these days." I took a seat beside her. "Besides, aren't they like family, too?"

She leaned into my side. "You know what I mean."

"Heh, yes, I do. But, if trouble comes, do let me know."

She looked at me, worried. "Basi, you're a father now."

I shrugged. "Still. It would hurt my heart knowing I could've done more if anything happened to you."

Kayla nodded and took my paw. "Fine."

A light breeze blew through and owls hooted in the distance.

"Thank you for letting us stay."

I squeezed her hand. "Honestly, anytime, Sis."

"We plan to head out tomorrow."

"Sure thing, again, no worries."

A shooting star flew across the clear sky.

"Do you remember that time when we chased Tula?"

She giggled. "Yes. Heh, you got in so much trouble."

"That's right, I did."

"Remember the Cloudy Canyon incident?"

"I was in trouble again. I have not forgiven myself for that. You were seriously hurt."

"But you always had my back. I'm still sorry I ran off."

Again, silence fell away to distant chirps and nearby scurries.

"Do you miss him?" Kayla asked.

"Father? Yes, of course."

"Do you think he'd be proud of us?"

"Yes. And, before you say it, that wasn't your fault either."

Kayla closed her mouth, nodded, and leaned into my side again while looking south. "Thank you."

LUTE – 14 YEARS

"ON MY WAY OUT, ABE!" I mounted my horse. "Let me know if you need me earlier tomorrow."

The nurse waved with his back to the door. "Sure thing. Honestly, you're good, but I'll send word otherwise."

I petted my horse's neck. "Okay, buddy. Yes, it's hot out, but let's go to Neo-Gen."

Up and around, my horse trotted through town. Everywhere I looked, tired eyes glanced at me with weary smiles. Roofs to store signs were still under repair, while garden beds needed replanting. The smell of sawdust and paint was unavoidable.

Having reached the outskirts of the Overland, I tapped my horse with my heel and rode for the next few miles west to Neo-Gen as quickly as my steed could.

"Oi!"

Vaerin waved as ze put a bag over zir shoulder. "Sir Lute, good afternoon. How goes Queen Kayla's memory recovery?"

"Steady, last time I knew." I dismounted my horse. "How's it going? Came to check-in on Neo-Gen's repairs."

"Thank you for your concern. However, we've already reported to others, but in summary, we can always rebuild."

I shook my head. "All that crystal...the Leaf Turners did a number here. How many of your homes were damaged?"

The R.M.N. shrugged. "Thirteen out of fifty-three isn't a concern." Ze looked off toward zir people as zirs continued repairs. "Those who died are at rest."

I flinched. "Sorry for your loss."

Ze bowed zir head. "Thank you. Also, Doctor Balfor already came through with medical supplies this morning." Ze walked west. "But we could use help with the cleanup. We are gathering debris here in the middle of the valley to repurpose when new opal from the north finally arrives."

I nodded, following zem toward the tall pile. "I'm sure the mines will have plenty." I tapped zir arm. "And, hey, maybe later we can buy a drink. Heard the tavern has cider now."

D'Lana smiled. "Sure. Don't see why not."

———————————

CLANK. THUD.

The overripe smells of pressed apples to apricots nearly overwhelmed the air of the crowded pub.

I set my mug down and slumped in my chair. "And that's why I'm exhausted," I said over the loud chatter of the crowded place.

Jacques patted my shoulder. "There, there. Been a long day for everyone."

I whimpered and rested my head on the tavern's wooden table. "Does it ever end?"

"Lute, c'mon. Ya actin' loopy, and yar drink is basically fruitjuice."

I spoke to the floor. "I feel like crud, honestly."

"Like yar brain won't stop hurtin'?"

"Uh-huh. I ache. Period."

"Yup. Same. Kayla better not be—"

"Enough," Jacques chided. "Don't embarrass yarself as we sit with Sephur here."

A rush of liquid poured from our pitcher, followed by the plunk of a set cup.

"Here," said Jacques. "Let's talk about **anythin'** else before we have to turn in for the night."

"I can drink to that," said Vaerin.

"Sounds good," I mumbled, sat up, and took another swig of cider. "Ah~ okay, how's 'anything else'?"

Jacques took a sip and set his mug down. "Helped deliver a colt today."

"Really?"

"Yeah, unexpected, but the stable hands found her adorable, of course."

Three bowls of hot potato soup were delivered to our table.

I lifted my spoon. "What's her name?"

"That, we aren't sure of yet." Jacques took a bite of soup.

"I see."

"How far in the Folk-kin did ya go?"

"Read a good number of pages."

"Is reading all you two do for her majesty to remember?" ze asked. "Memory jogging?"

"More or less, yes," I said and took another bite. "Jared took over hours ago though—ah, see? We did it again."

Jacques facepalmed. "This is pathetic."

"Meh, so we care, so what?" I shrugged. "Not facing the end of the world with a Dragon at the helm would be nice, wouldn't it?"

"Can't argue." Jacques nodded. "Our last confrontation, once again, was too close. And, I'm afraid it's not the end of our troubles."

Vaerin set zir spoon down. "Shouldn't we talk about such things outside of this establishment?"

"Here, it's less suspicious than in some dark alley," said Jacques."

"What's going on?" I asked and took a sip of soup.

The captain glanced between D'Lana and me before leaning forward. "My report...it's not entirely true that Jared and I didn't see anythin'."

I tilted my head to the side. "Oh? Well, don't leave us chompin' at the bit. What's up?"

"Across the Masana, I've found claw marks bigger than the biggest bird gouged into the ground. Even Tula reported there were others across the land. Residents there have been hurt, carcasses left behind, plus erratic bursts of deforestation were located, far from our battle last week."

"What do you think caused this?" asked Lute. "Or who?"

Jacques frowned. "That's what I don't know."

I set my spoon down, no longer feeling hungry. "Claw marks...how big? I mean, we've seen Dragon marks."

Jacques leaned back in his chair. "I've also found white tufts of fur in branches, whiter than any creature from King Basi's Territory. As Jared and I escorted Queen Moli to the castle, she spoke of frightenin' red eyes, bigger than she'd ever seen. I requested her majesty to promise not to tell Kayla, for

I'm afraid Kayla will spur off before she's honestly ready to confront whatever or whoever is doin' this."

Clank.

"By the stars...."

Jacques and I looked at D'Lana, whose sweaty brow and nervous eyes told us more than ze probably intended.

Ze swallowed hard, followed by a dry cough. "So, not only is Xenos still M.I.A, but...." Vaerin closed zir eyes and leaned back in zir seat. "My word, no."

"What? What is it?" Jacques asked.

Ze leaned forward with a sigh. "There's...s-something you both need to know, but I feel this may just be a long shot. Problem is, even I don't know what causes what I saw."

"Go on," Jacques insisted.

Vaerin chugged the rest of zir cider. "I feel horrible, but...when it happened to Xenos, I-I had promised. Ze promised ze would be okay and figure it out with Jared."

Jacques put his right forearm on the table. "I promise ya Jared didn't get to see whatever this is goin', or we wouldn't be here."

He and I exchanged a look. I gestured for him to go on and took a sip from my mug.

"But, if we are to admit to things," Jacques said. "We have somethin' else about Zar ya must know about too."

"I'm sure her majesty and her Guardians had good reason," said D'Lana. "But...um, may I go first?"

Jacques raised his cup. "Certainly."

KAYLA – 10 YEARS

"FORGIVE ME"—CONIPHUR Yalene set down zir cup—"when Sephur D'Lana and I got word of your lunch invitation to the castle, I was surprised. Thought you'd still be recovering, your majesty."

I unfolded my napkin. "Thanks, but I'm okay."

"It's been two weeks," said Jacques. "We wait on this news any longer, and I think there would've been a riot."

"News?" Sephur D'Lana asked.

Jared took a piece of bread to his plate. "Coniphur Yalene, Sephur D'Lana, you saved your people." He picked up his knife and the butter. "You created the fang and saved a ruler, not your own. Therefore, as Queen Kayla's court is underway, to invite you both as ambassadors for your community was logical."

A gray blush tinted zirs noses and ears.

"We have an elder who may be better served." Coniphur Yalene shook zir head. "I'm just a historian, but—"

Lute smirked. "We asked around, who could speak best for the community, and zirs all pointed to you two."

I took a deep breath. "But...before you say yes or no"—I rose from my seat—"I would...like to apologize. I destroyed the fang."

"*What?*" Both of zirs gasped in shock.

"I was scared of what I saw on the other side and could not let it get through." I trembled a bit as I remembered Zar's lightning.

"Wait." Coniphur Yalene looked at my gathered Guardians. "You all knew and said nothing?" Ze rose slightly from zir chair.

"We did." Jacques looked zem in the eye. "Can ya tell me if she told ya any sooner, it would have changed anythin'?"

Sephur D'Lana rested zir hand on Coniphur Yalene's arm as the historian sank back into zir chair. "I want to think not, but we had **hundreds** we could have saved."

"And you would have lost your hand at least and your life at most, Xenos," Sephur D'Lana hissed.

The R.M.N.'s friend whipped around to face zem. "You know I would have given my life to save one more handful, Vaerin!"

"Don't doubt it, but what about our people?" I asked.

Please, I'm so sorry...

"I—" Coniphur Yalene couldn't even look me in the eye. "No...you're right. You didn't know us and had yours to think of too." Ze clenched zir fork in hand.

My heart pounded in my chest as my knees buckled.

This is hard...I can't tell either the rest. Too soon...

The historian dropped zir fork and moved to refill zir cup with water. "The fang is gone. What's done cannot be undone." Zir arm shook, zir knuckles were bone white around the handle as ze set the pitcher down with care. "I thank you...for your confession."

I swallowed hard. "I'm—"

"Please." Ze raised zir hand. "I-I will be okay. Let us put this in the past and look to make our people's alliance as strong as possible."

After lunch, I stood before an empty, tan canvas hung on a stone wall.

Okay, let's see here...

I placed my hands on the cold surface and closed my eyes. My line of thought drifted to all the maps I studied, the material used, the symbols, markings, and, each important place and landmark I could recall, plus about how far away each could appear from one another. The task was detailed, so I took little breaks for a peek.

After a while, I lowered my arms and stepped back to see how my mental picture drew the map with dark brown lines.

"How are we doing?" Jared asked.

I shrugged. "Good...I think. I have the Overland down, and now I need the Masana next, but this may take a lot of time." I turned around. "How goes the cleaning?"

"I'm sure the *Court of Consuls* project will be done before you know it," said Jared. "I have created some additional light orbs to brighten the corners of the room."

"I saw, it looks pretty—"

"Oi, you two, we can't lift these heavy tables all by ourselves," Lute called from across the room.

"What? Are they made of brick?" Jared muttered.

We shared a grin before I snapped my fingers, and he used his magic staff to help move the wood furniture.

In transforming the great hall, four curved tables sat arranged into two semi-circle rows divided by a royal blue carpet from the entrance to the head table at the back of the room meant for my Guardians and me. The map in progress was behind the head table. On the right wall, servants cleaned and hung the two Territories' respective flags, leaving space for Neo-Gen's when all was official and zirs flag was made.

"Who made Masana's flag?" Jacques asked. "I like the reds used in it a lot."

"Created by the Shellfore house," said Jared. "The Johari home and native trees were sketched, then made from the layered golden-blue material."

I lowered my arms to take a break. "Brother and I talked about designs during the surprise birthday party. I like how it turned out too."

Miss Wanda decorated the other tables with deep blue cloths with golden trim. Meanwhile, Lute and Jacques brought in chairs of the same oak as the tables with silver velvet cushions.

For each meeting, the consuls will meet with my friends and me. Everyone will have a voice: the Masana Representatives, the Overland Nobles, and Neo-Gen's Ambassadors. In addition, all would keep their Territory's fellow subjects in mind.

"Whew, all done." Lute wiped his brow. "See you at dinner, Kayla!"

I clapped my hands. "Okay, looks great, thank you."

Jacques and Lute headed off to eat, but I stayed behind with Jared.

"Incredible work. The map is well done."

"Thank you, I wanted to make sure I didn't forget anything."

"Yes, of course, I like the simplicity. Nothing seems amiss."

"Good."

"By the way, earlier today, I overheard you telling Jacques your plan to give the Sword of Elaiobus to Coniphur Yalene?"

"Yes. I took the fang away. Plus, if that quartz stuff traps me again. Someone may need to wield it for me."

Jared nodded. "True, ze does not have a magical weapon like the rest of us. Plus, ze would want to make sure zir people are safe."

"Yup."

"Is there...something else?"

I let out a short sigh. "Yes, who is going to keep track of all of our magic stone stuff?"

"Heh, well, I will. This 'rock stuff' is pretty important."

I folded my arms. "Okay, but, Jared, you said you didn't know about smokey quartz. Renjor made me decide between two choices I didn't want to make in the cave because of the runes around my quartz anklet."

"Apologies, I will see to doing better. However, contractual magic is tricky. Once cast, it is not something even I can dispel. Always try to look for a third option if you can."

"Alright." I pointed to his staff. "Is that orb the same stone as Renjors?"

He placed his hand over the smooth rock. "Amethyst? Yes, it helps channel my energy used for magic. However, the opal of the Folk-kin helps you *tap* into yours, serving as a direct line to Elaiobus' potential itself. The difference between you and Neo-Gen is the diary's covers are pure and enchanted."

"And no one thought to tell me?"

"There was no need. There is but one Folk-kin, and you are connected to it. As for how the diary was made exactly is beyond my level of understanding right now. As for the smokey quartz, on the other hand, I only knew the Dead Mountains had to be avoided."

"But I was kidnapped."

"Unfortunately. Now, we know it is a place to possibly acquire it."

"Still, though. I'm not some impossible boss. I get tired." I shook my head. "Jared, do you really not remember Renjor?"

He frowned. "No. I have started doubting we ever have met."

One week later, before the others of the Court, Coniphur Xenos Yalene and Sephur Vaerin D'Lana officially signed on as Neo-Gen's Ambassadors to support relations. Zirs yellow and black flag was raised high, bearing the symbols of two purple hands cradling under a floating diamond star before a white crescent moon.

"With the Overland and her majesty's promise, may it be known, the western hills yonder from the settlement toward the setting sun are at this moment the Territory of Neo-Gen," Jared announced.

Applause filled the room. "Hear, hear! Rightly so!"

Jared stepped back with the decree in hand, and I rose from my chair and came forward. "Coniphur Yalene?"

"Your majesty?"

I held out my hands and materialized the Sword of Elaiobus between us.

"After talking with my friends and Guardians, I would like to present the Fang Bearer, Coniphur Xenos Yalene of Neo-Gen, the Sword of Elaiobus as a token of this alliance."

"It is an Imogen-Kythe weapon named after this world's energy and driving force," Jared added. "May it help Neo-Gen ward against the evils we may face."

Coniphur Yalene stared at the blade. "This is—I'm honored, your majesty."

I smiled. "I would like to thank you for helping my friends save me too."

Hesitant at first, the historian took the decorated blade from me. Once in zir hands, the lion beneath the hilt morphed. Its mouth opened and revealed a sun inside.

Sephur D'Lana put zir hand on zir friend's shoulder with a smile. "Incredible."

Coniphur Yalene smiled in turn. "Thank you, your majesty. I will use it well."

After breaking for lunch, designs passed for a trading forum between the Territories and our new allies. In the future, designated barterers would prepare their business outside, in the castle's front courtyard, while meetings were in session.

A couple of weeks later, agreements for a future mining operation were underway.

"With Lady Annika Eider's help, blue opal could be transported from the northern mountains," Jared offered. "Understand this is not an easy resource for us to acquire."

Sephur D'Lana rose from zir seat with Coniphur Yalene beside zem. "Yes, however, Neo-Gen is willing and has the means to an extent. As this esteemed Court knows it, Neo-Gen works dependent on this opal. We are willing to transmute and thus create appropriate aid should the Overland require it, much like now. Before that can happen, Neo-Gen asks the Overland to help us make the essential mining tools needed. From there, we could help with building a wall and future defenses."

"Such a wall could help to protect our peoples and could be made from limestone, transmuted with the opal to build faster," Coniphur Yalene added and came around the table to present a shard of rock. "Here is a sample."

"I believe the Foggy Mountains would be the best place to look for this limestone," said Lute, then he slapped a hand over his mouth. "Pfft~!"

"Oh, no," Jacques deadpanned.

Lute chuckled. "We should call it the 'Dragon Defense Decree.'"

I snorted and covered my mouth as others rolled their eyes. Meanwhile, zirs took a seat.

"Lute, no," said Jacques.

"Lute, yes?"

"No," said Jared.

"Sorry, but the triple D! It works."

"Ahem, jokes aside, preparations for this wall have to begin, said Jared. "Renjor's actions are still fresh on everyone's minds as Zar is bound to come. All in favor of the Mining Operations Agreement, say 'aye.'"

The vote was unanimous.

"With this agreement, what other matters should we move to next," Jared asked. "Ah, Ladies of Shellfore?"

Lady Akilah lowered her hand and rose from her seat with her sister. "We agree *whenever* the attack comes, preparing for it now is best. That said, we have a wall. So, my sister and I would like to make a motion to shift the discussion to military strength and training."

Hands rose in favor.

I nodded. "Then, let's move to that."

No matter the topic, no matter how fast time flew, the Folk-kin was always there. It rested on a white marble podium in front of the head table. It radiated a blue glow, opened on its own, wrote, and closed again after each law or decree passed. At first, the whole room hushed and watched. Now, we moved on as the diary went about its business.

"Oi, Kayla, pay attention," Lute whispered. "Ignore the Folk-kin, please."

"S-Sorry." I sat up straight, returning my focus on Lord Quild speaking of crop yields.

When all items were addressed for the day, my stomach threatened to growl and embarrass me. I was starving.

"Finally! The meetings are over for a while," Lute declared, standing to stretch.

Jacques got up next. "Chill, ya sound like a kid who got out of bein' lectured."

"Meh, whatever, man." Lute dismissed with a wave of his hand. "Say, Coniphur Yalene, whatchya doing? You are watching the Folk-kin almost every time it opens."

I rolled my eyes. "Jeez...there's no crime in looking at it."

Lute raised his hands. "What? I'm just saying."

Coniphur Yalene shrugged. "It's alright. Honestly, I find this to be a mesmerizing piece."

I smiled and walked over to stand next to zem by the podium. "Right? The diary is amazing. It transcribes—as Jared puts it—everything important."

"Everything?"

"Yes, the Folk-kin creates my story."

"Sounds more like a logbook if it records all the details...have you ever read it?" ze asked.

"A bit, but not really, no. I'm busy."

Neo-Gen's ambassador blinked and looked at me with a slight, furrowed brow. "And you're okay with being so busy?"

I put my finger on my chin. "I...actually, I'm not sure."

"I keep tellin' her it's okay to take a break," said Jacques. "The new defensive wall is well underway since construction started a couple of months ago."

I folded my arms. "Yeah, I keep saying I can't."

"To be fair, that sorta sounds like you, too," said Lute.

Jacques raised his hands in surrender. "Fair. Let's take some personal time." He brought his hands together with a clap. "Renjor can't feed into our anxiety."

"Do come to Neo-Gen when you can, your majesty," said Coniphur Yalene. "I can see a few Calphs wanting to play or have lunch with you."

"Another idea is going into town and visiting the bakery," Lute added. "But that's me. I'm ready for dinner, heh."

I grinned. "Sounds like fun, thank you."

XENOS – 21 YEARS

"TASTY AS ALWAYS!" THE hospital's resident, Lute Gibe, patted his stomach while the rest of our group agreed. "It stinks Sephur D'Lana headed home already since ze is going to miss dessert."

"Ze had to go and take care of Dissapha—*yawn*—Xyphir, who is down with a cold." I blinked purposefully and shook my head. I caught myself staring at my plate and pinched the bridge of my nose as I leaned back in my chair. "By the Designs, I am tired."

"Ha." Lute Gibe lightly punched my arm with his fist. "Big changes will do that."

Captain Volt set his cup down. "Would ya like to stay overnight? I'd hate for ya to fall off ya horse or somethin'."

I picked the rheum, gunk, from the corners of my eyes. "Yes, actually, if it's not too much trouble."

Her majesty shook her head. "Not a problem at all. We have guestrooms."

"Thank you. It's been nonstop since the mining approval six weeks ago, and I've groups near ready to execute zirs schematics for the wall. That is if—*yawn*—the Lords and Ladies approve the plans during next week's updates."

Queen Kayla set her fork down. "Looking forward to it."

Once we parted ways, a servant showed me to a modest guestroom. I shut the door behind me and gently set my gifted weapon against the vanity on my right. It was heavy to bear but an honor to carry. I took in the fresh smell of rose and lavender potpourri on the washbasin and leaned on the furniture to pull off my boots.

"Hello, dear."

I dropped my boot in hand and spun around. "You."

"Shhh~"

Dressed exactly as before, the Kizin came forward.

153

"H-How did you—"

"Oh, I'm not here. My friends"—Renjor tapped her forehead—"they have a way of getting into *special* minds." She pointed to my chest. "If you know what's best." She pointed to hers. "You're going listen to me."

I blinked. The witch's vision disappeared right when pain lurched and dug into my skull.

"Ah~" I violently shook my head.

<It was a matter of time. All spells do. So much time.>

"Y-Your voice—get out," I hissed.

<How 'bout no, and we have a lil fun?>

In the mirror, my vision went red. I pounded my fist on the wall next to the vanity. "Get out of my head!" I grabbed a small vase and threw it at the mirror.

Silence.

My sweat turned cold. I collapsed onto the bed.

<Are you done, Genecian? Or is 'Xenos' peachy with you?>

I screamed into my pillows so no one could hear me.

<It was her fault, you know. Genecia is gone because of her.>

I covered my ears. "Lies!"

<Ah~ welcome to the club!>

"The queen has done nothing."

<Who do you think released my benefactor?>

"Released?" I shook my head hard. "Liar."

<She didn't tell you?>

"Stop."

<I wouldn't lie to you. Trust me.>

Queen Kayla's gift radiated a soft blue glow from the corner of my eye, calling to me. Renjor's taunts grew into screams by the time I reached the Sword of Elaiobus. I grabbed the grip, unsheathed the weapon, and sliced at the air out of desperation.

The mind games went silent.

"Have I struck it down?" I whispered to myself. "Did...did her majesty know?" I looked up and down the blade. "By all the stars, what was this weapon made of?"

Exhausted, my pulse still pounded in my sleep-deprived head. I sheathed the blade and kept the weapon close while I got ready for bed and put on the provided nightwear.

"At least I didn't prompt anybody to come here," I whispered.

I laid under the covers, yet barely slept.

The following morning the room looked dull. After dressing in my standard uniform, I glanced around at my mess from last night. Frowning at the glass shards everywhere, sad and guilty for things in such disarray, I jolted to the sudden knock at my door.

"May I come in?" Miss Wanda asked from the other side of the door.

I stayed at the foot of the bed. "Um, yes, please."

"Coniphur, I wanted to make sure your—my word," she whispered in shock. "What happened?" She closed the door.

"Ra—" My lips sealed. "Ra—" My throat trapped my words.

<Nice try.>

"Coniphur Yalene, what's going on?"

I rubbed the back of my neck. "Uh~ sorry, d-don't mean to worry you, b-but there were—"

"Did something attack you?" Miss Wanda knelt to look for, what I assumed, to be clues.

<Go with it. Or explain it like a crazy person. Up to you.>

I coughed. "Ahem, y-yes, it was so weird. A bird flew in as I opened my window."

"A bird?"

"Yep, two. It was like watching Calphs play a wild game of tag. I shooed them out, however, and didn't want to worry anyone." I offered my hand.

Miss Wanda looked up at me with sad eyes before standing back on her feet with my help. "I'm surprised you didn't call for someone."

I let go of her hand. "Apologies, I should have. In the unlikely event this ever happens again, I promise to call for help."

She brought her hands together before her. "Promise?"

"Yes, yes. Now, please, I'll clean this up, okay?"

"No need." Miss Wanda looked at the Sword of Elaiobus upon my bed. "I'm glad Queen Kayla gave you the honor. Speaking of her majesty, will you be attending Lute's birthday brunch? It's a casual thing."

<What a babysitter.>

"Begone," I spoke under my breath.

"Coniphur?"

I took a sharp inhale. "S-Sorry, not you. But please send my regrets. I have other matters to attend."

"Of course. Now, we can't have glass on the floor. Please leave the door open as you leave. I will have someone come in to address it, alright?"

"Thank you."

"Have a safe return to Neo-Gen, Coniphur Yalene."

Once the door closed after her leaving, I took a seat on the edge of my bed.

<Now what, Xenos.>

I brushed my hair back with my right hand. "Renjor, leave." I picked up the magical Sword.

Alone in silence, there were no more quips. In relief, I headed home.

Calphs were giggling and making crowns of dandelions when I arrived. In my passing through the valley of the western hills, there were those picking fruit or working the field while a few others were in the middle of expanding zirs homes with the new shipment of opal and limestone. Some called out to me and waved. Despite the fresh air, I returned the gesture but kept going, feeling sluggish. I dismounted my horse, tied the lead to a post near my home, and went around to my circular door.

A hand clapped onto my shoulder.

"Ah~" I spun around.

Vaerin held up zir hands in surrender. "Just me, ca'hala."

I slapped a hand onto my chest. "Mo~ jen kli no, Vaerin."

Ze lowered zir arms. "Heh, sorry, Xenos. Didn't mean to scare you—say now, you look exhausted. Need to rest?"

"Yes, I have to. Meetings about the wall and mining over at Fermuru Hyphia's home start like in an hour."

Vaerin tapped zir tablet made of wires and glass framed with opal. "Alright. I need to get to another meeting with the weavers. I'll be your alarm clock."

"Thank you."

Twenty minutes later, at best, I rolled off my futon and answered D'Lana's relentless knocks at my door. Couldn't shout at zem, though. Ze and I were the last ones to arrive. Once there, we were handed a wooden cup of warm tea by Hyphia's partner Nilo.

Talks about the latest successful mining trip went in one ear and out the other. Speeches about how grateful zirs were for Lady Annika Eider and Queen Kayla's aid meandered. Couldn't blame anyone's chipper mood, however. The opal trade and treaty helped improve our way of life here. Our housing evolved from survivalist tubes to dwellings akin to cottages, boosting our morale substantially. However, my heart sank regardless. I didn't feel present or of the same mind as anyone else there. Despite the chatter, the sole thing keeping me awake was the tea refills.

Fermuru Hyphia passed me a roll of parchment. "Per our last meeting, I calculated five pounds of blue opal to every one hundred of limestone will be plenty to raise a wall strong enough. Happy to report we have almost collected enough by transporting crates of opal"—ze held out a carved, palm-sized pendant with rune inscriptions around it—"with our Dragon bone amulets to and from the snow mountains."

ᚻᚠᛁᚷᚠᛏᛁᛟᚠᚹ ᛋᛗᚲᛏᛗᚻᛏᚱᛁᛟᚠᚠᛏᛗᚻ ᚻᛁᚴ

ANOTHER FRIEND RAISED zir hand. "Also, we finished calculating a clock tower as a gift for the town. We hope it will raise morale."

On the parchment, the words might as well have been pictures. "L-Looks good. Thank you."

"Coniphur Yalene? Are you alright?"

I looked aimlessly, unsure who spoke. "Huh?"

"Heh, forgive zem. Ze a lot on zir shoulders," said Vaerin.

Fermuru Hyphia pursed zir lips. "I can see it. Too many roles and we lose sight of who we are."

I rose from my seat. "P'nya, night has fallen, neighbors. Mere sleep is what I need."

"I'll take zem home," Vaerin offered. "Be back soon to finish."

Once home, I took my Gieci off my forearm and put it on my small table. I slipped off my uniform jacket, hung it up on a coat rack on my right, and untucked my shirt. I kicked off my boots and decided to skip dinner, crashing into bed.

———— ╫╫╲╲╲╫╫ ————

"TWO HOURS, YOU, J'FLI," I muttered.

<*Ah, ah, language. It's not like we didn't have a fantastic conversation.*>

I rubbed my eyes. "And, as I keep telling you, over and over, you're a lying sack of manure."

<*And here I thought you'd like your gift. You **want** revenge, right?*>

"It's been weeks, so give it up. I'm not ever putting that necklace on."

<*Oo~ Ouch. You don't want power?*>

I grunted and grabbed the Sword.

<*You wound me——*>

Silence.

I exhaled and shook my head. "Note to self, hug the blade next time," I mumbled and sighed. "Okay, thank the Designs, I live alone. No one needs to see me coddle this weapon like a plush toy."

Once dressed save an unbuttoned shirt, I studied the mark she'd given me.

ᚱᛗᚾᛁᚷᚨᛏᛇᛊ ᛊᛁᚷᛁᚵ

IT GLOWED PURPLE, WHERE the left side of my chest met my shoulder just below the collarbone.

"Curse, you, witch," I muttered.

After decoding what was seared into my skin with the Atsain, I discovered the symbols' translated to *Tethered Sigil.* I wanted to tell Vaerin or anyone about it, but such was her spell, which throttled my voice each time I tried and linked me to her calls.

What's worse was the 'power' the witch tempted me. A so-called gift gleaming red and, frankly, appeared ominous upon my table. A small pendant of two teardrop rubies—the top blood red and the other pale pink—welded at the tips. A rough, dark iron ring surrounded the abstract hourglass, suggesting one could flip the rubies around a silver axis.

"AS IF I'D EVER TAKE it," I scoffed.

After buttoning and tucking in my shirt, I rolled my right sleeve and strapped my Gieci back on. After all that's happened, the weight of it was a comfort. I pressed the top square button and removed my data cube from its compartment.

I twirled the opal-diamond transmute between my fingers. "Everything about me and ever was...."

The data included my notable achievements, dissertations, diplomas, etcetera.

"Yet, I ended up here." I closed my hand around it. "Don't think I need you anymore."

I put the chip on the table and buckled the Sword of Elaiobus to my hip. I checked my short hair in the mirror, left to saddle my horse, and put Fermeru Hyphia's plans in my bag.

"Morning!"

I looked to my right and waved. "Hello, Vaerin."

"You sleep better?"

"Hardly enough. Had to crack some final details. You?"

"Yes, oh, also Xyphir and I finished the wooden wind chime set I told you about last week."

"Oh? I'm happy to hear that." I stifled a yawn. "Sorry, I forgot, but I'll look at it later, okay?"

"Sure!" Ze pointed over zir shoulder. "I'm running behind, so I'll catch up."

I mounted my horse. "Sounds good. See you at the meeting."

The trip felt short. My mind but a haze floating among all the clouds overhead. On auto-pilot. After giving my reins to the royal stable hand upon arrival, I pulled off my saddlebag, put the strap over my shoulder, and entered the castle.

When the guard closed the door behind me, I almost gasped.

"Oh, shoot, I wonder..." I slipped to the right, turned to press my back against the wall, and dug through my bag. "Hope I didn't forget the—"

"What about Zar?" Queen Kayla asked from around the corner.

"We will get there," said Lute.

"*What?*" I hissed and slapped a hand over my mouth.

"How can I? It's awful Zar is alive because of me."

I let my hand drop to my side. I wanted to yell, but my voice wouldn't speak. My lips wouldn't move. My whole body trembled, yet my feet felt cemented to the ground.

< Told you, Xenos. >

I peeked around the wall and held the side of my head near my left temple. When Sir Gibe and Queen Kayla were out of sight, I bolted to the one place I hoped would be private.

< They want you on a leash. >

"No."

< Yes, they do. >

"What good would—no!"

I reached the stables and hid in my horse's stall.

< You done? >

A cold sweat beaded across my brow.

My brown horse counted his hoof and huffed a whinny. From scraping rakes to pouring feed, the stable hands worked, yet none noticed me. With clenched teeth, I gripped the Sword.

<Come now, you know the truth.>

I sniffed. "This is but a trick."

<Honestly...>

"Leave me be."

<What do you plan to do? You're too tired to keep me away.>

The stall wall thudded to the beat of the back of my head. "They—*thud*—had **every** chance."

<Exactly. Now you're getting it.>

I drew in a labored breath and closed my eyes. "I-I don't know what to do."

<Go home. If you want real power. You'll find it still waiting for you.>

I rose to my feet. "If you harm a hair on my friends' heads—"

<So, you do care about Neo-Gen. Go home.>

KAYLA – 12 YEARS

THE SOFT SUNLIGHT DANCED through the tall windows of the courtroom—

"Finally!" My cry echoed in the stonewalls.

I slapped the pages and pushed my chair with the back of my knees.

"Isn't it a bit early to make this much noise," Jared asked.

I looked up from where I stood and found him and Jacques walking in.

"Good morning and good timing"—I wiped my tired eyes, returned to my seat, and pointed to the diary page—"Miss Wanda already told me it was about lunchtime, but I figured out what we could use to find Xenos."

Jared's blue eyes scanned the last page I read and furrowed his brow. "A data cube. That is perfect, but"—he pointed to the text—"what of this hourglass? I have never seen nor heard of this." He looked at Jacques. "Have you?"

"No. Through a joint search, nothin' about that came up."

I frowned.

Maybe...ze threw it away, or did ze wear it?

"By the way," said Jacques, "Lute will join us soon. He told me he had some stuff to put away first."

I sniffed. "Okay."

"Ya alright?" Jacques asked.

I yawned. "Not really. I'm tired, but it's awful how Xenos learned about Zar."

"How so?" Jared asked, took a moment to scan the next page, and frowned. "Oh...yes, that is quite unfortunate."

"Is there even a plan?" I slumped back into my seat. "For when we find Xenos?"

"We will figure it out." Jacques rested his hand on the hilt of his sword at his hip.

I rubbed my arms. "Still."

"What are ya gettin' at?"

I shrugged. "I don't know. I worry a lot. Doesn't help I've been reading **everything**."

When neither of my friends replied, I sighed and closed the Folk-kin. "You all told me from the start this was my diary. Am I supposed to pretend not to know the fibs and secrets? Private things? I meant to talk to you guys about this, but we've been busy."

"It was the price to get you to remember," said Jared. "I do not believe I ever found an instance where a Saqui truly read their story for the reasons you mentioned. Continuing this tradition would have been nice, but you know we had no choice."

I deflated further in my seat and rested my head on the table. "Jacques, I..."

"Look. I, for one, have nothin' to hide," he declared. "I stand by anythin' I might have said or thought."

I pursed my lips and sat up. "Alright, but—"

"But what?" Jacques waved for me to continue. "We gotta get goin'."

I could barely look him in the eye. "I feel guilty finding out you were born a girl by reading it in the Folk-kin, alright? Especially after how Lute found out as he did, and you didn't want to tell me." I felt Jacques staring. Shocked or mad, I wasn't sure while focused on the diary on the table. "I-I'm sorry." I folded my hands together. "The Folk-kin has shown me these secret sides a few times." I looked up. "So, I'd like to say I am sorry."

He took a long moment, then passed a hand along the back of his neck. "Ya right. I didn't want to, once. But, time went on and just...life, ya know?" He lowered his arm and shrugged one shoulder. "One thing after another. End of it all, yeah, it's not ideal. But, if I wasn't truly okayor was worryin' over what ya might have been readin'—I would've been more apt to read aloud in Lute's place. Frankly skippin' the parts I wouldn't have wanted ya to know about."

The pit in my stomach grew anyway. "I just...feel bad you didn't get to tell me in person. Are you sure—"

Jacques waved his hands in front of his chest. "Listen, seriously, it is okay." He pushed his black ponytail off his shoulder and stepped forward.

"Quick storytime. When I was ten, little things such as 'wearin' skirts make me feel weird' or 'I like rough housin' started stockpilin'. Folks took notice and supported me."

"And we are all the better for them doing so," said Jared.

Jacques grinned, casting his eyes down with a fond look. "Yeah…it wasn't all that easy, but I've had a long time to think, and I'm happy where I am and what I've done." He looked back at me and rested his hand on the hilt of his sword. "So, we are good, Kayla. I understand this isn't an ideal reveal or time to discuss, but I—we—are *more* than fine."

I ducked my head a little, bracing for the awkwardness. "Even with wearing bindings or bandages?"

The captain's eyes grew wide. He blinked deliberately, and then he relaxed with a chuckle. "Yeah, tho, if the Folk-kin were a person, I'd have words to share with them. Like, such details weren't their business." He looked up, tilting his head to the side. "Then again, such being a part of who I am…yeah, we're good."

With an appreciative sigh of relief, I smiled. "You're a good friend, and I'm happy we're okay. You were Jacques Volt when we met and still are."

He gave me the largest grin I'd seen from him. "Heh, thanks." Jacques took a step back. "Now then, the return of the missin' pages takes priority. Once we pinpoint the location, I recommend Jared, here, communicates with Annika to see how she's doin' and get her help on repairin' the Folk-kin once we have the pages."

"I have," said Jared. "I can guarantee she is aware, and the diary needs to be made whole. To be honest, I expect her to arrive when we need her most. Right now, we know the mission."

"And handle Xenos' trial," Jacques added, folding his arms.

I raised my hands. "Hey now, I understand this doesn't look great for zem, but let's keep an open mind."

"Understood," Jared confirmed.

"Oi!" Lute entered the room. "Did I miss anything?"

"I'll catch ya up," Jacques replied. "Kayla, what is the item we need?"

I put my hands on my hips. "Well, that's the tricky part. In the Folk-kin, Xenos' says ze had this 'data cube' from Genecia, zir personal records." I folded my arms. "Ze took it out of zir Gieci. I don't know if ze stored it somewhere else.

"Maybe the tower we were in for the last battle?" Lute guessed.

Jared nodded. "Probably, the tower has become zir home away from home, of sorts. That cube could help us create the tracking spell we need."

"Then, let's get to work and head on out." Lute turned on his heels toward the door.

"Oops..." I held my growling stomach.

Lute pivoted back around. "A~nd never mind! Hungry for some lunch?" he chuckled while Jacques facepalmed and Jared shook his head.

The chimes of the town clock struck five as we walked past the dining hall entrance for supper. The table was prepared with lit candles and silver dishware, complete with a mouthwatering meal of fresh fruits, cheeses, veggies, and thinly sliced, cold venison. After the butler pulled out a seat for me, he returned to the kitchen through doors on my right.

Lute passed the basket of rolls to me. "I have a question."

I took a roll and passed the basket to Jacques. "Sure."

"Rather than go to the tower, can't Jared seek the data cube with a spell, find it, and then we can move on?" he asked.

Jacques stabbed at his venison with his fork. "Can we eat then discuss further? I haven't eaten for most of the day."

Jared remained silent.

Lute put his hands in the air. "Fine, fine. I feel this is a giant oversight, is all." He pulled the platter of fruits next, closer to me. "Here, Kayla."

I took a few apple and cheese slices. "Thank you, and I know what you mean."

Once done with my selection, Lute pushed the large platter to Jacques. "Better yet, why in the world are you not snappin' your fingers to will it to appear?

Jacques picked up his cup. "Seriously? Food. First. I'm *hangry*."

The cube isn't alive, Kayla...and we're past 'privacy'...

"I. You're right." I snapped my fingers, and the cube materialized beside my folded napkin.

Jacques covered his cough with his forearm and set his drink down. "By all that I am, can't we get a moment?"

Lute grinned. "How about ten?"

Once lunch finished, we moved to the throne room.

I took a seat. "Jared. Go ahead."

"Yes"—Jared headed to the middle of the room and raised his hands—"let's start."

The room was dead silent. I leaned forward in my seat and watched the cube.

"Uh~"—Lute tilted his head to the side—"it's supposed to do something, right?"

Jared closed his hand and brought his arms to his sides. "Yes, it is not working."

Lute scuffed his boot on the floor. "Shoot—wait, didn't we get any reports from the Masana? Any clues? We're sure Xenos' location isn't the Dead Mountains?"

Jared shook his head. "That location does not make sense. It typically takes at least a full day by horse, and Xenos got there in, what, a matter of hours? This spell should have helped us. I mean, it is usually reliable."

"Tch, I'm blaming the Kizin," I scoffed.

Lute threw his hands in the air. "Then ze used zir super speed!"

"It's a great guess." I shook my head. "But, no."

Jacques nodded. "The Dead Mountains are west of Johari in the Masana Territory. The gazelles or jaguars would have seen Xenos and reported to King Basi. In turn, he would have had Tula report to us."

"Please explain," Lute asked.

I stood from my throne and came forward. "Speed and sighting others of speed are the Birds Tribe's specialty." I folded my arms. "To be honest, though, I kind of wonder how a gazelle would describe Xenos."

Lute ruffled his hair. "So, they could've seen zem."

"Again, Renjor is my guess," I said.

"Now that you know about her," said Lute with a look of pity. "On the one hand, I'm glad, and on the other, I am so sorry."

"What is the point of how Xenos traveled?" Jacques asked. "Ze essentially vanished. Great. Have we at least figured out what has caused zir sudden change?"

I raised a finger. "The witch taunted zem. That I know. Did we see her when we fought Zar?"

"Good point," said Lute. "I didn't."

Jared and Jacques shook their heads.

"Okay, well, let's think. During the battle, Xenos had my brother send a bird to deliver me the Sword of Elaiobus."

"I'm lost," said Jacques. "And?"

I walked closer to my friends. "I gave the Sword to Xenos as a gift after becoming an ambassador, right?" I looked at Lute. "I read the blade didn't stop Renjor from getting in zir mind."

"B-But ze helped us—" Lute slapped his hand over his mouth. "...Never mind, prolly too early for you to know."

"A-Anyway, Xenos couldn't speak," I continued. "Even if ze wanted to. Ze found out about Zar and was so, very much upset."

Lute rubbed the back of his neck. "Oi, that...jeez."

Jacques scowled. "Still doesn't explain the transformation." He looked at Jared. "Is this an illusion?"

Jared shook his head. "I do not believe so."

"No, but a bizarre hourglass pendant was given to Xenos, and Renjor spoke of power," I said.

"It may be behind this," said Jared.

"But that would mean ze put it on. Had it with zem in secret," said Lute, who then ruffled his hair, agitated. "How much pain...yikes."

"Again, ze might not have been able to tell anyone, though." I wiped away a stray tear. "I'm sad we didn't get to talk to zem about Zar in time."

The silence was heavy. Looks of regret, frustration, and concern fell across my friends' faces.

"Yeah, it's addin' up the more I think about it," said Jacques. "Vaerin warned us in the tavern the other day, Kayla. Now that we're caught up, we need to help."

"Then it's settled," I said. "We need zir side of the story."

"Let's save Xenos," Lute agreed.

Jared stepped forward. "I do not believe anyone here underestimates the urgency between retrieving the missing pages and bringing Xenos home safely. However, at this hour, we either plan for an early morning or start another search right away."

Lute waved his hands. "Oh, no, no way, too soon." He raised his right hand into the air. "I vote to rest and prepare for an early morning."

Jacques raised his hand. "I agree. It would be too dangerous to go runnin' off without more preparations."

I looked between them. "Don't see any other choice."

The captain folded his arms. "Like I said. It's risky. If it were me, ya wouldn't be goin' at all."

"I would not put it past our enemy to burn the pages if Kayla does not come," Jared warned.

Jacques nodded. "If Xenos has found zemself involved with the Leaf Turners, we don't know who may be listenin' or watchin'." He brought his hand to his chin. "If we ask for the Lords and Ladies to come, the town is defenseless...yeah, I'll need some time to figure this out."

Lute turned to me. "Here's the plan. Sounds like you're going to bed as we prepare for tomorrow. Doctor's orders."

I folded my arms. "Excuse me, you're not Doctor Balfor yet."

"Maybe not, but you have bags under your eyes, and it doesn't help anybody if you're not focused. If you want to come with us to search for clues tomorrow—"

"Do I look like I need your permission?" I asked.

"You may want mine."

I turned my head to find Miss Wanda entering the room, the dining hall doors closing shut behind her. "Forgive me, your majesty, but this snippiness is probably why Sir Lute is asking you to rest. You do look tired."

Lute gestured to her with a smile while still looking at me. "See? Amelia gets it."

I sighed. "Fine, Miss Wanda, can you, please, take me to a spare room? I don't think my bedroom is fixed."

"You're correct. It isn't yet, so I had a room prepared for you in the east hall upstairs."

"Alright."

"If there's an update, I'll have Miss Wanda get ya," said Jacques.

"Okay."

I left my friends, went upstairs, and kept going until I reached my destination. Once I shut the door, I sprawled across a modest bed.

With a snap of my fingers, the weight of the summoned Folk-kin fell near my side. I needed to keep reading, but I didn't open it for sleep weighed on my eyes.

I don't want to fight anyone. Hang on, Xenos...

KAYLA – 10 YEARS

PRETTY LEAVES OF GOLDS, oranges, and reds fell from their branches while green grasses had long turned bro—

"Cold! I hate the cold! I can't take any more of this cold!"

"Stop complaining," Coniphur Yalene chided. "You're a grown man now, Captain."

Jacques rubbed his arms. "S-Seventeen. S-Still cold. Don't care."

"Oi, lunch breaks are short between meetings, and we all get the library lounge is chilly, Jacky," said Lute. "The firewood is coming soon, okay?"

Jared looked up from his book, sitting on the couch on my right. "I take it training was a—"

"Cancelled. Couldn't take the bitter wind at all," said Jacques.

Lute snorted. "Oh boy."

I rubbed my feet back and forth across the rug and leaned back in the armchair beside the couch. "Sorry, Jacques. I would have created fire, but Miss Wanda told me to let others do it."

"Can't wait until his reaction to winter," said Lute with two thumbs up, rolling his eyes.

"Winter comes here, too?" Jacques groaned.

Jared returned to his book. "How could you stand Lady Eider's place?"

"Here, I'll give you a drum roll...." Lute made clapping noises, hitting the ground with his hands.

"Hmph, I wore my brown cape, thank ya very much."

"Uh-huh. Where is it now?" Coniphur Yalene asked.

"Ya were there! Ya burned it, remember?"

"Oh...it was *that* cape? It looked kind of..."

"Worn through?"

When Jared pitched in, Lute threw his head back and was in stitches. I tried not to, but I could barely stop my giggles.

"Why I oughta—"

Jacques lunged at Lute. The ambassador stepped away and stood on the opposite side of the large hearth. I laughed at Jacques giving Lute a brotherly head nudgy with his knuckles.

Trapped in a headlock, Lute couldn't stop chuckling. "Ah, I yield, I yield!"

"That's right, take it back!"

"Honestly, come on," said Jared. "We have a guest."

"Your majesty Saqui?"

A soldier came up to me, bowed, and presented me with a package. "This arrived at the gate. It is from a child who desired you to have this as a gift."

I held in my laughs and took the package. "T-Thank you."

"Of course, your majesty Saqui."

With one more bow, the soldier turned and left. With everyone distracted, I saw no reason not to open my present. It was a small, rectangular object in brown paper wrapping. I tore through the foil and cast it aside. The gift was a narrow, silver box with a black and gold lid with a smooth, marbling texture. There were no markings or emblems, and there wasn't a card to say who sent it. I wanted there to be one to send a thank you note for this pretty thing.

I opened the box.

Then heard Jared shout.

XENOS – 21 YEARS

"NO!"

The goofs and gaffs screeched to a halt. Advisor Jared rushed to Queen Kayla's side and ripped a box from her hands to toss it into the still unlit fireplace.

<And like that, the plan is working!>

I froze in place. Her majesty's eyes were entirely white, and she wasn't screaming. Deathly still. A fine golden-orange and black sand had flown out of the trap and swarmed about as an enchanted curse enveloped the queen's entire form.

Jared shook my shoulders. "Focus! The sand contains that quartz! Light the box on fire!"

I remained unmoving. Jared went over and shook the dumbstruck Captain Volt, followed by Gibe's shoulders. "Grr~ snap out of it!"

"Graah!" Jared knelt in pain and held his head in agony.

Before I could say another word, the Guardians' eyes rolled back simultaneously, and all three crumpled to the ground.

I remained unaffected. Yet my heart twisted in my chest.

<See? Told you I keep my promises.>

I looked at my hands. "W-What?" I hissed, turned to the library door, and took a measured step forward. "help...H-Help! Please, someone!"

<What are you doing?>

I dug my nails into my skull. "Renjor...you...get out of my head."

I balled my hands into fists and focused on my star-wind.

<Stop! We had a perfect plan. Don't you dare!>

"Silence," I cried, shooting a ball of fire at the cursed box.

No burning smell came as green and blue sparks flew from my white flames.

"Ambassador?"

Three shocked servants arrived with the firewood.

I waved them over. "Come here, please. I need help taking your Guardians to the hospital!"

Worried and confused, they dropped the wood but collapsed when they got close.

"Ah, stars," I hissed.

I moved closer and crouched in front of Queen Kayla's comatose form. I tried taking the queen's hand, but the sand lashed at me.

"Ow! Fight this, your majesty! I'm sorry, you have to," I pleaded.

<Stop it!>

I reached again. "This is my fault. No more. Queen Kayla is a child. Whatever the past was, it was just that."

<She must pay!>

"No!"

The buzzing sand kept swirling around her majesty, almost mocking me. I cradled my injured hand and tried to think of all the devices I could use.

"None of those things could work," I shouted. "This is—"

The mysterious substance swirled faster and caused a louder buzz. Upon hearing this buzz, an all too familiar pain in my head came shooting back.

<Leave her in the mist!>

"No, you dared trick me for long enough!"

Like a fool, however, the very weapon to free me from Renjor's grasp was on the other side of the hearth.

"No longer...*your* puppet," I cried.

<LEAVE HER IN THE MIST!>

I fumbled toward the Sword of Elaiobus, holding my head, and gritted my teeth, struggling forward. "I **will** save her and be rid of you."

<No— >

Once the blade was in hand, I turned back around. The sand struck me across my shoulders and face, but I kept reaching. With the queen's hand in mine, I pulled her from her seat. The substance's buzzes and lashes around the chair became furious.

"Oh yeah? Get out," I shouted. "Knock it off!" I let go of her majesty's hand and fired another ball of my star-wind.

The buzzes turned into violent screeches as the white flames enveloped the chair.

"What have I done?" I whispered and closed my eyes, waiting for Renjor to mock me. But nothing came.

I moved the queen to the couch. When all was quiet, the servants and other Guardians regained consciousness. Captain Volt's near-vacant expression appeared as though he couldn't even find the energy within to pick up his blade.

"This fire will burn until there is nothing but ash," I said. "I'll see to Queen Kayla, Captain Volt, and take care of things here. You lot need to go to bed."

Like shambling corpses, the group, thankfully, did what I asked and went off to rest. I returned to observing the cursed object's dissolution. My vigil ended after a few minutes, but her majesty was still asleep.

I tried to awaken her, but Queen Kayla did not stir. I checked her heartbeat and breathing. Fortunately, both were well and steady. Around her eyes and down her cheeks were pale blue to green, ombre streaks. I tried rubbing the marks away with my thumbs but failed.

I took her hand between mine and shook it. "Your majesty, you must wake up. I am sorry."

Nothing.

I gathered the queen in my arms, straightened, and headed out the door. Passing through the throne room, Vaerin joined us.

"By the stars and Designs, what is happening, and where are you taking the queen?"

We left the castle we headed for the stables. "I've little time to explain. Help me take the Saqui to our horses."

We made haste, reached our horses' stall, opened the gate, and headed inside.

"I will take her majesty to the hospital, and you make your way to Neo-Gen—"

Vaerin slipped in front of me and grabbed my upper arms. "Wait a minute."

"W-What?"

My friend frowned with scared eyes.

"Seriously, what?" I repeated.

Ze pulled forward a piece of white hair by my shoulders. "Look, it's grown. Also, your hands"—ze took a step back—"give her majesty to me."

I passed the queen over. My hands shook as my trimmed nails had yellowed and grown inches longer.

Stars...I forgot to turn it!

"Your eyes haven't stopped being red since I ran into you."

I spun toward the horse. "I-I'm fine. We need to go—"

"No. Tell me. What is happening?" Vaerin set the queen amongst the fresh hay, leaning her against a wall. "Don't push me away."

"I-I was given a gift."

"A gift that's **changing** you?" ze asked. "I-I don't understand."

I looked over my shoulder. "We aren't in Genecia anymore," I snapped. "Talking beasts who turn into fantastical people at will? Magic? I needed help to lead," I rushed into a lie. "I will speak to Jared to help control it."

Vaerin made a circle with zir hand around me. "Control your power or your appearance that's still in disarray?" Ze shook zir head. "You need to meditate, retrain your mind, or rest."

I balled my hands into fists as my knees locked. "Like I said, I will speak with Jared. Prolly a side effect. Plus, there's no time for more discussion."

Our horses neighed, frightened.

I threw open a saddlebag and pulled on my gloves to hide the nails. "Besides, I'll give myself a haircut later."

"Think of the Varkal, Xyphir, our people! Anything to calm yourself. I'd hate to see you put yourself in danger."

We ducked as Quartermaster Valen sounded close.

D'Lana peeked over the wall edge of the stall. "Is there anything I can do to help—"

Once the stable seemed clear, I grabbed zir collar. "I said we need to go."

"This...gift...didn't cause her majesty to—"

"**No.** Don't fret the others either, and I'll be fine too, okay?"

My friend's eyes flashed red before ze gave a look of pity. "...alright"—ze turned away—"let's move out."

"Good." I rose and went to my saddle.

The three of us headed down the main road. I took point with Vaerin and her majesty riding behind me. The sky was nothing but gray-blue clouds, and the townspeople had dropped their work, baskets, or carts as others slumped against the porch walls of their homes. Some collapsed, sitting on the dusty ground while children loitered around, grumpy and half-awake. It was eerie as store signs creaked among faint sobs and groans.

How...am I going to explain this to the others?

Once we reached the hospital, I dismounted, and my ca'hala passed her majesty to me before riding away. With Queen Kayla in my arms, I hurried into an empty medical room and placed her on a bed.

I grumbled, yanked the ruby hourglass pendant out from behind my shirt and turned the dial over. Now flipped to the top, the blood-red stone's deep color tediously drifted toward the pale pink.

Four days...Every four days?

I tucked the pendant away and rushed to open the stock cabinet doors for supplies.

Would...any medicine work in this case?

"Come on." I sorted through the containers. "Stars, I don't know!"

I slammed the cabinet doors, grabbed a cloth on the counter, wetted it with water, and added soap. My hand trembled as I wiped the rag on Queen Kayla's face, but the marks stayed.

I threw the useless thing to my left. The soapy cloth hit the door with a wet slop. The rag could stick there for all I cared.

"This is pointless...I'm such a fool." I buried my face in my hands.

My chest grew heavy with a dreadful feeling none could do anything for the queen, even if the others were here.

A gentle, icy cold touched the back of my shoulder. A soothing feeling washed over me.

"Breathe...."

I looked at my hands and breathed in and out—eventually, they steadied. Shortly thereafter, the nails retracted to normal.

"Easy now...that is it. You are alright."

I turned and met her concerned face. "Lady Annika Eider." I bowed my head in greeting. "Apologies. I am not well."

She gave a gentle smile. "You will be. I believe in you."

I glanced at a small mirror to my right, next to the cabinets. My once-frantic eyes were returning to blue. Only my grown hair remained, reaching past my shoulders. "T-Thank you."

Lady Eider took a step forward. "You calmed yourself, but I am sure it felt terrifying."

"It's an embarrassing state I find myself in." I rubbed my arms though my body ached. "I-I cannot afford to speak of it because of pressing, magical matters at hand."

She continued to smile and nodded. "Your secret is safe with me. I do hope whatever ails you, Jared, or a friend from Neo-Gen, can help manage your anxiety?"

I cleared my throat. "Appreciate it, but I doubt it."

With a wave of her hand, she gave me scissors. "Here. Will this help?"

"Yes, thank you."

"Of course...now then"—the sorceress' forehead furrowed with worry, placing her hands before her—"in meditation, I heard Elaiobus scream. Coniphur Yalene, what happened?"

I stepped aside so her majesty's mentor could see.

Lady Eider looked between Queen Kayla and me before her eyes narrowed. "The cuts on your face look horrible."

I touched my cheek. "Yes, and I still feel horrible too."

She turned around and faced me. "Please, explain."

"There was this cursed box. Queen Kayla would still be attacked by its violent mist if I weren't there to pull her majesty out." I snipped away a piece of my hair and threw it in the trash.

"Violent mist?" Lady Eider gasped with widening eyes. "Where did this happen?"

I kept my story short between the cutting of my hair.

"Then I set the box on fire and the chair, which, how did it stay self-contained?" I brushed wisps off the back of my neck. "Doesn't matter, I guess, but after igniting the bewitched box, there were green and blue sparks, but the mist itself was black and gold."

"Odd."

"What?"

"It is the color." Lady Eider gestured to the space around us before she placed her hand on her chest. "Our world's people, creatures, culture, and so forth all have sigils or trademarks of color. For example, mine is blue because I work closely with Elaiobus, for I am this world's sorceress medium."

I raised my hand. "Right there, I-I'm sorry, but is Elaiobus a deity?"

She shook her head. "No, Elaiobus is a living energy that creates stories."

I raised an eyebrow. "So it is, or not?" I scratched the side of my neck. "How you described Elaiobus—is it a god and you, its priestess?"

Lady Eider held out her left hand, palm up. "Do your priestesses speak to your gods?"

I shrugged. "We used to, but that Genecia is ancient history."

She smiled and shook her head. "I've never spoken to Elaiobus. Much like how creatures can feel a storm on its way, I read the signs as the story unfolds. As it is complex, I prefer to summarize the role I play, Coniphur Yalene."

I looked at Queen Kayla. "But, with all your privileges and capabilities, you didn't foresee—"

The sorceress put her hand on my shoulder and looked me in the eyes. "Despite how I appear, I am not perfect."

I cleared my throat. "I-I see." I took a step back. "Apologies. Please continue."

Lady Eider took back her hand and nodded. "Of course, as for these sigils, there are exceptions. For instance, both Lute and the Leaf Turners have shades of green, showing can have dual meanings." She shook her head. "In any case, I have not heard of this black and gold combination before."

"But, with all due respect, we must wake Queen Kayla up. Isn't there anything we can do?"

Her eyes cast downwards. "I am afraid not."

My heart sank. "What? Surely, you know something."

Lady Eider shook her head again. "Another card in play may have tricked us all. The black and gold combination baffles me—I do not see the connection."

I pointed to my right with both hands. "You don't know"—I shifted my weight to the other side, pointing my hands left—"or *won't* know?" I lowered my arms. "Perhaps you're not thinking clearly, and some rest will help?"

"Perhaps. Kayla is alive, but her recovery will take time." Lady Eider held out her right hand over her pupil's form. "I can sense her connection with Elaiobus is still there but greatly weakened. Who knows what could have happened if the mist had bombarded Kayla any longer? You did good work."

I ran a hand through my hair. "Assuming it's a curse caused by Renjor anyway, maybe the Kizin has an alliance or has powers we don't know. Are you sure we can't get help from anyone else?"

"When Kayla's predecessor abused their authority, Elaiobus' energy waned, then fractured into smaller pieces. The world you see before you, do you not think it is rather small? What lies beyond the horizon is nothing: no other cities nor populations." Lady Eider turned and held out both of her hands. "What you see, is it."

"Nothing else?"

She sighed. "Once, I had a theory the Leaf Turners were Elaiobus' defense mechanism. They went against the corrupt Saqui on their own."

"I sense a 'but' in there...."

"Yes, I have long dismissed that notion. This incident suggests the Leaf Turners are not working alone."

I balled my fists at my sides. "I see." I pulled my shoulders back. "Queen Kayla was the reason the Great Storm could not come here, but now she is asleep. It's foreboding, who knows, at best, a sign of a future attack. I want to protect her majesty, so my people can stay safe."

This is the reason I decided to follow Queen Kayla on her quest. I want to protect her for the sake of the Neo-Gen, my new home.

A flash of a vision. An open Folk-kin appeared to me. Why I was seeing the queen's diary, I knew not as its pages rushed through in a flurry on their own.

"...I want to protect her for this purpose," I whispered and jolted to attention to a prick of pain. "W-What was that?"

Lady Eider grinned with kind eyes.

I clasped my right hand around my left wrist. "Ah, ow!"

Not unlike a hot needle, a piercing heat ran along my shaking fingers. White lines appeared, and when they stopped at the base of my nails, the lines coiled around my fingers on their own. The pain vanished as quick as it came once the marks were completed.

I swallowed hard and held out my trembling hands. "What...by the Designs, what is this?"

LADY EIDER STEPPED forward. "Welcome. Guardian. To your new chapter."

It's a new start...a new story...That's why I had the vision.

I leaned back on a table and huffed a sigh. "Blazes...this place keeps getting crazier and crazier."

JARED – UNKNOWN

PLACED INTO HER BED, Kayla looked peaceful.

"Oi, she's to remain asleep for how long? There is nothing we can do?"

Lady Eider nodded and kept facing Kayla from the foot of the bed and held out her arms over the comforters. "Though I speak of theories, for one reason or another, Kayla threw herself into a deep sleep—to protect us from something."

"I agree." I stepped forward. "Her eyes turned white as she was bombarded with the mist. She might have seen a vision and reacted."

Lute brought his hands together and pressed his fingertips to his forehead. "Kayla, gimme a break. Why would you do this?"

"You are family and friends," Lady Eider reminded, lowering her arms.

"Makes sense to me," said Jacques.

Lute rolled his eyes and let his arms return with a slap. "Of course, it does, you coldhearted—gr~ah! I can't take this." He ruffled the hair on the sides of his head.

"Relax. Yar not helpin' actin' out like that."

"....sorry." Lute took a breather and moved to pace the room.

"Again, I hoped there was something to do," Coniphur Yalene repeated. "I feel horrible."

"There was no way you could have known," I said. "You did your best."

Lute took a seat near Kayla's bedside. "None of us were able to help you. You did what you could. No one can be mad."

Ze gave a small smile. "True...."

I did a double-take. "White? Really? No offense, but out of all the colors."

"Oh, yes, these"—ze smiled back—"as if I'm not pale enough already, right?"

"What are you, two—oh. Oh! Wow! Then that means?"

"Finish a sentence, Lute," Jacques teased.

I placed my chin in my hand. "Regardless, it appears you have proven to be something else."

"Doesn't 'Guardian' mean protecting her majesty?" ze asked, then pointed to Kayla. "Isn't this a bit...ironic?"

The three of us nodded.

Lute slumped his shoulders. "Evil, isn't it?" he deadpanned.

Jacques extended his arm. "Welcome, Xenos—that is, since we will be workin' together even closer now, can we call ya that, friend?"

"I-I don't know what to say," ze stammered with a grin and shook Jacques' hand. "I've—I mean—I was going to I-I...ugh, I'm at a loss for words. But, yes, Xenos is fine."

"Aw, no need to blush," Lute joked. "Seriously though, glad to have you."

"It is the best news to come out of all of this," I added.

"Really? I feared I'd look bad because I wasn't hit as hard."

"Listen, I'm just glad ya didn't get a, figuratively speakin', blow to the chest as we did." Jacques tapped the new Guardian's arm with the side of his fist. "Ya did good."

"Agreed, we should be thankful," I said.

"Yes, and none, not even I, saw this coming." Lady Annika clasped her hands together over her heart. "As for how long Kayla will be unconscious, I am afraid I do not know this either."

"Oi, you're kidding, right?" Lute sat upright.

My lady shook her head. "This peculiar weapon...I do not remember ever hearing about such a thing before. We should prepare for Renjor at all costs."

Jacques folded his arms. "That I can do. I can work harder with the Lords and Ladies of the Overland. Since the birthday trinket fiasco, I've found they're skilled and eager to protect their homes."

"I can work with Doctor Balfor and see to helping the townsfolk," said Lute, and he turned to Xenos. "Hate to ask, but did you have any heads up before Zar seized Genecia?"

Xenos frowned and scratched zir nose. "We first chalked it up to a severe thunderstorm which evolved into multiple tornadoes. Hurricanes and quakes came later. The disaster escalated to its end in a matter of days." Ze pointed to Kayla. "Focusing on her, since we don't know how long her majesty will be asleep, I have a way to keep her alive. Unless there's some spell in your handbook to keep her from going hungry, I will spur Neo-Gen to help."

MOLI – Appears 30 When Furless

I SHIVERED, AND MY whiskers stood on end. My whole face and shoulders were beyond cold though my back half remained warm under the high Masana sun.

I tilted my head to the side. I didn't know what to make of the sky-high blockade—a cliff face of whistling wind and white flurries at the border. I could barely see the Overland pine trees through the weather conditions.

On my fours, I raised my right paw to touch the frigid gray. The moment shards of white blistered across the tips of my toes, I retreated and licked them.

Odd...

I put my paw down. "That hurt."

"Queen Moli, what are we going to do?"

I looked over to Tula beside me on a rock. "I'm not sure. I can't get in."

Tula flapped her wings to pass the border, but the frigid winds pushed her back, taking a few tufts of feathers with it.

I turned around and stepped forward. "Are you okay?"

"I'll be fine," she tweeted with a low whistle and ruffled her wings. "What are we going to do? We were just on patrol when this storm started."

"I don't think we can do much, but hope it passes soon."

"Should we go tell his majesty?"

"Yes, let's go."

JACQUES – 17 YEARS

TWO POINTS.

~whip~

Three points.

~whip~

Bullseye.

"Great shot."

I leaned left and counted Jared's score. "Can't deny yar aim either. Impressive."

We moved toward our straw targets under the gloomy clouds in silence, albeit the snow crunching under my boots was deafening.

"Is the snow getting to you less?" Jared asked, withdrawing one of his ten throwing knives.

I picked out an arrow from the straw. "Still hate it. Miss the sun more than anythin.'"

Jared pulled out another blade. "How goes your journaling or calligraphy?"

"Can't say I've been inspired, but I've been able to get practice in here or there."

The crisp wind blew as we reset for another round.

"Any updates on her condition?" I asked.

Jared shook his head. I nocked my arrow and pulled back the bowstring.

"Captain."

I lowered my bow and looked right. "Squire Kirst."

"Captain Volt, any news?" the soldier asked. "It's been a month now. Surely there's good news?"

"Not yet." I put my arrow back in my quiver. "Jared, here, is regent. He will tell us if there've been changes. I've told ya this."

Fletch's shoulders slumped. "I know..."

"If ya feelin' weary, maybe call it a day today?" I suggested.

He bobbed his head yet with a frown on his face. "A warm fire sounds nice, sir, but my sister was found asleep in her bed—she won't wake up."

I sharply brought my head back. "W-What?" I stepped forward. "By all that I am, when?"

Fletch took a nervous sidestep. "S-Sorry, sir, I thought you already knew this was happening throughout the town."

XENOS – 22 YEARS

SPRING WAS DUE, YET snow fell as the dreary clouds remained.

I feel I'm in a snow globe...will it ever go past my ankles?

I patted the freshly-turned hourglass pendant under my shirt, knocked, and entered Queen Kayla's bedroom in the castle. "Sir Gibe is asking for your report."

My friend turned to me with zir tablet in zir hands, gave a quick glance, and returned to pushing buttons. "Stars, go sleep."

"I tried, Vaerin. At least no haggard appearances, right? Five hours is my current average, jeez." I walked forward, rubbing my arms. "I'll see to getting more firewood in here."

"The queen's vitals are steady, but it's been four months, and her coma doesn't look like it will let up any time soon." My friend lowered zir tablet to zir side. "I'm sorry."

Guilt twinged in my chest, but I pulled my shoulders back. "What of the others? Heard our weavers were able to transmute more V.O. gowns, thanks to the mining efforts."

"First aid is great, sure, but my team has yet to give me zirs afternoon report. However, I doubt much has changed other than an increasing number of people falling asleep." Vaerin continued to push buttons. "Five were taken to bed just yesterday."

"Do you think it has to do with her majesty being asleep?"

"I can't say for sure, but can't for the life of me figure it out."

"Is that why you're always looking at your tablet?" I scratched my shoulder. "Trying to do research?"

"There's only so much we can do without it. How many transmuted gowns do you honestly think we can create?"

I didn't stop walking until I was right in zir face. "I do not care how many. Our ally needs us. Residents of the Overland would starve without our help, without our tech."

There was a tense pause before Vaerin resumed tapping on the glass screen. "Of course. I will request more to be made, but do understand I cannot help further. 'Magic' isn't an explanation but an unlearned science. What do you think makes our gowns work? I will continue to investigate this strange coma for Neo-Gen. To protect us, if necessary, for we don't know if this phenomenon will spread."

I snorted. "Fine. Research away as long as our V.O. gowns continue to be created...please."

LUTE – 13 YEARS

"BY ALL THAT I AM"—I threw my mug of tea against a wall in my office—"four months of this stupid snow!"

There was a knock, and my door opened. "Sir Lute? Nurse Abe has a report on a new patient."

I breathed in and exhaled, not bothering to look away from staring through the window. "Be there in a minute."

Sleep, work, and repeat...

At first, it was two to three, but now five to six people fell asleep every day.

Doctor Balfor and her husband had been asleep for three weeks now. Each day since then, I walked into a room to assess new patients. Afterward, assistants from Neo-Gens picked them up, took them home, and dressed each in a *Vitals and Operations, V.O.* gown, unique wear transmuted to keep the wearer alive.

At least, that's what Xenos told me...

"Patient report?" I asked.

"Wryn Kirst. Forty-five."

My heart sank as I came closer.

"She was found collapsed on the floor with a large bruise on her head and a broken leg."

"She's Emil's tailor. Where was she found?"

Abe bowed his head. "In her place of work. It's speculated she was up on a stool, putting fabric away before she passed out from the curse. Hit her head coming down."

I wiped the sleepers out of my eyes with my free hand and pinched the bridge of my nose. "Right...who found her?"

"Neo-Gen Unit Two members, five minutes ago. Brought her in after trying chest compressions."

I shook my head. "I'm sorry. Zirs didn't bring her here for us to help. Wryn was already gone."

Abe took a step back with wide eyes. "B-But...."

I took a seat next to Wryn's bed with a heavy heart. "I know. I've never seen death here before." My vision blurred when I took her wrinkled, cold hand. "I didn't know her well, but...this hurts."

The nurse put his hand on my shoulder. "I agree."

I sniffed and rose from my seat after a few moments of silence. "She...should be buried. Let's take her to the castle."

Abe didn't say a word, nor did anyone in the empty halls of the hospital. Alone we traveled and pulled a rickety cart behind us to the castle gates. We didn't stop until we reached the lone oak tree in the western castle gardens. There, we laid Wryn down and left to return with shovels. The ground was tough, and the snow glittered on our shoulders as Abe and I laid the kind lady to rest. Once finished, I took a knee and placed a short stack of three stones to mark the grave.

I'm supposed to fix it...I'm sorry, friends...

"Sir Jared," Abe greeted with a wave.

Bundled in a heavy cloak and a wool hat, the wizard carefully treaded the remaining distance. I didn't say a word until he put a hand on my shoulder.

"Why?" I asked, returning my gaze to the grave.

"As you know, death is a stranger to nowhere and no one," Jared replied. "If you like, I am willing to go for a walk."

I rose from the ground and dusted off my pants. "Sure. Abe, would you like to join us?"

"Of course."

JARED – UNKNOWN

MORE SNOW TODAY...

Yet the snow had stopped accumulating long ago.

Another day...six months...

I made my way to the courtroom, where, upon entering, the new clock tower in town chimed three times. Inside, Lute, Xenos, Jacques, and the six Lords and Ladies of the Overland stood exhausted, waiting for me as regent to take my seat.

I sat in Kayla's chair and kept my staff at my side. "This meeting is now in session. Please report."

Lute stood first. "Doctor Balfor reports Queen Kayla is well. Four-hundred-sixty people are in bed." He took a seat on my right and slumped in his chair.

Jacques was next. "Thankfully, the wall is built. However, the castle has no recruits or army left. Yet, trainin' continues with us, the Court, and Neo-Gen." He returned to his seat as Xenos rose.

"While the food stores are more or less adequate, between the noble Blackfrost family and my alie, Dissapha Xyphir's efforts, the small, emergency greenhouses have been promising. For now, keep with the rations."

I cleared my throat. "Lord Quild, how is your area?"

The noble rose as Xenos sat. "Strong. The transmuted miracle that is Neo-Gen's gowns keeps our people safe."

"Good, thank you. Lord Blackfrost?"

He rose as Lord Quild sat. "Likewise, nothing to report."

"Ladies of Shellfore?" I asked.

The twins sadly stood from their chairs. "All is well," they solemnly chorused before they sat back down.

I rose and leaned on my staff. "As we know...it has been trying half a year. Our contact with the Masana Territory remains limited due to the curse's perpetual blizzard at the border. Only we remain able to stay awake and live as usual. So, of course, the Festival of Light is canceled, and Queen Kayla's eleventh birthday draws near. May I remind you we are doing our best in her absence, and I am proud of all of you."

Lord Blackfrost rose from his seat. "What of Lady Eider?"

I shook my head. "I checked in with her two weeks ago. Still searching for answers and helping keep an eye out for Renjor."

LUTE – 13 YEARS

I SCUFFED THE GROUND with my foot in the throne room. "It's not her freaking funeral."

My comment, unfortunately, made heads turn with a mixed bag of reactions.

Shoot...

"Lute?"

I turned toward the throne, where Jared waved me over.

I rolled my eyes and came over. "What, am I in trouble, old man?"

He placed his hand over the orb of his golden staff. "Listen here, our friends left awake want to be close to Kayla. They care too."

I repeatedly jabbed the air, pointing down. "*Seven* months is *seven* months," I hissed. "Where is Annika? *Where* are the Elemental Dragons? The Lords and Ladies have been *training* with Jacques, and for what?" I drew a sharp breath and let it out. "It's been too long, there's now a dumb clock outside, and it's her *birthday,* and her brother can't even be here."

"Shh~ do not insult Neo-Gen's gift," said Jared. "Zirs meant well to boost morale. Plus, you missed his majesty."

"What?"

"He hadn't seen her in so long, Lute. With my transportation spell as a workaround, I delivered King Basi through the storm to visit—Lute."

Having heard enough, I walked away.

"SORRY, I'M THE LAST to visit," I mumbled.

I slowly opened the door and walked in, not at all surprised the room remained clean with a lit fireplace. I closed the door behind me and walked to Kayla's bedside.

While dressed in the same silver gown, her face was peaceful, surrounded by her hair grown out to the edges of the mattress.

"Grr~ Oi, would you get up? It's been forever." I took a seat by Kayla's bed. "Everyone is either asleep or missing you. But, the worst part, you would mourn knowing Wryn has died." I bowed my head. "Sorry...just wake up already."

"Lute—"

"Ah, jeez"—I sharply turned toward the door—"Jacques!"

He stepped inside. "Sorry, was lookin' to find ya as the Lords n' Ladies and King Basi returned home hours ago."

"So?"

"So~ ya should've been there to send them off."

I slouched in my chair. "Don't care I missed a lame 'lunch party,' Jacques."

"Look, ya can be broodin' all ya like, but ya not goin' to do anyone any good if ya don't get some sleep or food."

I shook my head. "Not sure about sleep as long as she is like this"—I rose from my chair—"but, could use some grub."

After trudging to the dining hall with Jacques, our friends Jared and Xenos were already in their seats. The table still had leftovers from the party held in Kayla's honor.

I half-heartedly raised a cup. "To her—"

To the loudest clap of thunder, I jumped and dropped the goblet. The rolls echoed before another deafening crash boomed. I looked out the window on my left, but there were no signs of a storm.

Jacques threw his napkin down and jumped from his seat. "Everyone, grab your coats and come with me."

I bolted toward the dining hall doors.

"Is this a drill?" Xenos shouted.

Over my shoulder, ze was following me as Jared brought up the rear. "A gentle snow this whole time, and now it's thundering? Think about it."

A sky-high beam of crackling light and shifting colors, thick as the castle towers, had formed due north.

"We should move!" Xenos pushed a few buttons on zir Gieci. "Two unit leaders informed me the beam isn't giving off radiation. Initial reports suggest the flux of potential and kinetic energy coming off the beam is more like an enduring lightning bolt."

"Our enemies bid their time," said Jared.

"Send word to the unit leaders and Sephur D'Lana to take zirs positions along the town wall," Jacques ordered and rushed left, leading us to the armory.

Once inside, I strapped on my leg guards.

"Yeah, I feel far from ready," said Xenos, patting over zir heart.

I yanked on my gloves. "Do your best." I stepped closer to Jacques and helped fasten his brown leather chest plate. "With Kayla asleep, should we all go?"

"I'll inform Sephur D'Lana to send a unit back here to guard the castle," Xenos offered.

"Do it," said Jacques and turned to Jared. "Are ya good?"

"Yes, I will ride, bringing up the rear."

Jacques grabbed Avon's saddle and turned to us. "Perfect. Everyone, let's get goin.'"

With haste and Jacques taking point, we moved out. The clock tower bell chimes were mellow and sullen as the night wind whistled past my cold ears. Traveling through the town, Neo-Gen residents took refuge behind the wall, heading for the castle. We reached the square when the sharp clopping of hooves and nickering of several steeds announced the arrival of the Blackfrosts, followed by the Shellfores, then the Quilds.

Each noble pair gradually led their horses to ride around us.

Calistor and Almea Quild fell in line to ride beside Jacques in the front. Ada Shellfore rode on my right while her sister, Akilah, came upon Xenos' left. Finally, Tyford and Carmen Blackfrost brought up the rear with Jared.

"Be prepared," Jacques shouted over the cantering. "We may be in a fight for our lives!"

"No kidding!" I shot back. "This *is* what we prepared for."

"You know we can fight," Lady Blackfrost called.

"Commander, you know we're not leaders who stand behind," Lady Quild added and smiled at her husband. "These foul invaders shall feel the bite of our maces, won't they, dear?"

He raised his right gauntlet hand to cover his heart. "Love, they will not know what hit them."

From the direction of the transmuted wall covered with torchlight, I could hear the faint battle cries grow louder.

"Our preparations will stand," Lady Ada declared.

Lady Akilah picked up the pace. "May it protect our people."

"Eyes up," Jacques encouraged and looked over his shoulder at the rest of our group. "And be ready!"

A smile tugged on my lips. The guard pulled open the town gate doors, and our group moved through as Neo-Gen's units rallied and cheered from above upon the wall. We didn't stop outside of town until Jacques gave us the signal.

KAYLA – 12 YEARS

"WELL...I WOULD'VE READ the rest," I whispered and closed the crystal covers. I leaned back on the headboard of my bed as a tear ran down my cheek. "Poor Wryn...all of you...I am so sorry."

Afternoon sunlight made short rainbows along my walls. After a lingering pause, absently listening to the birds, I rubbed my eyes with both hands and dragged them down to my chin.

What am I going to do?

"Those missing pages must detail the rest," I muttered and looked back at the Folk-kin in my lap.

I wonder if the pages are about The Leaf Turners...

Though I had a nap earlier, my eyelids grew heavy from having continued to read—the one thing keeping me from falling asleep was my headache.

High-pitch shrills broke my trance. I looked about the bedroom with haste. To my horror, the diary's front cover had cracked. I picked up the book to study it closer, only to drop it back to my lap to block my ears from another round of shrill screeching.

"Stop screaming!"

A bright light pulsed throughout the Folk-kin's covers—the diary was flipping itself over and over, periodically shrilling—throwing a nasty fit.

"What do you want me to do?!" I cried, covering my ears for the fourth time.

While withstanding the noise for the fifth time, I realized the terrifying sounds were in my head as no one was coming. I pried the crystal covers open.

"D-Do you need me to continue?"

Once opened, the shrilling stopped cold. I thought I did the right thing, but the pages became too heavy to turn. Suddenly, the covers glowed like blue fire—the diary grew hot.

Frightened and burned, I dropped the Folk-kin. The covers returned to normal, and the diary closed on its own. Shocked, I stared at the book and could hear my heart thump in my head—my hands were clammy. I brought my knees to my chest and let all I bottled up inside go as hot tears.

"Kayla, we do not have time for tears."

I looked up. Lady Annika had appeared in my bedroom.

"What can I do?"

She came to my bedside and held out her hand. "Simple, retrieve the pages."

"We don't know where—"

My mentor waved her hand over the diary. "I do." The book rose in the air just to fall back down. "Hurry and come with me. We are running out of time."

I got up, walked around to the foot of the bed, and pulled a thick cotton throw off the couch to wrap the diary in. When done, the blanket warmed the moment I picked up the bundle.

"I hope that will do for now," said Lady Annika. "Please, Kayla, get dressed for travel and follow me. Xenos is counting on us."

With a snap, I changed my gown into pants, boots, and a blouse and followed her out the room.

"You know about zem?" I asked, shutting the door.

"Jared has kept me informed. I am troubled to report the best I can do is bring you all closer to inspect the Dead Mountains as quickly as possible." She turned to go down the stairs. "If there are any clues there, I would fetch them as soon as you can."

"Why not come with us?"

She headed down the stairs. "The quartz. It is a limit for my powers as well. It is draining. It is inert to use for magic but swallows it nonetheless."

With the help of a few guards given an urgent message, Jared, Lute, and Jacques soon met Lady Annika and me in the throne room.

"What's going on?" Lute asked, straightening his overshirt.

"Why did you not inform me of your visit, Lady Eider?" Jared wondered aloud.

My mentor gestured to me. "It is a dire emergency. Unlike the Coronation, this is worse."

I clutched the bundle close to my chest. "The Folk-kin won't let me read it. It's falling apart."

With a collective "what?" from the three of them, my tears welled up again.

"Urg!" I hastily wiped away my face, unable to look at anyone in the eye. "I hate crying, but I'm afraid. It's embarrassing."

Lute shook his head with a sympathetic smile. "No, Kayla, it's okay, honest."

Lady Annika stepped forward. "Remember, we all share one another's hope to prevail. Yes, I understand seeing the Folk-kin in such a state is of serious concern, but we have triumphed over dangerous situations before."

Jared leaned on his staff. "Let us prepare."

Lute showed off the holster on his leg and pointed to Jacques' sword on his hip. "Oi, I'm set. If I had a nickel for every night we had to get ready for bat—" he slapped a hand over his mouth.

"Ya *got* to stop doin' that." Jacques facepalmed. "Also, Jared, the Mountains don't bode well for ya because of the smokey quartz. Stay here as the actin' reagent, please. It makes no sense for all of us to go right now."

"Why the Dead Mountains," I asked. "Shouldn't we get Vaerin with us? What if—"

Lady Annika wouldn't listen. Instead, she took out a short wand.

"Wait, a wand?" Lute asked.

She twirled on her left foot, and her eyes gleamed.

Then.

It went dark.

JACQUES – 18 YEARS

A CRUMBLING OF STONE.

A thud of a landed jump.

A scuff of claws.

A heated growl.

Four paces away...

I opened my eyes. Sweat dripped down my cheek. My chest was tight, it hard to breathe. I, however, held fast to my sword, poised against my right shoulder.

A low chuff and a snort.

I peeked over my left shoulder, soon thankful the alarming red eyes were looking the other way.

Across from me, Lute wrung his hands around his collapsed quarterstaff, crouched behind a boulder, pressing his back against it. Beside him, on the other side, Jared sat, wrapping his head with a piece of torn fabric from his shirt.

I glanced at the wizard staff on the dusty red ground.

Snapped in two.

I directed with a silent signal to hold.

How could this go so wrong...?

KAYLA – 12 YEARS

RUBY RED. FROM THE ground to the walls, the prism room gleamed with the deep color. No windows. No doors.

"Been a while, brat."

On the cold floor, I turned around.

The illusion of Annika slipped away. Dressed head to toe in sleek, black leather armor save a helmet sat Renjor on a smooth crystal couch.

"Where's the Folk—"

"Come." The Kizin twirled her dagger in one hand, tapping the empty space to take a seat with the other. "You're missing the show."

I rose to my feet and brought up my fists, yet an engraved smoky quartz bracelet appeared, slapped around my wrist.

ᛗᚲᛁᚲᛋᚠᛏᚢᚱᛁᛏ ᛟᚱᛞᚹᛁᛏᛗ

"NO! NOT AGAIN." I PULLED at the chunky jewelry.

Renjor lowered her dagger. "Yeah, just don't. Come sit."

I charged for the back of her head.

"Oi! You okay?"

I slid to a halt behind the couch and looked side to side. "Lute—wait, he's not here—"

Renjor shushed me and pointed to the wall in front of her. "Don't be so loud. It's getting good."

A picture show playing within a diamond-shaped frame hung on a wall to my right.

Jared was bleeding from his temple.

I rushed around the couch.

"Hey, you're blocking my view—"

I put my hands on the window. There was a buzzing, and the show blinked to another view. Moments would pass before it would blink again to another angle.

"Again, get down."

My friends stood surrounded by the gray-blue shadows cast by the Dead Mountains in a valley. A creature lurked around as they tried to keep away as much as they could.

"Are you listen—"

"Run," Jacques ordered, and he, Jared, and Lute bolted and weaved around rocks."

"Get out of there," I cried.

"Hey! You break it, I break you."

I looked over my shoulder, lowering my fists. "You did this! Xenos, z-ze is scared. You—"

She crossed her legs. "Do you think any of them can hear you?"

"Dodge!"

A twisted beast bolted through from north to south, only to buzz right through east to west.

"Over here!"

"Oi!"

A bear-sized, wild dog howled. The creature had pointed ears, thick white fur, and grayish scales leading to large raptorial feet of thick, curved talons. Wire-thin red light tangled around and between a gigantic set of ram horns, holding together glowing ruby shards and chunks of black metal jutting out in a chaotic crown.

"Leave Jared alone—"

Krrrsh~!

My knees locked. "His staff! No!" I looked over my shoulder, turning halfway. "Leave my friends alone."

Renjor drew a circle with her dagger in the air, and the diamond's picture show went mute. "Had some unfinished business with you." She shrugged. "It's been a couple years, y'know? How *are* the fools putting up with you these days?"

I remained quiet.

She laughed. "Finally! The hero has learned to stop asking." The Kizin switched out her crossed legs and leaned back in her seat. "Welcome to the...well, it doesn't have a name. A Dragon's playground." She tapped her crimson brooch. "Home is where the heart is. Best untouched. Don't think about it too hard in that pretty head of yours. Like what I've done with my little nook?"

I didn't answer and folded my arms.

"Pfft, if glares could cut."

"Where is it?"

Renjor pointed at me. "There it is. Golly, you had me worried." She pointed over her shoulder with her dagger end.

A stem of crystal sprung from the ground on my left. The top of a table unfolded like a flower before the shape reformed and settled into a flat circle. The Folk-kin was on this table within the blanket I had wrapped it.

I rushed over. The diary pulsed green and had multiple cracks.

"While it's a tool, the book has also helped you regain your memories. Alas," Renjor sighed, "you can't get far without the missing pages, can you?"

"Then give them to me," I demanded.

She continued playing with her dagger without care. "You're in no position to make demands. The Folk-kin is tearing itself apart, much like Elaiobus was shattered, the book wants to become whole."

A chill ran down my spine. From the corner of my eye, Jacques dodged right, narrowly avoiding a bite.

Renjor snapped her fingers a few times. "Ah, ah, over here."

I glared. "I don't know why you're upset with me. Or understand why you kidnapped me back then or again today. I did nothing."

The Kizin pulled off her gloves. "You know? I actually hate it has come to this."

"No, you don't." I scowled.

"I do, honest." She held up her left hand, showing scars over the reddish lines coiled around her fingers. "I was like your Lukene once. A Guardian too."

I said nothing.

"...what, no le gasp?"

I shook my head. "Guardians don't hurt others to get what they want." I pointed to the book. "Give me the pages."

Renjor grabbed my left hand. "Again with demands. Arturan Vicitri would never—"

"V-Vicitri?" My knees buckled. "You mean the Saqui before me? You knew them—"

The witch squeezed right under the bracelet. "*Him*!" She looked at the screen. "Ah~ good show!"

I yanked my arm away and pushed Renjor back.

The Kizin hardly budged and gripped my chin. "My Heralded One. He should've been allowed to stay"—our eyes locked—"but since you're here instead, I want you gone so he can return." She roughly let go, stepped away, and walked around to the other side of the table.

"He told his story and left," I said. "That's how it works."

Renjor dragged her blade across the top of the table and pointed to my cursed bangle. "Your new contract. You have two choices. Save this world, or see your friends die. In short, *sign* the Folk-kin over to me."

"W-What? I can't!"

"Of course, you can. Arturan wrote in his all the time—at a cost—but still. Got the job done."

"Then...no." I shook my head. "You made Xenos take them. I know it. I read it."

"So, you know how it worked then?"

"Well, no—"

She smirked and placed her hand on her chest. "Years ago, when we met, I hit my *tethered* mark."

I pointed to my chest. "Right on Xenos."

"Exactly." Renjor brought her same hand to her temple. "The single setback was that blasted Sword of Elaiobus. However, I've been linked with zem ever since." She dropped her arm to her side and barked out a laugh. "Bullying the fool was delightful. Ze is so gullible."

"I read about the necklace. Don't tell me that creature is zem."

"Don't think I need to."

I drew in a sharp breath.

"See? You never quite knew zem, or how desperate ze was to protect zir people. Much like you, to be fair." A cynical smile graced her features. "But, I'm off track. Did you mean these pages, my dear?"

Renjor opened her left hand to reveal a small, black pouch stuffed with blue and gold pieces of paper. "By all means, you can have them." The criminal tossed them at me. "Can't do anything with them, so all I ask is for a simple signature. A resignation. Upon doing so, I will send you out of here."

"You're awful," I growled.

She chuckled, leaned over, and placed her hands on the table. "You know, the sight of suffering is amazing." Renjor gave a smug grin. "You're the Saqui now. You want your friends safe, right?" With a flick of the wrist of her dagger-bearing right hand, a ruby quill pen appeared out of thin air in her empty left. "Come on. You're out of ideas anyway."

I set the pouch down beside the diary. "No, I'm not."

The Kizin rolled her eyes and sheathed her dagger. "Really? Hello, the bracelet? What are you—"

I jumped onto the table and lunged forward.

Renjor sidestepped to the right.

I nearly belly-flopped onto the floor.

The witch cackled. "Adorable."

"Grr~" I got onto my feet and lunged again. "Let me out."

"Interesting"—Renjor sidestepped to the left—"overconfident as ever."

I threw a punch. "Meh, I do my best." And another as Renjor retreated backward around the room. "You will fix this."

"Why should I?"

"Because Vicitri ruined everything."

"Let's try this again." She stopped my punch with her right hand. "Why do you care?"

"I—"

"Didn't they just slap a tiara on your head? Why you?"

"I...was told—"

She let me go with a push. "Ah, *told*. What made you so stinking special?"

I stepped back and held my fists under my chin and arms close to my chest.

"When are you going to understand you're not?" The Kizin shook her head. "Pity."

"I don't need to believe you."

"Whatever story you've heard about your predecessor," said Renjor. "More so, a deception." She tapped her lips with the side of her pointer. "Let's bring you in on a little secret. He's just lost."

"Save it. Lord Colton and Lady Sierra told me your Arturan was gone."

Renjor shrugged. "And?"

"And, they couldn't rest in peace until I passed Elaiobus' tests. They told me they were forced to throw the Folk-kin out because of your Saqui."

She frowned and let out a sigh. "He's missing. Not dead. I wanted him to stay."

"You...liked him?"

Renjor began circling me. "When those pretentious **idiots** threw the diary out of this world, through the Realm 'Of Never and Ever After', I figured Arturan could stay, that Colton and Sierra had done the work for me. However, this...**chain**...thing pulled him away."

"Elaiobus saw it was someone else's turn."

The Kizin's eyes squinted. "When kicked out, by this world's perspective, he died. But I believe he is truly alive and well. I just need you gone and to find him."

"He was hurting those around him. Goodbye, I say."

The madwoman sliced the air with her dagger and pointed it at me. "This place **has** no rules. Rules didn't and don't exist. Whoever told you there were, **lied**."

I charged forward, bit her arm, nabbed her dagger, and dashed for the diary. "Well, thank you for your cooperation."

Renjor stood there seething, holding her arm.

I pointed the dagger at her. "From where I'm standing, the world adapted and changed to survive. It's no less wondrous, just in pain because of you."

"Ha! Lest we forget, the Folk-kin will break if you don't fulfill the contract," the witch scoffed. "Those Guardians of yours will soon be out of my way, and so will you."

"You won't win."

"What was that?"

"I've heard enough." I cut the air, and a tear formed.

The witch's good purple eye went wide. "Y-You——"

The cool breeze blew across my face and played with my hair. "I don't have to hurt you. I just have to get out."

"N—"

I dove forward with possessions wrapped and held in my arms. The cold room broke away to the rush of a warm breeze on my face. Renjor's yells faded to the wind whistling past as she and I fell.

"Got you!"

I opened my eyes and saw Lute's face.

"By all that I am, where have you been?" He set me down.

"D-Don't worry, I'm fine. Where's Xenos?" I asked.

Lute pointed to the left with his chin over his shoulder. "We think that's zem."

The furious creature was trying to bust through a rockslide trap. The beast's eyes peeking through the crevices flared red—all too familiar.

"It is..." I shook my head. "What are we going to do?"

"Lute, quickly! Come back," Jared ordered from behind us.

"Is everyone okay?" I asked after we gathered behind a boulder.

"Yeah." Lute gestured to his somewhat battered state. "Ju~st peachy."

I rolled my eyes and looked at Jared. "Still, are you okay?"

The wizard held onto the salvaged amethyst from his staff. "I cannot do anything here."

"Xenos fired a flaming ball from zir mouth," said Jacques.

"Which shot through Jared's shield and melted the middle of the staff," I said. "Renjor had your battle on this magic window—"

They blinked.

I waved my hands. "Never mind. Just know, I saw most of the fight."

"Okay, point is, Jared's gettin' weaker the longer we stay put," said Jacques. "We're pinned."

"Jared, if we distract Xenos, do you think you could make a run for it?" I asked.

"And do what?" Lute asked.

"We need Xenos back," I looked at Jared. "Take this pouch and the Folk-kin. Keep it safe, run, and recover."

Jared's eyes grew wide. "What is in the pouch?"

My heart sank. "The missing pages. Please take them."

He took a moment, then complied.

"You stupid mutt! How can you be trapped?" Renjor shouted in the distance.

"Again, the witch could nab him easily," Lute insisted.

"Not if we hold her off," said Jacques.

"Can you fix the Folk-in once safe, Jared?" I asked.

He shook his head. "Only Lady Eider can."

"Okay. You're shaking. Don't strain yourself, but leave when you can."

Jared smiled. "Here, I thought I was to give advice."

A snarling howl filled the air, followed by a deep bashing from behind the rocks. A graveling, repeating thud.

"Tell you what I did miss, though." I pointed with my thumb over my shoulder. "How did you manage that trap?"

"Timin' and a whole lotta luck," said Jacques.

"And I was the bait." Lute shook his head. "Never again."

Jacques exhaled, gearing up. "Anyway, we'll save Xenos and get out of here."

I nodded. "Yep."

"And keep Renjor busy as you confront zem? No."

"Got a better idea?" I asked. "Where's the Sword of Elaiobus, Jared?"

The wizard shook his head. "Not here. None of us took it on a mission to 'find clues.'"

I pointed. "And there you have it."

"So, in short, we might have to set zir tail on fire," Lute quipped. "Might snap zem out of it."

"I'm not going to hurt Xenos," I said.

"Oi, we may not have a choice," he hissed. "I'd like to keep my body in one piece."

I shook my head. "No, not with this bracelet around my wrist. I can't do anybody any good."

"Then hold fast onto that dagger," said Jacques.

"Oi, when were you going to—"

"Come out, Kayla! We aren't done yet," Renjor cried, peeking over the rock. "Time is up, heroes!"

Lute and Jacques leaped into defense mode with their weapons in the Kizin's direction. I stood behind them as Jared remained behind the boulder to our left.

Lute charged forward.

Jacques stood in front of me.

"Free Xenos," Lute declared, swinging his quarterstaff.

Renjor ducked and slid away.

In the trap, ze howled. The stacks of rubble shook.

The witch took a blow to the shoulder, spun, and kicked Lute's backside.

He recovered and swung the bottom end toward Renjor's middle, but missed.

I took Jacques' sleeve. "We can't kill her," I said. "We don't know how to set Xenos free."

"Yeah...but we can make it hurt."

"What?"

His knuckles turned white around the grip of his blade. "If ya only knew."

Renjor kicked off a smaller lump of rock and dodged his attack. "Two years, and you still aim for the front." She extended her arm toward me. "I believe you have something of mine."

The small orb in the wolf's mouth lit up, and the blade yanked away, almost slicing my palm. Renjor caught the flying dagger, spun with the momentum to her right, and finished her circle, unleashing a gust of wind. Lute flew back onto the ground.

"The inert quartz has nothin' on her," said Jacques.

I pointed. "It's the brooch—"

"Yeah, figures," Lute groaned, exasperated. "Thanks for worrying."

"It is a ward," said Jared. "If you can get it, she'll have no magic here, like me."

"Is the last Lukene still alive over there?" Renjor cackled. "Bravo, but the end will be the same." She lunged at Lute and pinned him to the ground with the dagger to his neck. "I'm warning you, your majesty. Sign the Folk-kin. With it free, I will have my Arturan Vicitri with me."

"Sign? What's she on about?" Jacques asked.

I balled my hands at my sides.

*Come on...think, Kayla, **think!***

She flipped her hair over her shoulder. "Not your concern, dear captain. Besides." She moved the blade to Lute's cheek. "It's the least your Saqui can do."

Xenos barked and growled. The trap's rocks rumbled and tumbled as ze repeatedly pushed.

"Don't worry, baby," Renjor teased in zir direction. "You almost got it." She looked at the seething Jacques. "One step and your buddy gets—"

Lute bit her wrist.

"Grah~!" She leaned back, grasping her injury.

He pushed her off and rolled onto his stomach.

"Hoo~what's with brats and bites!"

Lute scrambled away toward the dagger on the ground.

"Hey, over here," Jacques cried.

Lute low-tossed the dagger to Jacques—who sprinted forward, grabbed the blade, and chucked the weapon as far as possible.

Renjor pounced and put Lute in a headlock. "Why you!"

Jacques charged ahead with his sword held near his right shoulder.

With an enraged howl, Xenos busted free from zir rockslide prison.

"Hey, baby," the Kizin pulled Lute back. "Get her, will you?"

Jacques spun around and got between Xenos and me.

"Help Lute," I said. "I'll be fine."

"Ya said the bracelet is holdin' ya back."

"I know."

"Don't...worry. Just...choking," Lute wheezed.

Red eyes flared brigh. Claws dug into the dirt. The smell of wet dog, earth, and pine. Jaws snapped shut.

"Go, Jacques," I repeated.

Renjor raised a hand, extending her fingers. "Soon. Soon my dagger will be in my hands. I would make a choice, Kayla."

Lute elbowed her in the side and finally broke free.

Xenos stepped forward.

I returned to zem. "Jacques, put your sword down." I stepped toward my friend, raising my hands to show I meant no harm. "Come back to us, Xenos. You can do this."

Ze growled again, retreating backward a few steps as zir ears folded down.

Jacques kept close to me, wary. From the corner of my eye, Lute was brawling, trying to keep Renjor from collecting her weapon and buying us more time.

"You don't have to stay with her." I took another step. "Please. Don't be afraid."

Claws dug deep into the soil. Zir long tail beat against the rock behind zem.

"Do you understand?" I looked right into those red eyes. "Xenos?"

I received another growl.

"Kayla, ze isn't—"

"You don't like that name, do you?" I put my hands down. "You don't want to be known as 'Xenos' in this form."

"Jacques, either put the darn sword away or come help me!" Lute ducked Renjor's punch.

Distressed. Red eyes looked between the witch and me.

"It's me," I continued, scooting closer. "I know you're hurting." I knelt. "It's me."

Jacques sheathed his sword and took a knee on my left. "It's us."

"And we're sorry too," I added, holding out my right hand.

A large nose went to sniff. Red eyes blinked. With a low chuff, our friend shook zir head.

I reached for the knobbed ankle of zir right foot.

Ze growled.

I withdrew my hand but kept it palm up. "Don't worry. It was not your fault."

Ze chuffed again and stepped forward.

"What are you doing?" Renjor cried. "Hurt her!"

Thwack!

"Without your dagger, witch, you have no power here," Lute cried.

My eyes remained forward. "You got this."

Talons dug into the ground.

"I'm sorry about Zar."

A low growl, zir gaze wavered.

"And I'm sorry we didn't tell you," I said. "That I didn't tell you I freed Zar by mistake."

Ze threw zir head back and howled. I covered my ears, rose to my feet, and retreated a bit with Jacques.

"You are mine," Renjor cried. "You **chose** to join me!"

I shook my head. "Not true! I know it wasn't."

"Yalene, fight this," Jacques encouraged.

Deep whimpers and desperate huffs, ze shook zir head side to side then slammed zir head into the dirt. Ze raised zir right, front paw, and clawed the ruby crown off zir head.

"Yes!" I gave a clap and reached out to help.

Ze turned zir large head away from us and kept pulling.

Jacques held me back by the shoulder. "Let zem do it."

"Traitor," Renjor cried as the crown broke apart and fell into the dirt where it disappeared.

"Shut up," Lute demanded.

Red eyes welled with tears as they shrank. Fur retreated, and with a final howl, the raptorial feet vanished. The tail grew smaller before disappearing while pointed ears returned to normal.

Jacques took off his cape and tossed it over Xenos' shoulders as ze fell to zir knees in a pair of shredded pants. A flash of purple letters on zir chest caught my eye.

Her curse...The Tethered Sigil is still there.

Yalene feverishly shook, wrapping and clutching the cloth around zem.

I came forward. "Xenos?"

"I'm s-sorry too," ze whispered. "You slept because of me. So many were hurt."

I offered my hand, and eventually, ze took it.

Next, I placed my other hand over zir and gave a small smile, though ze didn't look up to see. "Xenos, I remember you."

Ze continued shivering. "I-I tried not to listen."

I held back a gasp. Zir Guardian tattoos were missing around zir fingers. I looked at Jacques, but he shook his head.

Right now, it doesn't matter.

I coughed and gave a smile. "We know, Xenos. We aren't mad at you."

"Yes," said Jacques. "Welcome back."

Xenos buried zir face in zir hands, letting me go. "How are we going to explain this to Neo-Gen...my people."

"We'll figure it out," said Jacques.

"Let's talk later, okay?" I promised. "I don't have all the answers, but we have to—"

"DAGGER! *WATCH*—"

Shh~unk!

Lute's voice echoed in the valley.

Jared fell to his knees.

I blinked.

Renjor lowered her throwing hand and reached out with her other.

The dagger tore back out.

I blinked again and shook my head.

Jacques chased after the flying dagger, yet I could barely hear his battle cry.

I couldn't speak and barely registered the presence of Renjor fighting against the captain and Lute.

I couldn't move.

"You will *pay*!" Lute declared.

Clashes, shouts, and battle yells, yet I focused on Jared's kind eyes.

Red...

Twinkling shards of red crystal and light caught my attention, flying away from his breaking body.

"Jared...you..."

His staff...it was broken.

I looked at the quartz bracelet as my sight blurred.

The wizard smiled as blood dripped from his wound. "You are the one"—he coughed—"who needs to finish their story."

I remained stuck, digging my fingers into the dirt. "We can save you." My tears wouldn't stop. "I can't do this. Not without you."

"There....are others out there...those who can help you."

The red light reached Jared's waist.

"N-No, w-wait, please!" I lurched forward closer and held onto his shoulders.

"By all that I"—he cupped my cheek and wiped my tears with his thumb—"am, do not cry."

I fell deaf to the world.

The shards fluttered away into the twilight sky.

My friend was gone, leaving the Folk-kin and the pouch behind on the ground.

A thud. I turned around.

Lute and Jacques fell to the ground, breathing heavily on their sides.

"I told you," said Renjor, picking at her retrieved blade. "You had two choices."

I gritted my teeth and screwed my eyes shut.

??????????????????????

"ONCE UPON A TIME..."

Kayla looked from side to side. "Where am I?"

"...there was a child," a young voice echoed around her in a crumbling hall filled with blue books.

"Who stood in this once empty hall with untold stories to tell," a teen voice added.

"Their name was Elias," a little voice said next. "They didn't have a quill. Nor paper."

"So they spoke," a deep voice followed. "And crisp paper formed in their hands."

"So they danced. And the first quill whittled itself in the air."

"So they sang. And ink dripped down from the walls, and Elias contained the ink in a jar of stars."

A child about five years old with wide brown eyes appeared to Kayla's right. "Elias then got to work weaving their stories."

A tall teen with two ginger braids appeared to Kayla's left. "One day, the Forces of Time stopped their work. Elias wielded together their many pages and formed a special book with crystal covers. The last act."

A freckled twenty-something with hazel-gray eyes appeared in the middle. "Time stopped the harmony. Yet, the final story was never done. Eternal Stories are never done. Never was an Ever After. Each of us has a story, fellow Saqui. Fellow, kind soul."

A brown hand with a beaded bracelet around the wrist rose first. "It was my turn."

A slender hand, missing fingers, raised next. "Then mine."

A little hand followed. "Then mine. Now it's yours. Elias has passed the quill to you."

A redhead tilted. "Are you done with the Folk-kin?"

A trembling followed by a shake and smash shook the infinite hall, but the group stood in the crumbling wake of falling blue books.

The child began to vanish. "Are you going to let a mere shackle stop your story? Are you done?"

The first teen vanished next. "Will you get to work?"

"I-I...yes, yes, I will," said Kayla. "My friends need help."

"Are you sure?" A sweet voice asked in the dark, worried.

Kayla nodded. "I'm sure. I'm not done."

The final voice was calm. "Then, believe in yourself."

XENOS – 23 YEARS

"YOU HAD TWO CHOICES."

The hairs on my neck stood on end as my stomach churned.

Kayla remained on her knees with the Folk-kin in her hands. Whereas, across from me, Jacques and Lute remained on their sides, bleeding.

"Hmph, well, if you're going to sit there, moping." The witch dusted off her leg armor. "Let's have a story. You remember touching the glowing white bark?"

I shivered as an icy chill ran down my spine.

"—staging as the voice of the Aniran Tree was *fantastic*—"

"Ya...heartless wench," Jacques groaned in pain.

Kayla remained silent, perfectly still, with a bowed head and hands at her sides.

Renjor touched her temple. "Oh yes~ to telepathically speak with others. That brilliant willow was part of a large forest back in my day, you know. It was **disgusting**. If it weren't for Lady Carrie, all of those blasted Trees would've been gone already."

Lute sat up with gritted teeth. "You're lying."

Renjor put her hands on her hips, ignoring him. "Now, as much as I want to take credit for you losing your memories—"

"She's lying," he yelled over her. "Don't listen, Kayla."

"Am I?" The Kizin put her right elbow into her left hand and put her pointer to her chin with a feral grin—"seems this group is bone dead stupid." She turned to Kayla and raised her hand. "Now, if you sorry lot wouldn't mind, I'll take the Folk-kin now—"

"No, you don't," I cried.

I shot a star-wind fireball at Renjor's dagger but missed her blade. Instead the blaze flew in Kayla's direction.

A loud crack. The breaking sound of glass.

223

The dagger stopped midair and flew backward.

Kayla rose to her feet when the Kizin caught her weapon, and the bracelet fell to the ground in chunks.

"What have you done?" Renjor gasped, pointing her finger.

"Sorry for spacing out there." Kayla touched her temple. "I was...given an important reminder."

"What?" the witch spat and took a step back.

Kayla pointed to the Folk-kin in her arms. "I'm not done with my story."

"We will see about that," Renjor seethed.

"Why so worried, Kizin?" Kayla asked, casually dusting off her knees. "Nervous that you don't scare me anymore?" She pointed to the quartz remnants. "And you needed that fear, didn't you? Keeping me back depended on it."

The witch gave a nervous laugh. "E-Even if I don't get the diary today, your blasted Folk-kin is crumbling apart this very moment, and now you want to play ball?"

"I will stop you." Kayla gave the Folk-kin and pouch to me.

Ironic...

"You should *not* be able to do this," Renjor growled, shaking with rage.

"You will leave my friends alone." Kayla raised her hands as the Kizin continued staring at her.

Like a rolling carpet or waves, rocks, and dirt heaved and surfed, delivering Jacques, Lute, and myself toward another boulder.

"Oi~! Let us fight!"

"Don't ya dare!"

I clawed the dirt, not wanting to move away, but my injuries stung, crippling my efforts.

Renjor cackled. "Boys, sit this one out. It's ladies' night!"

Once behind the boulder, a blue shield enveloped us and the rock.

"You *will* stop hurting them," said Kayla, taking on a front-fighting stance.

"Hey! Let us go," Jacques demanded, pounding the force field with his right forearm while keeping pressure on his bleeding side with his left.

"You're insufferable, your majesty," Renjor grumbled with a sigh and took a left side-stance, raising her fists.

Kayla directed her wave with her arms, riding upon a dense collection of earth. Such tactic evaded the Kizin's lightning strikes, yet any attempt to capture Renjor with the soil met a blast from the witch's dagger.

"This is pointless, Saqui!"

Amid the debris of another failed attempt, Kayla seemingly dove into the dusty ground only to shoot back through the soil with significant momentum.

Right behind Renjor.

Her majesty did a backflip while in the air. Her foot kicked the Kizin's face along the way. The second Kayla landed, she hurled herself forward.

"Let us help!" I urged. "Jared mattered to us too."

I was bout to strike the shield but noticed the cuts and scratches over my forearm and hand were healing.

I tapped Jacques' shoulder. "Hey, look, your injuries."

A glow caught my left eye.

The amethyst. The orb shone blue behind Jacques and me with pieces of the broken staff floating back together.

"Kayla didn't snap for this," said Jacques.

My jaw dropped. I patted the captain's shoulder and pointed to Lute reaching for the levitated, reassembling staff—whose eyes glowed blue with determination.

"You will sign it!" Renjor demanded.

I turned back to face the fight. With a flick of her wrists, the witch unleashed a whip of green lightning attached to the dagger.

Kayla dodged—jumping and bending her body away from the crackling energies.

Renjor cracked her whip over and over until the Saqui threw herself into a forward somersault. Kayla grabbed the energy whip with her left hand and yanked.

Caught off guard, the Kizin flew toward her majesty.

Kayla leaped forward, met Renjor halfway, and knocked the witch to the ground with a mighty right hook.

Renjor absolved her whip and shot a barrage of purple and silver light bolts.

Her majesty blocked the incoming attack with a granite shield and countered with a levitated slew of rock arrows.

With Renjor busy dodging, Kayla manifested and levitated a large slab of black granite before her. She jumped into the air, punched the block with one fist, and sent the block flying.

The Kizin was quick to blast the square slab into pieces but missed Lute's charge from behind—who struck her across the back of her head with the repaired staff, sending her flying several feet.

"I said you'd *pay!*" he cried.

Unable to hold it, the healing force field dissolved.

"Idiot! It's not a club," Jacques shouted, picking the bundled Folk-kin and paper-filled pouch from the ground.

Kayla pointed at Lute from the ground. "You! Questions."

Lute stood between her and Renjor, gripping the late wizard's staff in his hands. "Later. Questions later."

Renjor rolled onto her back. "So, we're at an impasse." She laughed. "So...what now?"

"You will never be in my head again," I cried and charged at Renjor with star-wind in my hands. "Accept your fate!"

The Kizin shakily raised her dagger once more.

"Watch out!" Lute warned.

I dodged the attack and fell backward onto the ground.

"Careful," Jacques warned. "Don't be a fool!"

"Humph, traitor," said Renjor and sliced the air with her dagger for her brooch began blinking.

"Don't you dare leave!" Kayla wiped the sweat with her forearm and slammed her right fist on the ground, heaving for air.

"No"—Jacques wiped his eyes with the back of his hand—"we've delayed returnin' the pages long enough!"

I ran toward the witch, who rolled into her tear and vanished at the last moment. "T'léyna, not again!" I kicked the dirt.

JACQUES – 18 YEARS

KAYLA BURIED HER FACE in her hands in grief, and a low grumble trembled from the ground. The quake rippled across the land and up the shaking mountainside.

Tears stained all our faces when I pulled her to her feet. I offered her taking the diary and pouch of papers from me, but she didn't take it. I took back my offer and retreated a few paces while she kept looking at the ground.

"What are we going to do?" Xenos asked.

"This isn't right. We should go after, Renjor," said Lute.

"Hello? How?" I asked. "You're the one with the staff now. Got any ideas?"

"I'm not instantly a wizard."

I gave the Folk-kin and pouch to Xenos. "Well, how were ya able to heal the staff?"

Lute furrowed his brow. "Heal? I dunno. It just...it called to me. I was mad and hurt, but I knew we needed what he left behind."

"It's good you have it," said Kayla, lifting her head and wiping her eyes.

"I will make sure Jared receives the highest honors when our mission is done," said Xenos. "Lute, off-topic, sorta, but your eyes glow blue like Jared's. Did you notice? I'm curious if you know spells now, or...?"

Lute shrugged, bewildered. "I don't know."

The mountains trembled and quaked.

"Er...Kayla, are you making the ground shake?" he asked. "If not, let's get out of here."

We turned and headed east as none could argue.

"Once we reach the Masana, then what?" Kayla asked. "Jared told us Annika was the one to fix it."

Xenos shook zir head. "Wait, Lady Eider said the Folk-kin was made from the same blue opal."

"Okay, so?" Lute asked. "Are we too late? Jared was the only one who got a hold of her, or she'd come to us."

"Allow me to take it to Neo-Gen," said Xenos. "Lady Eider is too far away, and no one here knows how to reach her castle fast enough, right? Plus, we have no other way to contact her."

I kept walking. "Jared may be gone, but surely there's somethin' at home, in his room, that could help us contact her if Neo-Gen cannot fix the diary."

"I agree," said Kayla. "Searching his room might be our best shot."

"But, it's a book," said Lute. "Paper and covers."

"The essence should be the same," Xenos argued. "Please, this is the least I could do. Let me make this right. I'll run ahead to Neo-Gen. Meet me at the throne room."

I nodded. "Go."

Blue runes of zir special state glowed, changing zir human sprint to that akin to a cheetah. Xenos sped ahead, carrying precious items in hand.

A loud crack echoed among the peaks, and rocks tumbled.

"We need to go! We need to go now," I hurried, jumping and evading the rocks. "Let's go! Come on!"

"We know," Lute cried.

Kayla ran ahead. "Let's find Zebras. See if they can help!"

"What's the likelihood of that?" I shouted.

"Any better ideas?" she asked.

"No, but again——"

"I'll try transporting us," said Lute.

"Clear this first, then try," I ordered.

We leaped from the end of the Dead Mountain pass and landed and rolled across the tall grasses, cutting it close.

Coughing, we rose from the ground, banged up and dusty.

The Dead Mountains continued quaking, cracking, and sifting in waves until the terrain was nothing but piles of rubble.

"If that can happen, who knows where else," I said.

Kayla pointed to empty, black patches in the sky. Across the savanna were stampedes of gazelles, water buffalo, to wildebeests.

"It's official," I said. "We're out of time."

"I hope Xenos is okay," Kayla wheezed. "I still see zem heading south."

"It's a day ride from here," said Lute, wiping his face.

"Not with Jared's transport spell."

"Which he doesn't know," I said.

"Hey, I can try," said Lute. "It's not like I didn't observe, or we haven't seen Jared do it a dozen times."

Kayla touched the golden staff then Lute's arm. "All magic is about focus."

I held onto Lute's shoulder. "Better hop to it."

Our friend closed his eyes and took a deep breath.

"Er, you need to touch the amethyst orb—"

"Ah, right, sorry."

Lute grasped the orb with his full palm.

"Jared touched it with his pointer—"

"Oi!"

"Just do it," I ordered. "World's endin—"

"Then both of you, shut up."

Lute closed his eyes, drew another long breath, and touched the top of the orb with his right pointer.

Moments passed. Nothing.

"Come on," Kayla whispered.

The orb then lit, and the familiar bubble ballooned around the three of us.

I smiled. "Then Jared tilted the staff forward—"

"To drive it, I remember," said Lute, peeking.

He angled the staff, and we took off like a bandit. A wobbly bandit.

I think I'm going to be sick...

XENOS – 23 YEARS

"AH, GET IN YOUR HOMES!"

Everyone in Neo-Gen was running for cover when I arrived as star showers streaked across the cloudy twilight sky with the full moon tinted red.

Wait, I need your help! Fermuru Hyphia, Vaerin, Xyphir!

My exhausted heart wrenched in my chest. Upon arriving, I dropped the bundled Folk-kin with the pouch and fell forward in a heap.

Please...

Due east, a curtain of rain fell singularly around the Overland.

A touch on my hand. I opened my eyes.

Vaerin rolled me over and helped me sit up. Ze peered down to the cracking Folk-kin, picked up the pouch, and its torn shreds inside glimmered blue in zir hands.

"This is...opal-charged...w-we need to fix this, don't we?"

I groaned with a weak nod.

Vaerin looked to zir right. "Hey, over here, you three!"

My friend...I'm sorry...

"It'll be okay, Xenos," ze whispered. "I'm sorry for your ordeal, but I'm glad you're safe."

Am I too late? When...will Renjor take over again?

"Me too." I coughed and clutched the sleeve of zir arm. "The Sword?"

Ze held my hand. "In your quarters. The other Guardians gave it back to me."

Seedlings and sprouts around the greenhouses withered to nothing. The grass turned brown at an unnatural rate as trees snapped under the heavy wind.

Hands, I knew not whose, helped me to my feet.

"Here," said Xyphir. "You used it once."

A roll of thunder trembled overhead as ze returned the sheathed Sword of Elaiobus to me.

"Maybe you can use it again?"

"Your olie can barely hold it," said Vaerin.

D'Lana rose from the ground with the diary and scraps in hand. "Ca'halas," ze shouted. "I need you! If we cannot fix this, or transmute and repair what I have, we spell our doom once again!"

A door on my left opened, and Fermuru Hyphia rushed out. "Over here, hurry!"

Escorted to a chair inside, my sibling, Xyphir, gave me a blanket and put the Sword of Elaiobus by my side. I leaned back on the cool, crystalline wall of the home and closed my eyes. A sharp scent of pungent yet refreshing oils startled me alert when a wet cloth dabbed across my skin.

"Colutia Remka," Vaerin greeted. "Can you help us?"

Our colony's highest-ranking and oldest member stood hunched, to my right, with zir oak cane in hand.

If ze couldn't help, none can...

Xyphir put a cup in my left hand, wrapped zir hands around mine, and helped lift the drink to my lips.

"What do you want zem to do?" Fermuru Hyphia asked.

"The scraps need to be transmuted together and be put back into the book," said Vaerin.

Colutia Remka walked over to me, zir bubble braided hair dragging by zir ankles. "It's but a book," ze said, stopping in front. "Coniphur Yalene, her majesty cannot do this?"

I shook my head and swallowed another mouthful. "No, Runemaster. Much like how an opal cannot ask to become an emerald."

Vaerin put the book in Fermuru Hyphia's hands and gave the pouch to our Colutia. "Please, Captain Volt and Sir Gibe told me of their predicaments. Now that we have these items, they must be transmuted."

"Very well. Stand back."

The Runemaster held out zir wrinkled left hand, and the markings, all up and down zir arm, glowed in spirals.

One by one, a scrap fled the pouch and reassembled in the air like a puzzle. Friends stood ready to fetch completed papers lest they fluttered to the ground.

"How do we know the order?"

"They are numbered, fortunately, Dissapha Xyphir," said Fermuru Hyphia. "Ca'halas, hand them to me. I'll sort them."

Once the pouch emptied, ze fetched the last of the pages, turned on zir heel, and went to a table near my right.

Meanwhile, Colutia Remka lowered zir arm and leaned heavily on zir cane. "They cannot be returned to the covers. I do not have the strength."

Fermuru Hyphia walked over and bowed zir head. "Runemaster, we are grateful. Let me get you settled on a chair."

"It's getting worse out there," a helper fretted. "Where's her majesty?"

I shivered. "Castle...I need to get there."

"P'nya, but you can't head off in your condition," said Xyphir and helped me take more sips of water. "Sweet Arinamo, how did you even run so long in your rune-state?"

I let my head droop forward and took the Dissapha's hand. "I had to. Didn't want us in more danger."

Ze gasped and held up my palm. "Your fingers."

When...did they come back? The run?

My sibling dropped my hand. "H-Have you left our Unity, my olie?" zir whispered.

I shook my head. "Never, my alie, I earned these. Dubbed as a Guardian of her majesty."

"Between wearing gloves during the long winter, I suppose no one noticed or was too busy." Xyphir leaned forward and helped me finish the cup. "Did you get to choose?"

I swallowed hard and nodded. "I was alarmed, but, yes, I did, for the greater good in the Greater Design."

My alie retook my hand. "For the Greater Design."

"Ca'halas, friends," Vaerin announced. "Hate to cut into more world-ending drama, but I have a solution."

"A Dragon bone shard?" Fermuru Hyphia asked. "Did you dig through my things?"

"Yes, sorry, I did say world-ending, didn't I?"

I choked back a dry laugh.

"So, what's your solution?" Xyphir asked, rising to zir feet.

I couldn't quite see past the many shoulders. However, several stood around the table where books thudded as pages rustled in search of something.

"To restore the pages into the covers, the Guardians and her majesty will be in the castle, right?" Vaerin asked. "But, listen, it's storming out, and none of our horses are going to be fast enough."

"Sephur D'Lana, what are you carving?" Colutia Remka asked.

A foot stomped. "Wait," said Fermuru Hyphia. "I recognize those—you can't just pop into the castle—"

"World. *Ending*. And yes, it's technically breaking and entering, but hang up your moral code just once, my ca'halas."

"But, Sephur D'Lana, you're going to pop into the castle, and then what?" Xyphir asked.

"Improvise. Shocker, yes. Now, find a marble, a bit, a sliver, *some* sort of opal, people. Come on, let's move."

"But, who will accompany you? My olie is beyond exhausted—"

"Xyphir," Vaerin hushed. "Understand I'm taking zem there. Strap the Sword of Elaiobus to zir side if you must. Ze must see this through."

"But—"

A crack of lightning struck, and the wind howled. In minutes a blue-white shine emanated from the center of the table.

"Done, this has to be it," said Vaerin.

"Sweet Arinamo, give us one reason," Fermuru Hyphia demanded. "You're asking us to let a near invalid recklessly get to the castle with an untested Dragon bone shard."

"I can go," Xyphir offered.

I pushed myself off the bench. "No. It has to be me."

Vaerin made zir way around the others and held out zir arm. "This is why."

Colutia Remka rose from zir seat, stepped forward, and Vaerin gave zem my hand.

The Runemaster studied the coiled markings around my fingers. "Through suffering, you found strength in your resolution. Through determination, you found your self-worth"—zir wise eyes looked up to me—"so you're on the right path, Coniphur. Keep rising."

I took back my hand as my vision blurred. I couldn't stop smiling. My muscles ached, yet my heart was full. "Thank you."

"Yes, now, let's save what we can," Vaerin encouraged.

LUTE – 14 YEARS

"I'M GONNA HURL!"

"Hang on, Jacques!" The golden staff vibrated in my hands. "I'm trying to steer." The transport orb flickered. "I need to focus!"

Grasslands upheaved and cracked right and left. Trees bent to the wind or snapped. We swerved to the left around tumbling rocks and debris.

"I just need a moment!" he pleaded.

We swerved right and weaved through stampeding wildebeests.

"We don't have a moment, Jacques," I insisted.

"Close your eyes," Kayla suggested.

"Ya know I've tried—"

A wildebeest struck the side of the orb and knocked us to the left. We somersaulted, rolling like a ball. All of us were screaming.

"Let it go," Jacques cried.

I dropped the staff, the bubble burst, and we tumbled out.

The blustering wind howled. I rolled onto my back. Missing puzzle-piece-patches of the sky disrupted the falling stars, and the moon was blood red. I pushed myself to my feet and grabbed the staff.

I pulled Kayla to her feet. "We're at the border," I shouted and went to help Jacques get up. "Let's go!"

"We can't just run all the way there," said Jacques.

"And I can't focus in this wind!"

Kayla pushed the staff to my chest. "You have to try!"

A crack of lightning flashed above us.

"That isn't Zar, is it?" she asked, looking up.

I shook my head; Jacques covered my ears with his hands.

"What are you—" I jerked back.

"Focus!" he said, covering my ears once again.

I closed my eyes and held up the staff.

We need to go...we need to go...

"You can do this," said Kayla.

Take us home...

Soon my feet left the ground. Grinning, I tilted the staff forward, and we propelled ahead like a bird taking off.

I opened my eyes and laughed. "There we go!"

"Keep it steadier if ya can," said Jacques.

My tired grip trembled with the staff. "No promises."

VAERIN – 22 YEARS

WE TUMBLED INTO THE empty ballroom.

"What a rush! Got the bag with the goods?"

Xenos wiped zir brow. "Pfft~ yes, Vaerin."

I put my Dragon bone shard in my breast pocket and adjusted Xenos' arm around my neck. "C'mon, let's go."

We hobbled across the floor and pushed the door open.

"Hello? Miss Amelia Wanda? Sir Haley? Anyone?"

"Hello?" Xenos croaked, adjusting the bag strap around zem.

I set zem down on the steps before the throne and looked around, even up the stairs. "Where are they?"

"We may be—*cough*—early."

I pointed at Xenos. "You are whiter than the snow, don't tell me Hyphia was right to keep you home."

Ze shook zir head. "N-No, I have to be here."

Doors flung open, and her majesty, Sir Gibe, and Captain Volt rushed inside through the foyer.

"Never again," the captain lamented and wretched into the pot of a nearby plant.

Her majesty collapsed flat onto her stomach nearby me while Lute wobbled for the steps and fell to sit beside Xenos on my left.

The castle shook.

"We don't have time for churned bellies!" I shouted.

The young queen brought her hands by her head, pushed up, and crawled toward the stairs.

Sir Volt dragged himself over, half limping, holding his stomach.

A splintering crack ran up the side of the walls to my right.

I grabbed Xenos' bag, pulled out the tied stack of unbound pages, and dumped out the bundled Folk-kin. I pushed the book forward and yanked the corner of the blanket last minute from around the hot diary covers.

The Folk-kin slid a short way across the floor. The crystal covers pulsed between blood red to sapphire blues and swirling purples as blazing-white gouges split the front.

Her majesty covered her ears in pain, hearing something I could not.

I tossed the blanket behind me and hustled to stand a few paces behind the Folk-kin. "I beseech you all. What do we need to do?"

Jacques looked at the diary on the floor, and his eyes shined a powerful red, followed by the markings around his fingers.

Lute was next, who shined a brilliant green.

Xenos, a hopeful white.

My jaw dropped. I couldn't move and fell deaf to the world around me.

A mystical wind lifted the diary into the air. Jacques rose from the stairs with renewed strength, reached out with his right hand, and stepped forward.

I shook my head, yanked the string from around the restored pages, and held them out.

He didn't take them. However, Lute rose and moved forward, reaching out his glowing left hand.

The gouges were closing.

Chunks of roofing crashed around us.

Yet, Lute didn't take the pages either.

"Will someone take these?" I begged. "Xenos?"

None answered. Xenos sat up, stood, yet also ignored what was in my hand.

The cracks were gone, and the fighting colors tempered, clearing up.

The short stack flapped in my hand, but I remained as I was.

Her majesty's mark on her left arm and her eyes radiated blue. She rolled to her side, stood, and reached out to me.

The pages fled from my hand and swirled around her to form a circle from behind. The broken diary rose over the heads of the Guardians and flew to stop before her. The covers parted, and the white-hot pages flipped through in haste. The papers in my grip pulled free and zipped forward into place in rapid sequence.

The book slammed shut. Queen Kayla wrapped her arms around it tight and fell to the ground along with her Guardians.

My heart pounded in the surrounding silence. I exhaled, then took several gasping breaths. When did I stop breathing? The once-crumbling roof stopped and rewound back to where it had been. The splintering cracks healed as if they had never happened. I rushed to the foyer, ran out the doors, and paused upon the cobblestone courtyard.

The moon? Normal. Clouds? Gone. I ran through the castle gate. The town was fully reconstructed and dry, anew though stopped my heart.

Am I...home?

I looked over my shoulder—the castle remained unchanged from the outside. Alas, this wasn't, somehow, Genecia. I shook my head and continued running.

Bright lamps, sidewalks, bushes, trees, and sturdy park benches lined the wide, paved road. New homes with natural stone cladding and glass windows stood taller than before, complete with polished knobs and painted numbered doors.

When I reached the fountain, I sighed. It was the same as always. Splashing cool water on my face, I jumped to find the structure changed into a circular one. It was taller, and the stone's cut was smoother and polished. A statue of a curvy woman holding a shallow pan with water spilling over the edge stood in the middle. I smiled, reminded of the beautiful one in front of the opera house in Genecia's capitol.

The clock tower tolled with silvery bell tones akin to windchimes. I turned and witnessed the hour and minute hands reassemble piece by piece, shining a light blue glow of their own. Though Neo-Gen's gift stood tall, the swinging myriad of steel bells was new. I closed my eyes and deeply breathed in the fresh warm air.

Thought I'd never hear such a sound again...

"Sephur D'Lana?"

I jumped. A slender man on my right stood in a three-piece, tailored suit with a top hat.

I took a quick step back. "W-Where did you come from?"

He took off his hat. "It's alright. It's me, Lord Quild."

Not quite home, indeed...

"Apologies, have you seen my Almea, by chance?"

"N-No, I—"

"Sephur D'Lana?"

I spun to my left.

A young brown woman in an elegant sage green gown with silk bows appeared on my left.

She fiddled with the handle of her lacey umbrella over her shoulder. "No need to be startled. It's just me."

I tilted my head to the side. "Lady Shellfore?"

She tucked one of her many copper-black braids behind her ear. "That's right. Ada, to be precise. Have you seen my twin?"

I shrugged. "I'm afraid not—"

"Sister, over here!"

Across the way, on the opposite side of the square, Lady Akilah ran toward us dressed in an embroidered vest over a blouse paired with high-waisted trousers.

In her sprint, another person randomly flashed into view one by one. People in skirts to coattails to bonnets populated the town square.

"What happened?" was heard over and over.

"Have you seen my dog?"

"Have you seen my aunt?"

My this, my that, none appeared scared, nor seem to remember.

The sisters embraced.

"When I came to, you weren't there," said Ada. "I'm glad you're okay."

"Do you know what happened?" I asked. "Did you see the moon turn red? Feel the ground shake?"

The Ladies shook their heads.

"We were on a walk, the last I remember," said Akilah.

Lord Quild stepped forward. "If you were separated, I'm sure Almea is somewhere." He gave a short bow and turned to leave. "Best be off."

"Be safe," the twins chorused.

"Certainly."

Watching him go, I dug my fingers into my hair and couldn't stop smiling in relieved delight. "This. This is crazy."

~The Restored Entries~

LUTE – 13 YEARS

"JARED! DO YA SENSE anythin'?"

The old man pulled back his reins. "The pillar of light appears to be at the border, but I am unsure what to make of it."

"I do," said Xenos. "He's returned."

Thunder rolled, and lightning cracked the sky.

That's odd...

"Should we get King Basi?" Xenos asked.

"His majesty has to protect his people," Jared replied. "Besides, if we cannot get past that pillar, what do you think the king will be able to do, let alone how do we explain this?"

"At best, his majesty's subjects retreated to their homes or headed east," I suggested, stroking my horse's neck when thunder rolled. "Oi, that said, why doesn't it surprise me Lady Annika hasn't come to help?"

"We can do this without her," said Jacques.

"She has her role as this world's sorceress-medium," Jared reminded. "I would prefer her out of harm's way."

Right...

A violent, loud clap of lightning resounded above our heads. Our horses reared back—I fell off into the freezing slush and ice. I braced myself, prepared to get a hoof to the face.

"Ya! Go home!" a man cried. "Git! Go!"

I lowered my arms. Lord Quild had put his horse between me and my steed. Calistor dismounted once he sent my horse away and sent his in turn with a firm slap on the rump.

The noble turned and held out his hand. "Are you hurt?"

"No, but thank you."

I got to my feet before he rushed to his downed wife to give her a hand as her horse galloped off.

"You okay, honey?"

She dusted the snow off herself. "I'm fine."

He pulled her into a hug. "Good."

Jacques dismounted and let Avon go freely back to wherever she felt safe.

"Xenos? Jared?" I called. "You alright?"

"Jared's with us," the twins chorused as their thoroughbreds left them behind.

Both Blackfrosts aided zem onto zir feet. "We have Xenos!"

"Ah, great, a living snow person," I teased. "Always wanted one."

Xenos ruffled the snow from zir white hair. "Really? Now?"

"Thankfully, no one's hurt," the twins replied together, holding hands.

"New detection," Xenos announced, looking up from zir Gieci. "Something is coming!"

I spun around. The beam's colors transformed into consistent glowing green and purple.

I took a step back and looked at Jacques. "Oi, what was that about not needing Annika's help?"

"Jared," he said. "Return with haste and put a Vrastia shield up around the castle."

"How long do you expect him to hold that?" Tyford asked.

"It can last as long as he's alive," said Jacques. "or not badly wounded. Jared, include the town if ya can muster it."

"On it." Jared turned and activated his transport spell around him.

"Prepare yarselves," Jacques ordered, unsheathing his sword.

Before Jared could move, a force struck the ground and sent us flying backward. I slid and tumbled across the churned snow before coming to a full stop against a tree.

Ow...

"Hello, boys."

From my place against the tree, I had the perfect view of Renjor, having landed atop a large disc of glowing red light, dressed battle-ready in black.

"My, my...." She looked from side to side, peered over her shoulder toward the Masana, and then held out her free hand to capture some snowflakes. "What a mess." She lowered her dagger, and the disc faded away, leaving a wide spot clear of snow.

"What have you done?" Jared asked, struggling onto his feet with the help of his staff.

I got up and dusted the snow off my arms. I withdrew my shrunk weapon from its holster on my hip and extended the quarterstaff to its full length.

She put her hands on her hips. "Me? My dear, Lukene, lil ol' me has done nothing." She gestured around her. "You ran out of time. This snow? All due to *her*, I assure you."

"Dear? Jared, do you know Renjor personally?" Lord Blackfrost helped his lady onto her feet.

"Aw, you didn't tell them?" the witch sneered.

"Sir Jared, what is the meaning of this?" Lady Quild demanded.

Jared stood as he was and did not move or say anything.

"What is going on?" I whispered to myself.

"Discuss this later," Xenos insisted. "This Kizin is trying to distract us."

"Aren't you the smart one?" Renjor teased. "Then again, I already knew that."

Ze frowned but remained silent.

Renjor rocked back and forth on her heels. "Aw, cute—"

"What have you done?" Jared repeated and got in her face.

The crazed Kizin laughed. "Here's the best part. I don't answer to you." She pushed Jared back with her hand and came forward. "Now...Let. Me. Through."

Jared studied the beam of light over past Renjor's shoulder and stepped back. "Oh no."

"What is it?" Lord Quild asked.

The old man didn't bother looking at us. "We are in trouble."

"Something's coming through," Xenos cried. "Get ready!"

Frightful, screeching cries heard across the valley where we stood came in waves as thunder rolled overhead. From high in the sky, an enormous beast descended. When the monstrous, purple-black creature landed, the swirling pillar of light shortened into nothing.

Zar...that must be him!

I covered my ears when the Dragon let loose a mighty roar. Red tears of light ripped along the border in the air on either side of the creature, from which glowing green Leaf Turners poured out and clamored toward the Overland.

Renjor cackled. "Ah~ my darlings made it." She held out her hand to Jared. "As the Overland sleeps, we will take the Folk-kin now."

"Never." Jacques pointed to his blade. "Kayla's story isn't yars to mess with."

"It is today, dear captain."

The ground trembled under the Dragon's step. Zar inhaled, opened his maw, and released a tremendous roar.

I crossed my arms in front of my face, squeezed my eyes shut, and braced for impact, expecting the worst to come...instead felt a gentle hand on my forearm.

I relaxed and slowly let down my arms. With an innocent, playful smile, Kayla stood waving at me.

I reached out to her.

A tap on my shoulder.

I opened my eyes with a jolt.

"Oh, good, yar awake. Here," said Jacques, offering his hand to help me up.

She was a vision...figures...

Jacques snapped his fingers. "Hey, focus, it's thanks to them"—he pointed with his thumb to his left—"we stand safe as well."

The six Lords and Ladies of the Overland Territory stood surrounding us with their hands in the air, backs facing us, each still as stone. A blue ribbon of light coursed between them, connecting each other in a big circle. A white dome had formed over us like we were transported to a separate room.

"What's the big idea?!"

My eyes switched to the center, where Renjor spun around, wide-eyed and shocked.

"Well, now, this was unexpected," said Jared.

Xenos raised zir hand. "Uh, could someone fill me in?"

"That brat!"

Jacques pointed the tip of his blade at Renjor. "One **twitch** from yar dagger, Kizin, and yar head is mine."

Though protected, the ground trembled under my feet while muffled anguish wailed outside.

The psycho scoffed. "Pfft, I wouldn't worry about me. The world is about to break around you." Her gaze settled on Xenos. "Might as well jump ship."

"Shut up," ze spat. "You are—"

I could feel Zar's roar from the other side.

Renjor grinned and closed her good eye as her shoulders dropped. "Fools..."

I held out my quarterstaff. "Jared, mute that witch. Better yet, Jacques, get rid of her, and let's be done with this."

Jared pulled me back by the shoulder. "The Leaf Turners will still come."

"We have to do something! Kayla is at the castle," I argued.

"Ya think we don't know this?" Jacques shot back.

"She's stalling," Xenos panicked.

What?

I looked over in zir direction. "We know, buddy."

"Silence," Jared demanded.

We froze for a long moment. I, for one, wasn't sure what to say.

"Sweet Zar, move this plot along," Renjor groaned. "Your macho-cheesiness is irritating as you've been standin' around looking 'cool'. Can I have the Folk—Ow!" The Kizin rubbed her head. "What was that for?"

Jared tilted back his staff. "Keep talking, and I will zip your mouth shut."

I gestured between the two magic users. "Oi, do it."

"Empty threats," Renjor sneered and looked at me. "A threat to others maybe, but not to me."

My shoulders dropped as I looked back and forth between the two. "Oh, come on."

Jared winced and brought his left hand to his temple.

I tilted my head to the side. "You, okay?"

The town wall is hardly protected with me here." He gave me a pained look. "My strength should be focused on a Vrastia shield."

"And not on anythin' else," said Jacques. "Ya have to save energy."

Renjor smirked. "Very good."

Jared leaned on his staff. "And my connection to my shield will be better once we lower this one we are in."

"In short, we can't stay here long," I figured. "We should get ready."

Xenos unsheathed the Sword of Elaiobus. "Ready! I've been *itching* to use it."

"Oh, she just gave the blade away?" Renjor grumbled.

"Shut yer trap!"

The witch rolled her one eye. "Fine, Captain. Then have *fun*!" She flicked her wrist with her dagger in hand and phased from the scene like a coward—disappearing through a quick distortion in the air right before Jacques' sword passed through her shifting form.

He spun around and looked side to side, yet kicked the dirt. "Graah!"

"Do you think she'll slip through your shield?" Xenos asked.

Jared stepped forward. "I let in whom I want. And Renjor is not on the list. That said, we cannot afford to fail."

Jacques shook his head. "We won't. I don't believe any of us will let that happen without a fight."

Jared nodded and turned toward the white shield around us. "Lords and Ladies of the Ones of Reflection, stand down and prepare to fight!"

The nobles' arms slowly returned to their sides, and the dome around us descended like melting wax. Snow blustered inside, and the frigid wind returned. The twins put on leather gloves while the Quilds brought out identical flails with three iron balls of spikes, but the Blackfrosts were...odd.

"Oi, why the decks of cards?" I asked.

"Jared will tell you talismans are my family's specialty," Lord Blackfrost bragged as he shuffled. He pointed to his wife. "Her moon cards have healing powers. I have the sun cards to help fight back."

I smirked. "Good man."

Xenos' Gieci flashed green from the corner of my eye. "What is it?"

Ze pressed a couple of buttons. "It's Sephur D'Lana. Zirs are in position, at the ready to assist, Jacques."

"Tell zem to hold, for now, Xenos," Jacques ordered. "Everyone else? Get yar head in the game. Blackfrosts, help clear the way for Jared to reach the castle wall if ya can. Neo-Gen units can only fire so many times."

Now he tells me...

Groans followed by creaks and wails. Defaced creatures with large eyes of purple light surrounded us, and these had claws.

Lady Ada Shellfore moved and stood back-to-back with her sister Akilah and struck a fighting pose.

"Jared, move to the town gate," Jacques ordered. "Stay safe and focused on the Vrastia shield."

"We will cover you," said Lady Blackfrost.

She and her husband guarded Jared as they hustled for the gate.

"Ah!" I jumped back, feeling a swish on my right.

A Leaf Turner who missed me retreated.

Jacques picked up his blade. "Focus, Lute!"

"Careful," said Lady Akilah. "They are shifty!"

Jacques charged forward and sliced with a downward diagonal swipe with his blade but missed. He then swung and slashed upward, cutting through the glowing bone-shard. Shattered, the Leaf Turner unraveled into fleeting smoke with a howling wail.

"Aim for the glowin' shards," he ordered.

Xenos on my left shot zir star-wind, blazing four at once.

"That works, too." I knocked another Turner back—targeting the bone-crystal on its shoulder. "Ack!"

Jacques ran by me. "Hit harder!"

I spun around and struck another down through the chest. "On it!"

In a series of punches, the twins worked in sync, nabbing as many as they could. Ada did a high kick to the head, locked arms with her sister, who mirrored it with a kick of her own.

"The Vrasita shield has yet to come up," Akilah cried.

"Keep at it!" Jacques ordered.

I batted away with my quarterstaff, and Lady Quild charged past with a battle cry, circling her flails above her head, and tore through one enemy after another.

Calistor bashed yet another across the chest. "Great follow-up, Almea!"

"Thank you, honey."

"I always loved watching you fight."

Jacques chopped straight down. "Focus ya lovebirds!"

"Get ready, guys," I cried. "More are coming!"

Dozens emerged from the portals and streamed like a raging green river charging down the untouched-snowy hill.

"LIES~!"

Their cries echoed throughout the valley.

I took out two more with an uppercut of my staff. "Ah, the shield is rising."

The blue, translucent Vrastia shield raced down the sides of the town wall and ballooned over the Overland. The barrier forced the Leaf Turners climbing the wall to retreat and spur toward us in a sweeping U-turn.

I ran to the rear. "Xenos, with me, they're circling back to here!"

Ze parried, ducked, and wove, wildly hacking and slashing the Sword of Elaiobus.

"Use your star-wind," I urged.

"Did. Twice," ze heaved out of breath. "Cooling down."

"Oh, great."

An orange beam of fire and sparks whistled through the air and struck another Leaf Turner down.

"Good aim, Tyford," Jacques cried and stabbed two more.

Lord Blackfrost whipped out another card from his deck and chucked it. The magic ignited mid-flight, and another shot flew into the swarm.

I struck down another spirit. "How"—I ducked—"in the"—I knocked heads—"world?"

Jacques and I were pushed back-to-back.

"Train with us and spend less time on books."

"O-Oi!" I knocked two away yet was scratched across my left arm by a third.

"Lute—" Jacques fell to his right knee, struck on the shoulder.

Carmen swept in and pulled a crescent-moon card from her deck. "Mend!"

Blue sparkles fell, her card vanished, and Jacques charged forward anew.

My jaw dropped. "Was something put in my tea or..?"

"Focus, Sir Gibe," Carmen chided and ran off to help others.

Lord Blackfrost whipped another sun ray card to my right. "Keep going!"

From the corner of my eye, Ada side-kicked through another bone-shard. Her twin swerved and punched a couple other enemies.

Xenos fired another shot but missed.

Almea rushed forward and swung her flail, starting from a low left and upward in a diagonal.

"Go heal, Xenos," I cried.

Ze fled to Lady Blackfrost. All I could see of her power from a dealt card was a silver light.

Tyford moved up to guard zem. He flung more sun ray cards between his fingers, sending out a spectral force of dazzling arrows of orange light which slew multiple ghosts in a row.

Carmen held a half-moon card. "Revitalize!"

My aches rapidly faded to nothing; I could breathe easier.

"Thank you, " Akilah cried. "I feel much better." She punched another Leaf Turner through the shard on their shoulder.

"Nice," I said, raising my hand.

She grinned. "Thanks."

We high-fived and proceeded to take a few more out.

"There's no end to these guys," Calistor yelled.

Almea requested, "More assistance on the left."

"Code: Fire Rain," Jacques ordered.

"Sent," Xenos replied.

The star-wind units of Neo-Gen quite literally rained fire from above, dousing clusters of Leaf Turners into nothing.

I spun on my heel, then jumped to my left, nearly slipping, just as an arrow whizzed past me.

"Ack," I cried and batted another head in. "Jacques! Are there any more 'codes'?"

He dodged, then thrust his blade through yet another. "No, I promise."

"Good!" I shuffled to the right and covered Shellfores' six with my quarterstaff. I rapidly struck three Leaf Turners' bone-shards. One in the forehead, one in the shoulder, and the other in the chest.

On the border, Zar roared a higher pitch and beat his wings. The enemies' glowing purple eyes switched to a shocking red.

"Sweet Arinamo! Scary," Xenos cried and blasted another punch of star-wind.

A shower of more arrows set ablaze cascaded around us from atop the wall.

I swung two enemies across their heads.

Jacques slammed his blade across the chest of two more.

"Should we keep count?" I teased.

Lord Quild got swiped across the face. A bloody gash appeared over his cheek as his head snapped to the right.

I flinched. "Never mind."

Lady Blackfrost jumped in to heal Calistor.

The ground shook. The rain fell harder, nearly blinding.

"Retreat!" Jacques cried. "Go help who you can! Move!"

Under the protection of the archers, we fled toward the gate.

BASI – Appears 32 When Furless

THE PREDAWN LIGHT CRACKED the night under the rolling clouds.

"We are fearless," Moli cried. "We are the Masana!"

My queen and I ran with all our might. We strove to rally Tribe members the moment the towering storm blasted onto the southern border. Upon arriving, I dug my claws into the dirt. My lungs were on fire, yet a great shiver ran down my spine. My whole face was freezing, but there was no time to spare. Swarms of green, clawed terrors flanked Zar's large backside. The Dragon resembled an enormous horned lizard with curved talons.

A high roar pierced the sky. The ground trembled when the monster rose to his hind feet.

"Protect Johari!" I roared.

Grasses trampled under the trumpeting Elephant Tribe, whose stampede struck the monster from both sides.

The long neck followed by the monster's maw curled back, and a blast of green lightning and fire shot into thunderous clouds.

Lionesses swiped, bit the purple and black hide, retreated to avoid intermittent shocks zipping along the scaled skin, and then attacked again.

Flocks of cawing and shrieking Birds and screaming Monkeys swarmed the mobs of green nasties. They pecked, clawed, and grabbed floating rocks into the enemies' chests, foreheads, or arms. They destroyed each Leaf Turner, one by one.

I swiped, ducked, rolled, and roared. Blood trickled down my temple, and deep scratches covered my legs and paws. I couldn't, didn't, and never would give up. Crippled or dead, I needed to fight for my kingdom's sake.

Tobi...keep your sister safe, my son...

Gigantic wings beat the sky, knocking Birds to fellow Beasts back as harsh winds washed over the battlefield in waves.

My bones cracked as I sat up. "He's taking flight!"

"Do we try to push through the blizzard?" Moli asked.

I pushed to get up. "We can't." I stumbled. "Bird wings were cut in the attempt." I slowly rose to my four paws. "We keep fighting." I turned to the Lioness nearby. "Pounce as many nasties as you can! We have to keep going!"

LUTE – 13 YEARS

TAKING A FIGHTING RETREAT, I entered the shield and passed the front gate with cuts and bruises. Lady Quild tumbled inside, carrying her husband, his arm over her shoulder, as the injured Shellfores hobbled in last.

Lady Blackfrost rushed forward and healed the twins and Calistor, placing identical full-moon cards on their foreheads. "Repair!"

I looked at the swarms of Leaf Turners pounding away at Jared's shield. "Oi, how many people did the former Saqui tick off?"

"What now?" Xenos asked, hustling across the muddy road. "Sephur D'Lana reported ten confirmed dead, and the town is surrounded!"

Jacques exhaled and wiped his brow with his arm. "Zar has been tearin' us down with this weather and Jared is hopefully standin' strong in the town square."

"At least they can't get in for now, right?" I asked.

"We can't let our resolve die here," Jacques encouraged.

"Zar needs to be dealt with soon," said Lord Blackfrost. "I can't rely on Jared to hold the Vrastia shield forever."

I jumped in place. "Wait!"

"What is it?" Jacques asked.

I turned to Xenos. "You wanted to use the Sword of Elaiobus? Gimme the Sword."

The Coniphur appeared taken aback. "H-Huh? B-But why? What are you planning?"

I made a grab for the weapon. "Give it to me already."

Xenos dodged my advance with a sidestep to the right and turned away. "Would you stop? You're going to cut yourself!"

"Oi, I said give it here! The others have protected us from Zar's blast. Now, it's our turn to lend them our strength to support them as Guardians.

When Kayla first got this weapon from the Elemental Dragons, she was told it was more of a shield."

Jacques got between Xenos and me. "What's yar plan?"

"I saw her, Jacques. When the Lords and Ladies created the shield back there, I *saw* her."

My friend pulled his head back in surprise. "I thought it was just me."

"Same here," said Xenos.

I put my hand on Jacques' shoulder. "Listen, if I were to guess, we'll need space. Let's get back to Jared."

We hustled to the town square as quickly as possible under the deafening Dragon cries and his thunderous blasts against the Vrastia shield.

"Oi," I shouted and ran ahead. "Jared, we need your help!"

The old man remained at the fountain, the orb of his staff shining bright.

I slid to a stop beside him. "Oi, I have an idea, Jared."

"What is it?"

"That's what we all like to know," said Jacques.

I turned to face the group catching up. "We need to close the portals allowing the enemy to come through. It's not alive, and Kayla would strive to do the same thing."

"Leaf Turners aren't alive either," said Lady Quild.

"Exactly," I said. "We cut them off from what has to be a power source and the spell driving their shards—"

"We don't know it's a power source," said Xenos.

"But it makes sense," said Jared.

"What about Zar?" Lady Ada asked.

"After we dispel the Leaf Turners, I can raise the shield back up," said Jared. "That is until we figure out the next best option."

"But," said Jacques. "Kayla is not here."

I smirked and pointed to the Lords and Ladies of the Overland. "They are the Ones of Reflection."

"I see. You want them to act on Kayla's behalf," said Jared, catching on. "To utilize the Sword of Elaiobus."

"That's right." I folded my arms.

"We are not her," reminded Lady Blackfrost.

Carmen's husband stood by her side. "Even if we try, the best we could possibly do is set the enemy back for a while."

"Still," I said. "You're the best we got, milord, our best chance." I reached out to Xenos. "Hand. It. Over."

Ze shook zir head. "Kayla entrusted it to me. I will remain the one holding it as we carry out your plan. My Ryna Blessing, while channeled, could stand up to these monsters."

The muffled cries of angry spirits continued in the distance as Lord Quild stepped forward, leaning on his wife, and turned to face the other four. "I want the Leaf Turners to rest in peace, do we not?"

"Guardians! Fellow Lords and Ladies, let's give it our all," Lord Blackfrost declared with fire in his eyes and a raised fist.

Xenos stepped forward. "Hold it! When the shield drops for us to fire, what's stopping Renjor from walking inside the castle and taking out the Neo-Gen team?"

Shoot...

I pointed at zem. "Excellent question."

Jared frowned. "Nothing. Inform zirs to barricade the castle at once."

"W-What?!" I stammered. "We should head back!"

"We do that," said Jacques. "We can't last forever."

Our silence gave way to the sounds of enemy forces' screams.

I covered my ears when lightning crashed against the shield.

"Let's move," Jacques ordered.

Under Jared's directions, Xenos stood in the middle with the Sword of Elaiobus as the six Ones of Reflection stood in a circle around zem. Jacques, Jared, and I moved apart to form a triangle around the ring.

Meanwhile, Vaerin and zir units set up defense points around the town square to prepare for when the shield would dissolve.

"This better work or we will be sittin' ducks, Lute," said Jacques.

"Then let's not miss," I shot back.

"Xenos! Raise the Sword of Elaiobus," Jared ordered, and raised his arms to the sky. "Everyone, stand tall and steel yourselves. My friends, lend us your resolve to protect this world. Do not underestimate the strength of a goal backed with a unified mind!"

I closed my eyes to focus, meditating with everything I had, hoping our collective force was enough.

After standing with closed eyes for several moments, my whole body warmed up. I peeked a tiny bit. The coiled marks of a Guardian on my hands glowed as strings of energy bled from and between my fingers. They started green at my hands, matching my tattoos, but were a glowing blue as they left me. The threads meandered near the six and wove among us. I reclosed my eyes with a smile, and, with a gigantic whoosh, a great heat was upon my face. In time, the muffled cries and pounding on the shield in the distance faded.

When the wails of the Leaf Turners went silent, I opened my eyes and let out a long sigh. The six Ones had collapsed to the ground, all fast asleep still in their circle. I fought a yawn, feeling sluggish. Drained, my legs were shaky, and my hands were trembling.

Xenos dropped the Sword and fell to zir knees.

Moments later, Jared fell to his knees next, leaning against his staff.

"Oi, old man, the shield you need to—"

The roars of the chaotic Dragon increased, jarring us back to reality, forcing us to cover our ears.

New bellows met Zar's roar.

"Wait..."

Streaks of orange-red fire and golden light blazed across the darkened sky, all clashing against irregular forces of lightning crackling violently back.

It's not one Dragon...they came!

"Oh...shoot," I muttered.

Dysart of Darkness...against Zar's evil, he's going to become massive!

"Xenos, notify Sephur D'Lana that all units should move and help transport those injured to the castle," said Jacques.

"On it, I'll go help too."

A hand touched my shoulder.

"Lute, are ya still good to move?" he asked.

"Y-Yeah, I can still move, but—" I pointed to the display above.

"Yikes. Yeah~ it's quite a sight." My friend pat my arm. "Let's go get a better view and make sure at least part of yar plan worked."

Jacques and I hustled back to the outskirts of town and watched the Elemental Dragons in fierce combat. The awe-inspiring spectacle of different colors blurring and tearing away at each other almost made me forget who was creating such streams of power. There were rumblings and gushing of rock and water. The ground shifted under my feet but didn't break. The battle raged, and when the clock tower chimed six, Gia of Fire knocked Zar backward with his tremendous tail. The Dragon of Lightning disappeared through another—much smaller—distortion in the sky. The instant Zar left, a streak of golden light zipped after him like a shooting star, followed by what looked like a rippling, black cloak being sucked through.

"Dysart was *huge*," said Jacques. "We can finally see the blue sky again."

In time, Gia and all the remaining Dragons landed before us—the wind from their landing blinded me for a moment.

"Hello, Guardians. It has been a long time," Gia greeted.

"We were lucky," said Jacques.

"Luck?" Shan of Water tilted her icy head to the right. "How so? The Leaf Turners are formidable as spirits."

"They're tough," I agreed. "We were able to win with everyone's help."

Nan of Earth shook her head. "I'm afraid not. I still feel them under the dirt. They're simply biding their time."

"What?" I gasped and looked down, picking up my feet.

"Don't worry. It isn't as though a random hand will drag you down," she assured. "My point is, while the Lords and Ladies have done their best representing their Saqui, only Kayla can truly dispel the bitterness these spirits harbor in their hearts, which holds them from ultimate peace."

I nodded. "Uh-huh."

"Lute," Jacques warned. "Don't do it, man—"

"Why?" I asked. "Why her?" I pointed at Nan. "Why not you?" I pointed at Shan. "Or you?" I turned to Gia and folded my arms. "Speaking of, where have you been? *Any* of you?"

All three Dragons exchanged a glance.

"You're angry, young Guardian," said Nan.

"A bit." I mocked a bow. "Respectfully."

Shan lowered her head, eyes glowed pure white, and an orb of clear water formed over her. Within the sphere, a picture show from her perspective played.

"Memories," she said. "We were at peace."

"Or 'retirement' as humans would say," said Gia.

What appeared to be Dragons chasing and flying through the clouds, hovering over mountains, lush trees, and clear streams flickered within the liquid.

"Where is that?" Jacques asked.

"A sliver of what used to be. A *Fractal*," said Nan. "A piece of our shattered world, far away from what we know now."

The beautiful place switched to deep gray clouds hanging over a frozen land.

"It's snowing there, too?" Jacques asked.

"My friends and I sensed something was wrong," said Nan.

"So, we separated and traveled through various Fractals to gather what's been happening," Shan added. "When Gia and I stumbled across the alchemic world of Genecia, we felt Zar's presence, then sought to come here."

"Did you take too many left turns?"

Jacques hit the front of my shoulder with the back of his hand. "Lute, c'mon."

"Sorry," I sighed. "Can Genecia be saved?"

Gia shook his head. "It was falling apart, shattered like broken pottery when we visited. I don't think it can be restored. Fortunately, you've already established a colony here."

"Oi, that doesn't make me feel any better."

"But it is true, Guardian Lute," Shan replied and closed her eyes.

Her orb of water swished into a stream and retreated back into her.

I folded my arms. "Can't get a breather, can we."

Gia brought his hand to his chest. "Take this as a token of our apology for Kayla's absence." He removed a round stone about the size of a large melon from his necklace and handed it to Jacques. "No matter what, we should have arrived sooner. For that, we are sorry."

"What is that?" I asked.

"This is *Eleincense*. If you crush this resin, its special properties will burn like oil. Have a small censer burner in the queen's room, place lamps in the four corners of town, and understand breaking the curse will take time and diligence on your part."

Jacques nodded. "Thank you."

"You are most welcome," said Gia before his face grew solemn. "I am concerned; however, this may be the last time you see any of us."

"Oi, what does that mean?" I asked. "Kayla is going to want to see you again."

Nan thumped her tail on the ground and shook her head. "The Fractals have yet to be united. We need to survey those who may need our help and protect them from Zar."

Gia stepped forward. "Until the Fractals are one, from this day forward, we will strive to keep Zar from violence until our last breath."

"Fractals? Can you tell us more?"

Gia shook his head. "Be at peace, Guardian. Take the stone, and do not worry so," he assured, then leaped into the sky.

The other Dragons smiled knowingly, albeit sadly. Then each bowed their head in farewell and took off. Part of the cloudy-blue sky distorted once again before the Dragons went through to wherever their home was.

"SO THAT IS THAT," SAID Jared, back in the throne room. "We should check if King Basi needs anything."

"Hold it," Xenos demanded. "Jared, you have some explaining to do."

"If you are referring to Renjor, I am afraid there is nothing to tell. There is no point. What is done is done."

Xenos appeared ze was going to ruffle zir hair but shook out zir hands instead. "How are we supposed to drop it?"

Jared raised an eyebrow. "Are you questioning my loyalty?"

Ze shook zir head. "N-No, just, I don't understand."

"Some things are meant to stay in the past."

With that, Jared walked away.

I tapped the back of my hand on Xenos' arm. "Hey, it's okay. If Jared has his reasons, you can be sure they are good ones."

THE SMOKE OF THE ELEINCENSE wafted through the lid holes of a small copper pot on Kayla's nightstand. The all-spice smell hung in the air but was relaxing.

"So, it is what it is, Kayla," I said, sitting by her bedside. "We survived. Thankfully. Plus, Neo-Gen is training another unit, in case." I let go of her hand. "I still wonder if you can hear me, but I can't help talking to you." I sat upright. "Oh! Our Xenos and the old man have decided to pair up and make a safe house. Er, it's more of a tower," I rambled. "But you'll know what I mean...heh. The funny thing is ze strongly believes ze should **live** there and carry out observations and keep a watchful eye for any more Leaf Turner activity." I shrugged. "I don't know. That last part, I think, comes from Jacques' influence, in part about duty, or has something to—"

For the first time in months, Kayla stirred in her sleep and turned to her side.

I smiled.

It's working...

"Anyway, you'll understand why we need the tower. The danger is at our doorstep, every new moon as of late." I stood from my chair and fiddled with a couple of stems of Blackfrosts' bouquet on her nightstand. "Please, come back."

$$\longrightarrow \cancel{||||}\,||\,\cancel{||||} \longrightarrow$$

KAYLA – 12 YEARS

I CLOSED THE DIARY and frowned. The afternoon light was dim in the castle library. I stared at the blue front cover of the Folk-kin as the faint birdsong whistled beyond the glass window.

I raised my left arm and struck the diary with the side of my fist.

Why? Where were Gia and the Elemental Dragons?

ASHLEY SCHELLER

~THE ADVENTURE WILL CONTINUE ~

Don't miss out!

Visit the website below and you can sign up to receive emails whenever Ashley Scheller publishes a new book. There's no charge and no obligation.

https://books2read.com/r/B-A-BHQL-GEMOB

BOOKS 2 READ

Connecting independent readers to independent writers.

Also by Ashley Scheller

The Wielder Diaries
The Wielder Diaries: My Crystal
The Wielder Diaries: Shattered

About the Author

An educator by day and artist by night, Ashley Scheller loves to write stories if she isn't sketching new creations in her notebook. Residing with her family in Iowa, she enjoys connecting with her community about art, books, and games.

Scheller invites you to an exciting adventure and cannot wait to deliver the next installment of *The Wielder Diaries* series.

CPSIA information can be obtained
at www.ICGtesting.com
Printed in the USA
JSHW051929090723
44155JS00004B/51

9 798201 955649